INVISIBLE

ellen

SHARI SHATTUCK

BERKLEY BOOKS

New York

BERKLEY
An imprint of Penguin Random House LLC
375 Hudson Street, New York, New York 10014

BERKLEY® and the "B" design are registered trademarks of Penguin Random House LLC.
For more information, visit penguin.com.

Berkley trade paperback 978-0-425-27543-6

The Library of Congress has cataloged the G. P. Putnam's Sons hardcover edition as follows:

Shattuck, Shari.
Invisible Ellen / Shari Shattuck.
p.   cm.
ISBN 978-0-399-16761-4
1. Overweight women—Fiction.   2. Friendship—Fiction.   I. Title.
PS3619.H3575I58   2014   2013030313
813'.6—dc23

PUBLISHING HISTORY
G. P. Putnam's Sons hardcover edition / May 2014
Berkley trade paperback edition / May 2015

PRINTED IN THE UNITED STATES OF AMERICA

10   9   8   7   6   5   4   3   2   1

Cover illustration by Rita Carroll.
Cover design by Lisa Amaroso.

Penguin
Random
House

This book is for anyone who has ever felt they didn't count.

You do.

Your spirit shines as strong and as pure as any other.

1

Occasionally, though not very often, Ellen Homes would wonder how she had gained two hundred and seventy-three pounds and simultaneously disappeared. Not that she necessarily needed an answer, or even wanted one, because, simply put, being unseen was everything that Ellen Homes had ever wanted.

It was also all she could remember. Her mother, a noun she used for lack of an inoffensive alternative, had apparently at some point forgotten that she'd had a daughter. Ellen had a vague memory of the woman packing up her vodka bottles and glass pipe before leaving her alone in a grubby room of a halfway house when she was five. The only thing she clearly recalled from that event was gnawing hunger, and the joy of eating a cinnamon bun someone had eventually given her. But details of life with that woman, and especially that particular day, Ellen enthusiastically and effectively smothered, preferably under artificial nondairy dessert topping, or gravy.

Her memories of being found by the police, turned over to social workers, and the different foster families she'd subsequently been forced upon were also spotty and best forgotten. Ellen had ultimately been discarded in a group home. There, adults and kids alike had either taunted or ignored her. Preferring the latter, Ellen had assumed evasive techniques, avoiding attention by adopting a silent watchfulness and eluding all but the most necessary contact with others.

What Ellen did remember was how she sought out shadows to avoid the repulsion she met in the light. She found dark corners and attics to hide in. Hoarded packaged food, when she could get it. She learned to wear her straight brown hair longer, so that it covered the left side of her face, veiling her from the world around her and hiding the scar that permanently drew her left eye halfway closed and limited her vision. Since every human she'd ever met preferred not to look at her, a half step backward or an inverted slump was often sufficient to avoid potential scrutiny or even notice. Ellen became very good at being absent, even when she was there.

At nineteen she'd first noticed her complete visual absence. Ellen had tentatively offered help to a man staring with frustration at the bus schedule. He started as if addressed by a disembodied voice. His eyes, flicking past her, quivered slightly at the place her face would have been, and then he hurried away.

And Ellen had rejoiced, thrilled that a lifetime of cultivating the skills required for averting human interaction had finally paid off. The quality of being looked *through*, instead of *at*, felt so right.

Ellen reveled in her anonymity. She learned she could sustain her visual absence at work—the nighttime cleaning crew at a Costco—on busy streets, where people shifted their bodies away if she drew near as though shying from a cold draft, and best of all, in her tiny apartment, where she spent most of her time watching the neighbors from behind the embracing arms of closed doors.

Observing silently from the shadows may have begun as a crucial survival technique, but it had eventually grown into her most passionate interest. Real life enthralled Ellen—as long as it did not include her. The rare occasions she needed to be seen exhausted her. It was just too much effort, and opened the door to *participation*, the prospect of which horrified her more than running out of snack food or, unthinkably, bacon.

By twenty-four, Ellen had perfected her own invisibility to the degree that even her cat, Mouse, seemed only vaguely aware of her. Ellen and Mouse shared the one-room apartment and a love of caloric excess—especially bacon—but not much else.

The front door of that narrow studio apartment opened onto the main room, a dozen steps brought her to the kitchenette, which ended in a back door featuring a small window. Gazing through a triple layer of smog-grimed screen, dirty glass slats, and wrought-iron security bars, Ellen could see into a tiny courtyard smothered in gravel the color of bleached tombstones. It was a desolate spot. No whimsical water feature softened its echoing walls and there was an utter absence of refreshing greenery. Occasionally, Ellen would notice a weed that had strained its way upward through the sharp chunks of granite, but inevitably, its goal finally realized, the vegetation would take a look at the harsh environment, topped off by a minuscule patch of smoggy, dirt-brown sky, and die. She imagined that its last thought, if plants had thoughts, had been, *I'd rather be mulch.*

Across that narrow back-access space, she could look into the kitchens of the neighbors she so vigilantly avoided. In the window across from hers was a blanket, sun-faded and tacked up with nails she had watched the young couple pry from the molding, the fabric blocking her view into the only other upstairs unit with infuriating opacity, but on the ground level there were two apartments whose renters were so lazy and hopeless that they had never bothered with any kind of window covering, probably because, Ellen thought, it had never occurred to them that anyone would take an interest in their lives.

Because their lives weren't interesting, except, of course, to Ellen, who found constant fascination in how the occupants, whom she thought of as her pets, spent their hours. The girl in 1B Ellen called Heidi because, when she wasn't dressed for work—a cocktail waitress or a prostitute, to judge from the outfits—she wore her blonde hair in two braids that hung limply down the sides of her scrubbed pink face. The man in 1A, she dubbed T-bone because he was as thin as a rib and the bandanna he appeared intent on wearing until it rotted off was the color of raw meat.

A few months earlier, Heidi's midsection had started to swell. Her pregnancy, now at about eight months, Ellen guessed from the soccer-ball protrusion under her straining T-shirt, caused an interruption in whatever employment she did have, and now Heidi spent most of her time in the apartment, screaming at herself in a mirror or crying at her kitchen table. Ellen followed Heidi's antics with the enthusiasm of a sports fan during a play-off series. Tonight, with a bag of chips in one hand and a Tinkerbell pen in the other, Ellen made notes on one of the lined school pads so generously, and unwittingly, donated by her employer to her cause. "Heidi gets a beer," she wrote as she crunched a handful of cheddar chips into paste. "Debates over whether to drink it for ten minutes, then downs it in forty-five seconds." A minute later she added, "Throws up beer in the sink."

Shifting her gaze to the next window, she saw T-bone. The most interesting thing T-bone did was repackage big bags of marijuana into smaller ones. Tonight he was seated in his easy chair, smoking what Ellen had overheard him call a "Bob's Big Boy." The smallness of the space and the unmuffled solidity of the courtyard's walls sent any sound echoing up to her apartment, so it was easy for her to hear what she wanted to, and impossible to block out what she didn't. T-bone kept a sad potted plant on his windowsill, which he'd forgotten to water again today, a misdemeanor Ellen dutifully recorded. She had quite a collection of these notebooks, carefully labeled with the corresponding dates, and glancing at the shelf where she kept them, she felt a sense of accomplishment.

Slow night, Ellen thought as she closed her notebook, stuffing it into a large canvas sack. The impending entry to the world outside brought on a bout of compulsive, repeated stroking of her hair down over her left cheek. A habitual, unconscious warm-up, like an athlete stretching before a workout. She donned her faded black drawstring pants and loose smock shirt in preparation for work. She scowled at the sole of her left sneaker, the toe of which had come unglued from the canvas top, causing the rubber sole to flap each time she took a step. She needed to buy new ones, but that distasteful task could be put off awhile longer with the clever combination of ingenuity and half a yard of duct tape. After applying the appropriate technology, and field-testing it with a lap around the apartment, requiring a grand total of eighteen steps, to see if it would hold at least for the night, she dumped some dry food in Mouse's dish, snapped on her fanny pack, the girth of which she had extended with a child's belt, and checked to be sure that the front stairs were free of human occupancy before venturing out.

The short walk to the bus stop was clogged with people returning home for the evening but, as usual, the busy sidewalks cleared enough for her to pass. A small group waited impatiently for the number 12 bus to stop, its air brakes shushing out a harsh reprimand as it pulled to the curb. Ellen assumed her usual space in the queue, left open by people whose eyes swept past her with only the slightest shiver as their sight line crossed the place she occupied. She climbed the two steep, rubber-stamped stairs and collapsed onto a pair of open seats, effectively occupying one and a half of them. No matter how crowded the bus became, no other rider ever took what was left of the seat next to hers. She passed the time switching her attention from passenger to passenger as though changing channels in an attempt to find something intriguing, or at least educational, to watch. She tuned in first to a few seconds of a young man bullying his younger girlfriend, but quickly became bored with the girl's frightened passivity. She flipped over to an elderly woman performing a lonely monologue, then switched to a man leaping nimbly up the stairs onto the bus. He flopped onto one of the handicapped seats, set his gym bag on the other, and opened a paper. Pulling out her notebook, Ellen wrote, "Healthy guy sits in the handicapped seats." His infraction duly recorded, she returned her attention to the teen couple, the girl looking less frightened and more pissed as the boy taunted her. Ellen felt a shimmy of detached anticipation. Pencil poised, she settled on that channel and hunkered down to enjoy the show.

But she was distracted from the promising scenario when the doors hissed open at the next stop and Ellen heard a woman's clear voice call out, "Is this the twelve?" She perked up. The number 12 was clearly displayed on both the front and side of the bus. Hoping for the antics of at least an eccentric personality, if not a full-out lunatic, she waited eagerly to see what would unfold.

A mumbled, indifferent reply from the semi-catatonic driver seemed to satisfy the woman, and Ellen watched curiously as a white stick tipped in red tapped its way onto the aisle, followed by a young woman with dark hair cascading from an arrogantly orange cap. Though it was rapidly growing dark outside, the twenty-something woman wore sunglasses. Reaching one hand in front of her, she felt for an available handicapped seat. The man with the gym bag rustled his newspaper in annoyance as she brushed his shoulder, saying irritably, "These are taken. There's open seats halfway down."

With a disdainful smile that clearly said she knew he didn't belong there and thought people like him were descended from a long and undistinguished line of particularly disgusting silverfish, the girl groped her way on down the aisle. She was steps away from Ellen when the bus lurched out into traffic, sending her stumbling forward. She fell to her knees, one arm smacking on the empty seat next to Ellen. The girl reclaimed her balance and, holding the seat back to steady herself, struggled up.

"I'm fine!" she called out in an amused voice to the bus full of people studiously not helping her. "Don't bother about me, save yourselves!" With a light, derisive laugh, which she clearly relished, she slid in next to Ellen, making squishy contact with Ellen's overlapping thigh and midriff.

"Oh, sorry," she said, turning only partially toward Ellen. "Didn't see you there." Then she laughed again and pulled out a book, opening it to a plain, white textured page marked by a ribbon. "The face—pretty," Ellen noted without assigning the quality any particular value—angled toward her again, as though studying some fascinating object up ahead to the right.

She said, "Sorry to be a bother, but could you possibly let me know when we get to Grant Avenue?"

Ellen felt her neglected voice catch in her throat. She was being spoken to. Of course, the girl couldn't see her any more than anyone else, less actually, but she had felt her. "Uh, okay," Ellen muttered.

"I've always depended upon the kindness of strangers," the girl said in a sorghum Southern accent, then added from the side of her mouth, "But I wouldn't recommend it; most of them are bastards." Then she put her head back and a burst of laughter so hearty escaped her that Ellen felt physically assaulted and pressed herself protectively against the cold of the window. Unaware, or uncaring, of Ellen's reaction, the girl began to run her fingers over the blank white pages of her book.

Though Ellen was flustered by even the girl's partial, uninvited acknowledgment, the unabashed laughter resonated with her. She puzzled over it for the next few blocks, jerking whenever the blind girl would chuckle unexpectedly at something her fingers had converted from bumps to wit.

It wasn't, she thought, that she'd been "noticed," though that was novel. She knew it had only been the curious accident of physical contact that had enabled the blind girl to perceive her. No, what intrigued Ellen was that this young woman—topped off with a ridiculous hat roughly the size, color, and shape of a crushed traffic cone—was utterly unconcerned with the people around her, even the ones who stared blatantly. She couldn't see them, so they didn't matter.

The possibility of this was a revelation with the impact of a small, localized explosion in Ellen that cracked open a thin fault line of panic. Maybe she had wished for the wrong thing, and a thought struck her. *Maybe it's better not to see than to be unseen.* A strange jealousy gripped Ellen; cold green fingers slid across her rib cage and squeezed on her stomach. She could feel ragged fingernails piercing the well-developed organ.

Ellen checked her watch. As usual, she was an hour early for work, a precaution that allowed her to review the assignment list and get started while the rest of the crew was still stumbling into the locker room. There were easily forty-five minutes to spare if she chose to get off the bus two stops early; why shouldn't she? Suddenly overcome with a need to know more about this unique person seated next to her, Ellen blew the dust off her guts and cleared her throat.

"Next stop, Grant," she said.

The girl tilted her tangerine topper to one side, causing it to flop like a day-old daisy. "Yeah, that's what I thought. Thanks."

Ellen hoped her reluctant grunt would suffice as an answer.

The girl put away her book and stood up in preparation for disembarking, keeping a firm hold on the back of the seat in front of her. "Have a nice day," she said.

Turning to look out at the dusky gloom and strangely reluctant for the girl to leave, Ellen risked a connection. "Uh. It's pretty much night."

The girl slung her satchel over one shoulder and gripped her stick. She angled toward Ellen again, and leaned down.

"It's all midnight to me, baby." The laugh came again, so powerful that it triggered an aftershock in Ellen that levered open the fissure in her protective shield a few millimeters wider.

The stick tapped its way down the aisle, the air brakes hissed their discontent, and, as the Day-Glo cap bobbed out of sight, Ellen felt as though something had been stolen from her. Without thinking, she jumped up to follow the girl and, in her haste to make the door, her oversized bag smacked the newspaper of the bastard hogging the handicapped seats, ripping it in half. "What the f—?" he exclaimed, but Ellen was already off the bus, the closing doors almost catching her billowing black tent of a shirt.

The crowd was a mass of gray and brown as twilight stole the color from all lesser pigment, but the intriguing stranger's fluorescent hat bobbed above the muted waves of commuters like a beacon. As Ellen hurried to catch up with it, something else snagged the corner of her eye. Two men had peeled themselves from a doorway and started after the girl with the steady focus of predators. In their dirty jeans and baseball caps, they stood out in the upscale midtown neighborhood that was mostly peopled with men and women in business suits or parents in Lycra yoga pants and matching tops, jogging in place behind three-wheeled strollers as they checked their pulses against their expensive watches. With a nasty jolt, Ellen realized that she wasn't the only one interested in the blind girl and this struck her as grossly unfair. She'd been following her first and she didn't want to share. She hitched up her fanny pack and went on.

After three blocks, the girl turned off into a narrow alley, the two men followed, and bringing up the rear was an increasingly determined Ellen, who by now was thinking of the girl as her story and the two men as interlopers. This dead-end access to the surrounding buildings had no other foot traffic and ended in a brick wall with a large Dumpster pushed against it. It was clean and lit by a bright streetlamp. On either side of the alleyway, several large metal doors interrupted the patterned brickwork of high walls. The girl pulled a set of keys from her pocket as she tapped along. The men glanced back, surveying the busy avenue they had just left. Neither of them registered Ellen, hugging the brick a few feet from the corner, their eyes fixing instead on a cop car sitting stopped at a light. The traffic began to move along the main avenue, and the alley was once again hidden from the prying eyes of the city's finest.

The men returned their predatory attention back to the girl, and Ellen started cautiously down the alley after them. It was as though the window she usually only looked through had opened and she were venturing inside instead of watching from out. The tingly feeling was alien to her, uncomfortable certainly, but not entirely unpleasant.

All at once, the men stepped up their pace and the girl paused, tilting her head to listen, and then she hurried forward. As the men overtook her, she spun, clutching the strap of her bag. Ellen saw the flash of a knife and felt a physical pain in her chest as she gulped in a sharp, silent, terrified breath. In the next second the knife swiped neatly and the girl cried out and cowered, then straightened. She was left intact, but holding nothing but the strap of her bag, now dangling useless. As the men raced back toward the avenue with her satchel, she recovered and screamed after them. "Pathetic bastards!!" she railed furiously. "Police! Police!" she shouted, the words echoing even as they were repeated.

Ellen shrunk against the alley wall, stained the same soot color as the faded black of her clothes, her heart racing. The men sprinted toward her, their eyes fixed on the avenue and escape, only a few paces away. As they came level with Ellen, some limp emotion in her suddenly stiffened. Without planning it, she thrust a foot out into the path of the thief nearest to her. He went down hard, letting go of the stolen bag to catch himself, his hands slapping smartly on the rough cement of the sidewalk and scraping off layers of skin as he slid. Obviously unfamiliar with the buddy system, his accomplice did not pause, but rounded the corner and disappeared like a rat from an attic light.

The satchel was lying on the cement. Ellen darted out and grabbed it up while the thwarted purse snatcher was shaking his head and desperately gasping for the air that had been punched from his lungs. Gulping like a goldfish whose misguided leap for freedom had ended in a rude whack on the kitchen linoleum, he stared around, clearly stunned by both the fall and its cause. Moving behind him, Ellen stomped down hard on the instep of the man's sneaker and he wheezed a yelp—a choking, airless expression of pain.

"Beat it, asshole," Ellen screamed, her voice so rusty with disuse at that volume that the words came out in a low, throaty rasp. The asshole struggled to his feet, holding his scraped and bleeding palms out in front of him, and ran off without looking back.

Clenching the satchel to her hammering chest, Ellen collapsed against the rough bricks. Her whole body was shaking so violently from the unexpected confrontation that she worried she might disintegrate.

It took a full minute before she could hear anything except the panicked thumping of her heart, and when she could, she realized that outside her head it was oddly quiet. The girl had stopped shouting for the police and was standing still, listening.

"Hello?" the girl called out tentatively. "Who's there?"

"It's okay," Ellen gasped. "It's me, the lady . . . from the bus. I . . ." She sucked a huge lungful of air and tried to direct the oxygen to the sharp pain in her thudding chest. ". . . have your bag."

There was a moment of silence—then the girl said, "Really?" She sounded dubious.

Ellen couldn't imagine anything more "really" than what had just happened, but she couldn't be annoyed. She was having trouble believing it herself. "Yeah . . . really," she said.

"Sweet." The click of the cane brought the girl the few yards back up the alleyway. She stopped just in front of Ellen, who was, no doubt, easy to locate due to the fact that she was panting like a Saint Bernard on an August afternoon. "Are you all right?" the girl asked.

"I . . . think . . . so."

"What happened? I heard him go down."

"Um . . ." Ellen shuffled her feet uncomfortably and said, "I tripped him."

"Nice. I hope he scraped his face off. Thanks. I'm Temerity." She held out one hand, only slightly off course.

Confused by the gesture, Ellen realized she was still hugging the satchel and thrust it at the hand. Temerity took it, tucked it under her left arm and then extended her right hand again. "And you are?" she asked pointedly.

"Uh, Ellen," Ellen said. She took the hand between her thumb and fingertips and gave it an awkward shake. From the point of uncommon contact, she felt a creeping sensation spread across the skin of her wrist and up her forearm, as though a swarm of ants was following a parade route over her shoulder and across her back.

"Well, Ellen, can I buy you a cup of coffee or a beer or something to thank you?"

"No," Ellen blurted in horror, and then fumbled, "I mean, I have to go to work. I work nights."

"Where?"

"Costco."

"I didn't know they were open nights, not that it makes any difference to me."

"They're not, I clean."

"You clean," she repeated. "Do you eat?"

Ellen glanced down at her lumpy, overstuffed body. The prolonged conversation was making her increasingly anxious, and hollow. She needed food to stabilize herself. "Sure, sometimes."

"So, that's good." Temerity felt along the side of the strapless satchel until she located a small zippered pocket. Taking out a card, she ran her fingers over the raised lettering, then held it out. "Here's my number. I want you to call me tomorrow and I really want to take you to dinner, or breakfast, or whatever works for you. Like I said, it's all midnight to me."

In spite of the million-ant march advancing across her skin, Ellen gawked at Temerity in awe. "You eat at restaurants?" she asked.

Temerity's pretty face scrunched up into a sarcastic scowl. "No, I eat at libraries and furniture outlets. Of course I eat at restaurants, don't you?"

Ellen wasn't sure what to say. She wanted to know more about this woman, but the thought of making an actual social engagement spurred the anxiety ants into a fit of competitive flamenco dancing in miniature golf cleats. Uncertain of how to respond, she just said, "No, but, I mean, aren't you afraid that you'll, uh . . ." Her nerve failed her.

The head cocked to one side. "Make a spectacle of myself? Miss my mouth? Stab myself with a fork? Eat the toothpick? You don't have to be blind to make a complete fool of yourself, and anyway, who cares?" Temerity threw her arms out and spoke the last words so loudly that they echoed against the walls.

"I don't go to restaurants." Ellen felt ashamed to say it out loud.

Temerity let out an exaggerated sigh. "In that case, I can truthfully tell you the only thing you're really missing out on is the onion blossom at Judy's. So yummy, and impossible to make at home without a grease fire. Fine. Call me, I live here"—she pointed up—"we can talk about your dietary peculiarities then. If you'd rather, you can come over and I'll cook at home. How about that?"

"Maybe," Ellen said, anxious to get away now. "I gotta go."

Turning, Ellen fled from the first human who had offered her anything in almost six years. And who, ironically perhaps, saw her because she couldn't.

2

As she rushed back into the flow of humanity on the busy avenue, Ellen's stomach churned and growled. Feeling exposed and faint, she stood turning in place, trying to get her bearings and find something familiar. She spotted a hot dog cart parked in the pool of a streetlamp's light. To the hollow, burning shakiness inside her, it shone forth like the aura of a holy relic.

The vendor was engrossed in conversation with another man who slouched next to him, shrouded in the fog of his own cigarette smoke. The language they spoke was foreign, rapid, and weighted down with dense consonants.

Approaching warily, almost against her will, Ellen watched them. Neither noticed her, of course. But the gnawing need for comfort and some speck of residual courage prompted Ellen to use her voice.

Ellen moistened her lips. "One hot dog, please," she said.

The vendor neither glanced up nor interrupted the jumbled flow of his narrative as he produced a bun, slapped on the gleaming pink sausage and set it on the cart's stainless steel top. Without breaking stride, the man interjected the words "Three dollars" into his dissertation in the unidentified language—maybe it was Klingon, Ellen thought.

Ellen pulled the money out of her bag, laid it on the cart and hurried away, drenched in a sweat of relief that her voice had not summoned scrutiny. The first bite of the yielding, doughy bun absorbed the bitterness of fear from her taste buds, and the lusciously salty meat massaged her tongue. She swallowed, feeling the solid smoothness coat her stomach, and the heat began to ease. Four more bites finished the dog, but she felt only partly sated. Though she would have liked a second and maybe a third, the exchange with the vendor had required taking a risk, exacted a toll, and she'd been lucky to walk away unnoticed, so she didn't dare another. The possibility of being mocked or insulted in that rasping language required more fortitude than she could muster, ever. She reassured herself with the thought that soon enough she would be at work, the megasource for her dietary staples: processed snack foods. Turning, she headed back to the bus stop and caught the next number 12 bus after a short wait.

But this time Ellen found herself unable to perceive the other commuters with her usual emotional detachment, reducing them to illustrations in her personal comic book. She still studied them. A man in a suit was tapping his fingers nervously, a small hopeful smile playing across his mouth, and Ellen found herself wondering why he was smiling. Was he hoping something at work would get him noticed? Was he on his way to meet someone? A frightened-looking woman across from him, who constantly checked her silent cell phone, might have a child who was late coming home. Ellen was unclear on why these new, intrusive thoughts nagged at and unsettled her, but she did not like them. Ellen had always thought of the vignettes she loved to witness as her personal Polaroids, snapshots for a scrapbook without backstory or consequence. Return without investment.

Before the adrenaline surging through her body had a chance to release her from its barbed-wire grip, she reached her stop. She disembarked and headed across a parking lot the size of Rhode Island, then around the side of the giant block of a building. It was a quarter-mile hike that brought her, sweaty and gasping, to the loading docks. As usual, a massive semi was disgorging its contents and it was easy to slip up the access ramp, slink past the dockworkers, through the incessant *beep-beep* of the forklifts, and into the break room.

Two hairy men in jumpsuits sat at a table, drinking sodas and eating MoonPies, a treat that made Ellen's mouth water. Standing over them was a dark-skinned man in a cheap suit. His thinning hair was combed across the top of his head. This was Ellen's immediate supervisor, the night shift manager known as "the Boss." The title was an affectation he insisted his employees use to address him, something that thankfully Ellen, hired before his transfer to their store, had been able to avoid for four years. The three men glanced up as the door opened, blinked twice, then turned back to their conversation. The Boss was recounting a sexual conquest so lurid in detail that it would have earned him a slap from a hooker. As she passed them, Ellen heard the phrase "banged that bearded clam." Containing the sneering laughs of the men and the ugly pictures the phrase had summoned in her mind by mentally backing the images into a heavy metal cage with a bullwhip, she slipped through the door to the ladies' locker room, a square affair with a block of lockers in the center and benches along the walls around them on three sides. The fourth wall opened onto a restroom and a shower area.

Ellen went to her locker, dumped in her bag, took out the apron and rubber gloves that she kept there for her personal use, and then sat waiting for the men outside to disperse. The door swung open again, letting wisps of obscenity and laughter slip into the locker room along with a young Russian woman named Irena. The recent and perpetually terrified immigrant scuttled away from the lewd catcalls behind her, keeping her eyes down, and hurriedly gathered her things. She pulled out a battered CD player that she always carried and stuck the frayed earbuds into her ears. Ellen didn't understand why. She assumed that the music was one way to block out the world, and she could certainly understand Irena's desire to do exactly that, but for a frightened woman to not be able to hear what was going on around her seemed like an ill-advised choice. Yet when Irena opened the locker room door and was forced to pass back by the offensive trio, Ellen couldn't argue with the logic of canceling out their coarse commentary, though Irena still moved with the fearful slinking of a creature desperate to evade becoming lunch.

The men had vacated the break room when Ellen went back through. They had left their wrappers and cans on the table under a sign reading CLEAN UP AFTER YOURSELF! She went down a long, L-shaped hallway to get a cart and gather cleaning supplies from the supply room. Turning the corner onto the last leg of the hall, she found herself in an eerie semidarkness. The nasty overhead fluorescent lights were sputtering through their last death throes, and the resulting feeble flicker was barely sufficient to illuminate the short section of the corridor.

The harsh, acidic tang of ammonia and pine cleaners stored inside the supply room had given Ellen the habit of opening the door reluctantly, as though if she snuck up on it, the smell wouldn't be so abrasive. She eased open the door and felt for the switch.

From deep in the gloom, beyond the stacked metal shelving of toilet paper, scrub brushes, and floor cleaners, she heard whispered voices, one aggressively male, and the other female, pleading and afraid. Ellen held still and listened.

Keeping a hand on the door so that it closed silently behind her, Ellen moved into the darkness. She recognized the smarmy, innuendo-filled male voice, the kind of voice that never missed an opportunity to turn any comment into a sexual reference. It was the Boss.

"Come on, you know you like it," the Boss was saying in his creepy whine. "You want to keep your job, don't you? I know you have a baby and you're not really married. I could get you better hours. Just make me happy—nothing you haven't done before." The Russian accent tinting the young woman's plea to be released told Ellen that the voice belonged to Irena. No doubt the horny Boss had been able to sneak up on her because of the ever-present earbuds.

"Are you even legal?" the Boss asked, a cruel tinge to his voice. "I'd hate to see things get difficult for you. Everybody needs friends in high places." Ellen heard the sound of a zipper and then a sharp cry and a small scuffle. "Come on, I can be your friend."

Before tonight, Ellen would have blended in with the plaster and recorded the scenario with a nagging yet distant sensation of indignation, but now she thought of the satisfying slap of the bag snatcher's palms on the cement and she craved more of the same. Muted outrage and personal distaste for the greasy Boss welled up in Ellen, and she decided to disrupt this current attempt to misuse his puny authority, this abuse that was only one on a long list of his offenses that ended in Ellen's mind with three dots, as she'd seen in books when it meant the list went on and on. She backtracked to the door, grasped the handle, and threw it open as though she were just entering, letting it slam into the wall with a crash. She switched on the light and started rummaging through the cleansers closest to the door, on the bottom shelf, stooping down behind one of the carts. In a few seconds she heard the sound of a muffled sob and Irena's feet rushing past her out the door and then the slower, heavier tread of the Boss. Ellen could see his dark, scuffed lace-up shoes between the wheels of the cart as he came around the shelving. They paused, then turned away, and the door opened and closed. Ellen straightened up. Good, now she could get to work.

Wheeling the cart into the hallway, she spotted Irena coming back for her own cart, her startled face streaked with tears. Her eyes glued to the floor as she scurried past, a frightened mouse in a gray jumpsuit, scrambling for cover. There was no sign of the Boss, or the earbuds.

Wishing she had seen his face when he was deprived of his toy, Ellen moved on, working her way to the snack-food section to replenish her dwindling home stock.

Often, it was as easy as finding the packets that had been torn open, partially devoured and then stuffed behind other items on the shelves by shoppers who regarded the store's goods as a complimentary all-you-can-eat buffet. This smorgasbord without a waitress happened far more frequently than Ellen would have thought possible in a crowded store. Though the official policy of Costco was that any opened packages should be discarded, and this was partially to discourage the employees from damaging packages themselves, most of the managers overlooked their minimum-wage coworkers taking home the unsellable remains. Tonight's finds included a full box of Oreos—all that was left of a three-package value pack—and a torn-open assortment of individually wrapped Fruit Roll-Ups. Both nice, but Ellen knew she would want salty before sweet. The easiest thing to pilfer was chips. Ostensibly reorganizing the three-pound sacks of ranch-flavored Doritos, Ellen took a small trash bag from a pack on her cart.

As she snapped the white plastic in the air to open it fully, she glanced at the security camera mounted on the wall about fifteen feet up. There were exactly twenty-seven of these cameras placed around the store, and Ellen had memorized their locations. That and a few surreptitious trips past the glassed-in security booth, which housed the monitors, had helped Ellen identify precisely what was revealed by these watchful electronic eyes, and, more important, what they missed. Making sure that her cart was blocking the chip bag from the lens, Ellen produced a box cutter that she kept in her fanny pack, made a slit down the back seam of the chips bag, shook about a fourth of the product into the clean bag, knotted it loosely and placed it on top of her cart. Then, using a roll of clear packing tape, she closed the seam of the Doritos bag and repositioned it. It looked much like the others. With a self-satisfied grunt, Ellen read the words "Contents may have settled during shipping."

When her shift was over, Ellen would punch her time card and then spend an extra hour cleaning—off the clock. It was her way of paying for the items she took home. She knew they would never be missed, but she was a barterer, not a thief.

During break, Ellen went to a stall in the ladies' room, taking with her a liter of orange soda and a family pack of Xtra Cheddar Goldfish snacks. She was munching the last broken fin crumbs when she heard the door open and someone enter. Closing one eye, she peeked through the crack in the door to see Irena standing by the sink, sobbing with her face in her hands. After a few minutes, the woman splashed cold water over her face, wiped it roughly with the brown paper towels, and left. Ellen came cautiously out. She did not like that Irena had been mistreated. She gingerly prodded the part of her that felt good she had done even a small thing to deter it. It didn't

3

When Ellen arrived home at seven a.m., she closed and bolted the door behind her. That was the first step to casting off the nerve-scratchy sensation that always followed her in from the world outside. But the next step was to shore up her interior walls of defense, which required constant maintenance, and she never went wrong with bacon. Its heft and solidity, its very *fattiness*, somehow staved off the hunger-fear inside her in the same way the lock on her security door created a safety zone between her and the dangers outside. She unpacked the chips and cookies, opened a soda, and fried half a pound of bacon. While the streaky breakfast meat was sizzling on the tiny range, making a subtle, reassuring sound not unlike a distant, muted conversation, she checked across the courtyard to see if her pets were up, though rising early was not habitual for either of them.

Surprisingly, Heidi was awake. It looked like she had made an effort to dress for the first time in months, and she was nervously straightening up her apartment. She had opened the large kitchen window onto the courtyard and, as Ellen watched her through the security bars, she washed the dirty dishes that had been piling up in her sink and on the small table pushed up under the window, then

she scrubbed down the counters. Opening the back door, she swept
the floor, whipping up small clouds of dust spotted with flittering
bits of trash out into the bleak gravel. Cracking the window slats of
her own kitchen door, Ellen could hear Heidi's portable radio, balanced on top of the fridge, playing a hard rock station. Ellen sniffed
with distaste; the only station she cared for was the local college's
classical one, though she couldn't have identified a single sonata if
her life depended on it. She liked symphony music because it lasted
a long time and because it was like a soundtrack, with pictures provided by her own imagination. It took her places—around corners,
through forests, to castles and islands—places she would otherwise
never have thought to go.

Watching the unusual a.m. activity, Ellen ate her breakfast. She
put the bacon on white toast, thickly smeared with peanut butter,
and smushed it all down into a satisfying, soft yet crunchy mass with
pressure from her wide palm. The constancy of peanut butter was
something she could believe in. At one of her first foster homes, the
refrigerator and cabinets had been kept padlocked and the only
thing available was a jar of peanut butter and a loaf of harmless
white bread, nestled in its happy packaging—polka dots and bright
colors that clashed with the grim, cheerless kitchen.

Within a week of her arrival, Ellen had learned to open the door
to that house of horrors soundlessly and slink past the den, which
stank of unfiltered Brand X cigarettes and relentlessly belched the
stupidity of daytime TV. Avoiding the spots on the floor that creaked
and gave her away, she would cower in the kitchen as she quickly
made three plain peanut butter sandwiches. Taking her schoolbag
with its treasure of library books, she would escape up the stairs to
the eaves under the roof to pass a few hours as far from the miserable
housemother as possible. For Ellen, who avoided all meals in that

house, accompanied as they were by a cloud of rancid smoke and her housemother's constant stream of insults, those sandwiches had been her friends, had sustained her for the six months she'd slept on a mat in the attic before the social worker found the cigarette burns on the backs of her hands. The burns were the inevitable result of being noticed in that "home." White bread and peanut butter would never hurt anyone. Ellen wrinkled her nose at the memory of the smell of meals in that terrible place—cabbage, always cabbage, cooked into mush—that had infiltrated up to even the unheated space under the roof beams.

But the deliciousness of bacon reassured her, bucking her up and dispensing of memories of that distasteful environment. One piece of the bacon she saved out and threw to Mouse, who ate it with relish and then wandered about sniffing the kitchen floor as if the hickory-smoked treat had materialized through a trapdoor and he was sure to find another. Ellen was enjoying a yawn when she heard a car pull up to the curb outside her front window. She checked through a slit in the curtains, but instead of the expected grocery deliveryman, she saw a well-dressed couple, probably in their late thirties, emerging from a white Land Rover. They glanced nervously up at the seedy apartment building as though they feared it might vandalize their precious SUV. After fixing it with a hostile look, presumably to warn it off, they walked around to the other side of the building. That meant they were headed for either Heidi's or T-bone's front door. And Ellen thought it was a safe bet that these people weren't here to buy weed before eight a.m.

So Heidi had visitors. A second yawn was stifled before it could pry open Ellen's jaws. Sleep could wait, she thought. This would be good. Positioning herself on her stool by the back window behind the screen, notebook on her knee, Ellen heard the grating rasp of

Heidi's door buzzer, and watched Heidi rush to turn off the music and then stand in the middle of the tiny kitchen, which Ellen could see almost all of through the open door from her slightly raised point of view. Muttering admonishments to herself that Ellen couldn't make out, and spinning as though to double-check for any exposed contraband, Heidi shook her hands at the wrists, then disappeared from sight.

In a minute, she returned with the couple, leading them to her tiny table jammed up under the open window directly across from and below Ellen's viewpoint. The angle was so perfect that the scene might have been staged just for her. Heidi nervously served them coffee in mismatched mugs. Her hands shook as she offered them milk from a small carton and it sloshed onto the scratched tabletop.

Ellen angled her head so that she could hear as much as possible, and cranked open the window slats another inch.

The woman was saying, "It's not a problem, I'll get it." She wiped away the spilled milk with a tissue from her bag, which looked expensive, and then exchanged a look with the man—her husband, Ellen assumed, due to their matching gold bands. "Sit down."

When Heidi sat, Ellen had a view of all three of them—the couple across from each other in profile, and Heidi, between them, full on. As usual, the ridiculously small, stark-walled courtyard magnified their voices, so she could easily make out the conversation.

"So," the man was saying, "you're due in how many weeks?"

"Well, three, but who knows?" Heidi's forced laugh broke, making it sound more like a gasp of fear. She stared down at her fingers entwined on the table.

The woman straightened her perfect white blouse, and then said, "And the father?"

"He . . . was killed," Heidi replied, so softly that Ellen could barely make it out, but then Heidi cleared her throat and said more confidently, "In Afghanistan."

"Oh, he was in the service." The woman's voice sounded to Ellen as though she were pleased rather than saddened at hearing what was traditionally regarded as bad news.

"Yes," Heidi said. "He didn't know I was pregnant when he shipped out. I didn't know either, actually, until about three weeks after he was gone, and I never got a chance to tell him." She gulped. "He was killed two weeks later, and my letter was returned. . . . There was a bomb. . . ." Heidi trailed off, pressing her lips tightly together.

The woman reached out a hand and patted Heidi's shoulder awkwardly. Then the man spoke; it sounded as if he were trying to be gentle but kindness came unnaturally to him. "And you are certain that you don't want to keep this baby? Are you sure?" Heidi didn't answer right away, so he went on. "I'm sorry to be so direct, but we've been through this before. You can't imagine how painful it is to go through this entire process only to have the birth mother change her mind."

Heidi kept her eyes fixed just in front of her. She said, "I'm sure. I can't afford a kid, and I don't even have a job. I want to go back to school and, well, you know, have a life."

"What about other family?" the woman asked. "Your parents, or his, for example. Do you think there's any chance that they might try to claim this baby? You understand that they would have a legal right." She had named the relations with distaste, as though she'd been stung by those scorpions before.

This time Heidi's laugh was a harsh, hateful sound. "I haven't spoken to my father since I left Illinois three years ago. He didn't have much interest in being a father the first time around. In fact, I doubt he's sobered up enough to notice I've gone. My mom died. The father's parents?" Her mouth tightened. "I never met them, so I don't have any intention of telling them. I'm not really sure where they are anyway."

"What about the amount of money we discussed? Will you be willing to sign something that says that is final and you can't come after us for any more at a future date?"

The girl shrugged. "Why would I do that?"

"I need a solid answer," the man insisted, pressing harder for the response he wanted.

"Sure, yeah. Whatever." Heidi shrugged again.

Ellen wrote in her book, "Selling the baby."

"Do you have any questions for us?" The woman's tone was tense, but she lacked her husband's professional coldness.

"Uhm, well, I would just like to know that she'll be safe, you know. Loved."

The woman smiled and leaned forward, laying one hand on Heidi's knotted fingers. "We've wanted a baby for fifteen years. But I can't have any of my own. There are some medical issues. He—"

"The details aren't relevant," the man interrupted, and Ellen was sure that at least some of the medical issues were his. "What you need to know is that the child we adopt will be given every opportunity in life. The best schools, nannies, college."

For the first time, Heidi looked up. Not at the man, but at the woman. She said, "And . . . love?"

"And love," the woman said as though she were a salesman mentioning the excellent highway mpg of a car she was selling off the showroom floor. "She'll have lots of love and attention."

Yeah, right, thought Ellen, *from the nannies, while you're at work. Modern parenting: buy a kid and pay someone else to raise it.*

Heidi nodded. "I just didn't have the happiest childhood, and

I don't want . . ." She trailed off again, then cleared her throat. "And the doctor? Hospital?"

"We'll take care of all of that, as we discussed on the phone. As long as you deliver a healthy baby, we'll take care of the financial side and you can have your life back." Once again Heidi didn't respond, so the man pressed to close the deal. It was obvious to Ellen that he had a master's degree in negotiation with a minor in manipulation. "We don't have long." As though to illustrate this, he glanced at his watch. Then he looked up at his wife, and Ellen could almost see him gather himself to win this one for her. He straightened up and said with clearly restrained impatience that barely covered his slightly desperate bid to win this objective, "So, not to rush you, we know this isn't easy, but we need an answer as soon as possible."

There was a long moment while Heidi twisted her fingers around and around. Finally, she said, "Let's do it." Her voice sounded ruined, smashed, thinner and sharper than a penny left on the track and flattened under the wheels of a locomotive.

"Are you sure?" the woman asked sharply.

Heidi stood up and started to clear the coffee cups, though they hadn't been touched. "Absolutely. Get me the papers." As she turned away, the husband gave his wife a thumbs-up and what looked like a genuine smile. Reaching off to her left without even having to glance away from the scene below, Ellen pulled down the binoculars she had purchased from an army-navy store and focused in on the woman's face. Her jaw was rigid with frightened hope. She tried to return her husband's smile, but her lips were pressed tightly together and trembling, so he leaned over the small table and gave her forehead a peck.

The man pulled a briefcase onto the table and opened it. A thick sheaf of legal documents was laid out. Ellen squinted down through the binoculars, spinning the focus wheel until she could see the writing. All she could make out were the names, printed in bold across the top: SUSAN SMITH NEWLAND, ESQUIRE, AND EDWARD NEWLAND, ESQUIRE, 583 WINSTON AVENUE, HIGHLAND PARK. Lowering the glasses, Ellen copied it into her book.

So, they were a team of sharpshooting lawyers and Heidi was the fish in a barrel, a fact that became more apparent as the conversation turned legal and difficult to follow, which translated to boring. Ellen yawned again and decided to go to bed. She brushed her teeth and changed into pajamas. While she was still nestling into her mound of blankets, she heard the Land Rover start up. Sneaking a look over the sill, she looked down at it. Through the windshield she watched as the woman put her face in her hands and started to shake. Her husband stroked her back, looking lost, then lifted her face and smiled encouragingly at her, speaking rapidly. Ellen was pretty sure he was stressing his confidence that the buck was in the bag, so to speak. *So what?* she thought as she settled back down. It was probably lucky for the kid these people showed up, lucky for Heidi because now she would have the money to go back to school and quit moping her life away. She should be ecstatic.

But through the still-opened slats of the back-door window, Ellen heard the rise of a strange drawn-out wail, broken by wet, gasping breaths. It wavered, fell, then began again.

Ellen's gaze went to the card that Temerity had given her, fastened to the wall with a pushpin, and she wondered if Heidi would ever stop making that terrible noise. It was indulgent, Ellen thought critically. She was tired and she needed to sleep. Heidi didn't want the baby, fine, but don't turn it into a melodrama.

Yet, deep in some forgotten room of Ellen's chest, of which she had previously been unaware, an unsettled restlessness stirred. The fissure that Temerity's laugh had split open was widening to become a pathway that was allowing things intrusive and unfamiliar to slip through into lost corridors. It didn't occur to her to feel sorry for Heidi. Besides the fact that Ellen was adept at blocking emotion, not to mention the fact that having no one to empathize with left her a bit fuzzy on the overall concept of empathy, the girl's problems were her own doing after all. And everyone had problems, all you had to do was pay attention to see that, and paying attention was what Ellen did best. It was more like . . . well, she thought uneasily, it's that it wasn't a soap opera melodrama, Heidi wasn't a bad actor reading overwritten lines, it was her life, and Ellen was . . . invested in it. Someone was messing with her pet, and Ellen did not like it.

4

Before she could dismiss her irritation enough to go to sleep, a noisy car, the muffler missing or at least barely clinging to life, pulled up to the curb outside. A door slammed, feet stomped up her stairs. There was a tap at her door. "Delivery!" a voice called out.

"The money is under the mat!" Ellen responded, pulling the blankets up under her chin. Sitting up had dislodged Mouse from his spot between her calves. He shook himself and mewed an annoyed objection at the air. The boxed groceries were dropped next to the door and she heard the envelope with the exact change, plus a two-dollar tip, being opened and then the receding footfalls of the deliveryman as he went back down the stairs and drove away.

Ellen opened the door and dragged in the box. She put the milk and the ice cream away and left the rest of it to be unpacked later.

As she let herself fall heavily onto her mattress in the corner of the one-room apartment, she looked again at the card. What would happen if she called? she wondered. Probably Temerity wasn't even there now. Probably she had a day job, like most people, though she wouldn't care what time of day it was. *It's all midnight to me,* she'd said. Ellen smiled. She liked that. She liked the cavalier way the girl had said it and she wanted to hear her say it again. She got up and Mouse hissed lazily, then lowered his head, exhausted by the effort, and let his eyes close to slits.

Clutching the phone tightly, Ellen dialed the number. It rang twice and then she heard "Yo, waz up?"

"Uhm, hello?" Ellen ventured. "Is this Temerity?"

"Is, and am." The ironic laugh confirmed that it was indeed the blind girl.

"This is, uh, Ellen. We, uh, met last night. I don't know if you remember me."

"If I remember you? Two muggers attacked me, stole my bag, you Jackie-Channed the mofos and returned my stuff. I'm blind—I don't have amnesia. That kind of thing sticks with you."

"Oh." Ellen couldn't think of what else to say.

"So, can you come over tonight? I'm making pasta sauce, so it's a good night if you eat pasta. You said you don't go to restaurants, but you didn't specifically rule out Italian."

"I eat pasta," Ellen said, pressing her tongue against her teeth at the mouthwatering prospect of lasagna, one of her favorite frozen foods. Her number one favorite food, of course, being bacon.

"Great. You have a working knowledge of the alley where I live. My door is the third one on the left, just ring the buzzer marked 'Bauer' and I'll let you up. You work tonight?"

"Yes, but not until ten."

"Then I'll see you at seven." There was a brief pause, then a blast of laughter. "I love saying that. Okay, I won't see you at seven, but I'll hear you." There was a click on the line. "Got another call. Later, babe." She hung up.

Ellen stared at the phone in her hand, befuddled and uncertain if someone had actually just referred to her as "babe."

Returning to the mattress, she found that she was too nervous and something else—was it excited?—to sleep. She twisted and turned so often that Mouse gave up and thumped with annoyed muttering to the sofa, where he curled up into a ball roughly the size of a trussed turkey and began to snore. Lulled by the rhythm of it, Ellen drifted off.

She awoke with a start to find that it was already five o'clock. Rising, she took a quick shower in the stand-up stall that had been designed for a race of people far smaller and more compact than her own. Going through her usual contortions, she wet, lathered, and rinsed the considerable surface area of her skin, even washing her hair, though she had already done it twice this week.

It was as she was unpacking the rest of her groceries that she found the letter. It wasn't addressed to her by name, rather to one Cindy Carpenter, but it had Ellen's unit number on it, written in a beautiful longhand. She turned it over and studied it curiously. Her mailbox, at the base of her stairs, occasionally yielded grocery store promotions or the few bills she paid each month, but a personally addressed letter was unique. The mailbox latch was broken and sometimes a renegade envelope would fall out onto the stairs. The deliveryman must have picked up this letter and tossed it into the box with the groceries.

Should she open it? Return it? Could she live with not knowing what was inside? Did the fact that it had her apartment number on it—slightly smudged—make it her business? It was a quandary. Even as she held it, Ellen could feel its contents buzzing inside as though the white paper were stuffed with electricity.

She could write "no such person at this address" on it and leave it to be picked up by the man in gray, but what if it was for one of the other residents and they didn't get it? Cindy Carpenter. Could that be the person who lived here before her? But she had been here for six years. Maybe Cindy Carpenter was the elderly lady who lived in the unit downstairs from Ellen, the only one with proper curtains. The most intriguing question of course was, what was inside?

Ellen opened the package of Oreos she'd brought home last night and started feeding them into her mouth like quarters into a slot machine, washing them down with a creamy mug of half-and-half. The letter lay on the abbreviated kitchen countertop, and Ellen could almost hear the low hum of high voltage whirring frenetically inside the white envelope. She ate a third of the cookies, then picked up the envelope and a knife.

Sliding the blade under the flap, she worked it back and forth, tearing it only slightly. When she finally had it open, Ellen unfolded the single sheet of paper. In the same formal script used to address it, it read:

Dear Cindy,

I'm not sure how to begin this letter, so I'll start by introducing myself. My name is Janelle Beaufort. You've never met me, but you knew my brother, Sam—he talked about you in his letters home. I'm sorry that it took so long for me to get in touch with you, but all I knew was that you lived in Morningside and that you worked at the Milan Grill. When I went there, they said you had left. It wasn't until I found the strength a week ago to go through his army duffel bag that I found your full name and address. As you might imagine, our family has been thrown into a state of shock and sorrow over Sam's death, so the delay in writing to you is, I hope, forgivable.

So Cindy is Heidi, Ellen thought, remembering Heidi telling the shark couple that the baby's father had died in Afghanistan. She went back to reading.

> *I understand that you didn't know my brother for very long, but I also know that he had real feelings for you and was hoping to pick up your relationship when he finished his tour of duty. Perhaps it is an imposition to contact you now. You don't know me, and maybe you don't want to, but I would like to meet you. If you had genuine feelings for Sam, which I believe you did, based on your letters (I apologize for reading them), then I'm sure you have also been thrown by his death and perhaps we can find some comfort in meeting and remembering my brother.*
>
> *That's all I will say for now. I've included my phone numbers, both work and home, and address so that you can contact me if you choose. Please don't feel pressured. I am the manager of the furniture department at the downtown Macy's. My husband, Jimmy, and I live in Englewood Estates.*

It was signed "Janelle" and, sure enough, the phone numbers and home address were included.

Ellen wiped a few Oreo crumbs from the counter and laid the letter down carefully. She looked again at the address, wondering, if this Sam had written to Heidi—now Cindy; that threw her slightly—then why was the apartment number wrong? Ellen was in 2B and Heidi-Cindy was in 1B. Peering at the number-letter combo more closely, Ellen saw that what looked like a 2 could possibly have been a fancy 1, the way it was written in the fading art of longhand. It could have been read either way, which produced yet another new idea in Ellen, bringing the total for the last twenty-four hours to a dizzying total of three. And the third new idea was this: it was almost as though fate had wanted her, Ellen, to get this letter. Her mission, however, if she chose to accept that there was one, was unclear.

Ellen looked out the window down at Heidi's apartment. The mournful wailing had stopped while she slept, but she could see Heidi-slash-Cindy slumped in a kitchen chair, her shirt pulled up over her bulbous stomach, tears dripping onto the stretched skin and dribbling down the sides, raining on what must surely be the dead Sam's baby.

Turning to the clock, she saw that it was almost six, which sent a jolt of panic into her. Could she really go to dinner with a blind girl? Or anyone, for that matter? Her life, both simple and redundant, allowed her to avoid being confronted with many choices, and now she found herself faced with two decidedly difficult decisions: whether to go meet with Temerity, and what to do with the letter. Maybe it would be better for Cindy never to read it now that she'd made up her mind to give the baby away. On the other hand, she didn't really look very happy about it. Not knowing why she cared, and unaccustomed to the phenomenon, Ellen moved restlessly around her small domicile, feeling the same desperate, trapped panic as the one time she'd been unable to escape dodgeball at school. Horrified at both the attention and almost feral cruelty on the faces of her classmates, she had curled into a ball on the ground, only to be stung by balls and taunts until the class was called in and she'd snuck, unnoticed and unmissed, to hide in the janitor's closet until the final bell.

But Temerity's confident laugh rang out suddenly in her memory and stopped her in her tracks. Ellen had a new thought, not an idea exactly, which would have brought the day's grand total to an unprecedented four, but almost.

Maybe if she made one decision, it would also solve the other. With a tremor of apprehension, Ellen mostly made up her mind to go meet Temerity. She would tell her about the letter and seek her advice on what to do with it. For the possessor of such a valiant laugh, directing a single piece of paper to its proper place—no matter the mayhem in its message—would be Twinkie cake.

5

Ellen stood outside the huge metal door of Temerity's fourth-floor walk-up and changed her mind for the tenth time. Deciding, definitively, that closed doors should stay that way, she began to slink away, feeling relief and something else, something hollow. . . .

A heavy latch grated and Ellen spun back in alarm as the door swung partially open. "Welcome to the hangar," Temerity proclaimed.

Still huffing from the climb, Ellen did not answer, focusing instead on bracing herself to run. But she didn't. In a strange stupor, perhaps brought on by oxygen deprivation, she watched herself raise a foot to step through the door, and froze, her foot suspended in midair as Temerity stood back and revealed the space beyond. Compared to her own cramped room, the loft in which Temerity lived seemed a wide-open prairie over which hawks circled in a cloudless sky, making Ellen feel like a field mouse on a platter. It was relatively free of furniture, which made sense, Ellen supposed, though the presence of a television in a seating area confused her. Maybe she just listened to it. There were large windows across the entire far side of the loft, hung with sheer white drapes, thin enough to allow the light but opaque enough to preserve the privacy of its occupant from the prying, seeing eyes of anyone in the facing apartment building across the street. Underneath those windows sat an elegant grand piano and two chairs.

"You have curtains," Ellen said lamely.

"Yep. I might not have eyes, but I have a body, and men will be boys, as I'm sure you know."

Temerity was wearing jeans and a sweater, both dark blue. Her dark hair was pulled loosely back in a ponytail and she wore no shoes, only socks; one was pink and the other green, but the thickness, Ellen supposed, was about the same. As she crossed back over to a kitchen area, separated from the rest of the loft by nothing but a graceful L of granite counters with a row of stools on the outside, Temerity called out, "Well don't just stand there, come on in. You want a glass of something?"

Ellen wondered how Temerity knew where she was, but when she started hesitantly after her hostess, stooping defensively against the imagined raptors circling above, even she could hear the squeak of her rubber soles, one muted by duct tape, against the polished wood floor. "Water, I guess."

Temerity opened a cabinet and pulled down a glass from a neatly organized row. She filled it from a purified water faucet by the sink and held it across the counter. "Come and get it!" she called. Ellen shuffled over. Reaching across, she took the glass and then sat tentatively on one of the stools facing the kitchen. The smell of Italian sausage in rich tomato sauce made her knees weak. "Sure you don't want a shot of scotch or something in there? I'm having wine."

"No, thanks," Ellen said. She had tried getting drunk once, on some sweet liquor swiped from the return bin at work. After an hour or so of feeling dizzy, she had vomited copiously while sweat seeped profusely from every pore of her body. Poisoned, she had been sure she would shrivel and die. It had not been a fun night, and she had woken the next day feeling as dehydrated as salted jerky on asphalt.

"So, Ellen, I know that you work at Costco, and that you're a major badass. But that's it. What about family? A boyfriend, husband, kids?"

"No."

Temerity pulled a pasta pot from below the counter and began to fill it with tap water, using one finger to measure the depth. "No to which? Husband? Kids? Family?"

"No . . . all," Ellen responded.

Temerity's brow furrowed. "You have no family at all?"

"Only child, orphaned."

"Oh, I'm sorry. Hold on a sec while I pull this foot out of my mouth."

Ellen was surprised at the pathos in the girl's voice. "It's okay. I don't really remember much about my mother." She stopped, then mumbled, "And what I do, I wish I could forget."

"So you grew up, where, in foster homes?"

"Mostly a group home. Until I could get out on my own when I was seventeen."

"What was that like?"

Ellen shivered. She'd worked so hard to block it out. "Not good," she finally said.

"From what I've heard about the foster care system, you're not the only one glad to leave it behind you," said Temerity.

"What about you?" Ellen asked. The interest in her own life was making breathing difficult, like a wet blanket thrown over her face.

"Oh, me." Turning her back on Ellen to face the stove, Temerity patted the counter next to it until she located a bottle of olive oil. She screwed off the top, sniffed it, and then poured a dose into the pot. She repeated the procedure with salt. "Let's see. I was born here, my parents live out in the suburbs, about an hour away. I have a brother who lives with me, and I have a dog."

At the mention of the words "brother" and "lives with," Ellen shot up from her stool.

Misinterpreting the scrape of wood against the floor, Temerity asked, "Are you afraid of dogs? You don't have to worry about Runt. He's a bah lamb, and he's not here right now, my brother took him out for a walk."

"He's . . . he's coming here? Tonight?"

Temerity put her hands on her hips. "If you're really that freaked out, we can put him in the bedroom."

"No, not the dog, the brother."

"Mmm. I *could* put my brother in the bedroom." Temerity tapped her short fingernails on the granite countertop. "But I'm not sure he would stay."

"I thought . . . thought it would just be us," Ellen sputtered, her panic rising as she plotted her escape. She could say she left her stove on, that she had to work early, that she was due to be abducted by aliens, anything.

"He lives here. Is there a problem? Is this like the restaurant thing?" She put a lid on the pot and came to stand across the counter from Ellen. "Okay, maybe you'd just better tell me what to avoid so I don't have to try to figure it out with my keen sense of observation." She snorted a little and then slid her hand across the smooth surface until she located her glass of wine marooned on the smooth stretch of granite between them. "Maybe this will help," she mumbled and took a sip.

Ellen felt strangled by her utter absence of conversational skills. "I . . . uhm, I'm not very good at talking, explaining. I . . ."

"Why not?" Temerity asked, swirling the ruby liquid and burying her nose in the wide glass to breathe in the scent.

Ellen shrugged, a lost gesture. "I guess because I don't do it very often. Well, ever, really."

Temerity looked thoughtful. "Okay, let me get this straight. You don't talk very often."

"Not usually." Ellen knew her voice sounded high and unsure. She cleared her throat, but it only made it feel tighter.

"Why not?"

The deep breath Ellen tried to take shuddered in her clenched chest.

"What was that?" Temerity demanded. "Why are you afraid?"

"I'm not," Ellen lied. "I mean, I don't really want to talk to anyone, so I don't, but that's not . . . that's not why I don't."

"Okay then." Temerity shifted impatiently from pink sock to green sock. "Come on, help me out here." She pointed to her eyes, the irises were so dark brown that it was hard to see if there were pupils there. "I can't read your expressions. You have to broadcast them. Think of it as subtitles for the deaf."

"That's just it," Ellen managed to squeak out. "*No one* can read my expressions."

"Okay. Why not?"

Ellen prepared to go, with a leaden heart. She hadn't realized how much she'd invested in this little visit. Disappointment seeped up through her feet and legs, saturating her body with a flood of heaviness. Strangely, though, she wanted, she *needed,* to tell this girl the truth. So she broadcast it. "Because no one can see me. I'm invisible." She braced herself to be asked to leave, told she was crazy, laughed at—always, she'd been laughed at.

But a strange light was stealing across the pretty girl's face. She sipped her wine again, thoughtfully, her brow twisted in concentration, as though deciphering an unfamiliar language. Finally, she spoke. "I think I understand," she said, and then with delight dribbling off of the words, she added, "How *marvelous.*"

And then she laughed, smacking her palm against the countertop as she hooted with laughter. The familiar slap of humiliation reddened Ellen's face as she turned slowly toward the door.

"Freeze!" Temerity shouted, pointing one finger at Ellen with surprising accuracy. "No way, you're not going anywhere. This is the coolest thing that's happened to me since you hobbled that parasitic worm last night, and that was so cool it was friggin' arctic. Sit your butt back down!" she ordered. Ellen sat, too stunned to disobey. "Well, that explains quite a bit, especially about last night. Right. Okay, now we have to make an important decision."

Assuming she meant the brother, who might return any moment, Ellen said, "I can just go."

"Bullshit." Temerity laughed again, and the joyful abandon in the swear word made Ellen oddly cheerful. "No, I mean, should we have penne or spaghetti?"

"Spaghetti," Ellen said, having no idea what the other one was. "Definitely spaghetti." She felt heady, dazed, surreal and, for once in her life, drawn to stay. But she was also wary, as jumpy as though she'd had too much coffee. This brother . . . She should go, she thought, but she didn't. Without thinking, she released her hair from behind her left ear and smoothed it down over her cheek.

"This is excellent." Temerity licked her lips in anticipation. "Okay, so I felt you, so you are really here. What about dogs, cats, cameras? Are you invisible to them too?"

Astonished by the candor of the question, Ellen tried to answer as honestly as possible. She thought of the cameras at work: No one had ever challenged her about any of her borrowing, so she thought not, though she was still careful. "Well, I'm not sure. I mean, I can't really remember having my picture taken."

"Not even at school?"

"I always skipped out of school photos; there wasn't anyone to buy the pictures. And anyway, I was still . . . there . . . then. People could see me, sort of."

"Mmmm. And what about animals?"

"My cat can hear me, but he never looks at me, so I think it's the same as people."

"Other people can hear you?"

"Well, yeah, if I make the effort, but it's kind of exhausting."

"Okay, so, when my brother gets here, this'll be interesting, and I'll tell you why." Temerity licked her lips again and rubbed her palms together. Ellen would have thought she was mimicking a cartoon villain, except, of course, Temerity had never seen a cartoon. "He's always been fascinated with people and how they behave. He notices more than most people. We always joke that he sees twice as much because he stole my sight in the womb. We're twins actually. His name is Justice."

"What do you mean, more than most people?" Ellen had a quick image of a person with X-ray vision and crossed her arms tightly over her chest.

"You know, some people would call it nosy—I do, anyway—but he's really just curious, no . . . 'observant' might be a better word.

Fascinated by little things, especially how people behave or react to each other. He pays attention to details and subtleties and really listens. Most people don't listen or see because they're more worried about what everyone else thinks of them, if you understand what I mean. Should we just wait and find out what happens?" She snickered with glee. "Ooh, I'd love to scare the bejesus out of him. He gets me all the time, except in the dark. I've got the advantage then. You could sneak up behind him and say something like 'Boo!'"

Ellen felt uncertain. She'd never been a prankster and she didn't really think she was built for sneaking. "I'm not sure."

"Well, you will be soon, 'cause I hear him coming!"

Ellen spun toward the door, but it remained closed and silent. She realized, too late, that Temerity's hearing would be exceptional. "But I don't want . . ." Ellen fumbled, starting to panic. And then she heard a faint scuffling, the sound of a large dog's paws on stairs. A few seconds later, keys jangled.

Ellen couldn't breathe, what if he could see her? She didn't want to be discovered or displayed. Searching frantically, she spotted another door on the far side of the open loft and, assuming it was a closet or a bathroom, something, anything that wasn't out in the open, she started clumsily for it with no thought other than to hide in darkness. The dog barked on the landing, the lock tumbled, and Ellen began to lope awkwardly, making a beeline to the escape route. Unfortunately, that line intersected the seating area, which consisted of a sofa, coffee table, and two armchairs on a large area rug. Ellen stepped on the corner of the rug and it slid across the polished floor like ice, sending her skating through thin air. She waved her arms wildly, tried to save the forward fall with a wide step, caught her second foot on the now bunched-up carpet, and went down with a thump onto the plush, woolly fabric.

Except her head, which smacked against the corner of the wooden coffee table. From Ellen's point of view it went like this: panic, flight, surprise lateral ice-skating, whoosh of air, sharp stab of pain, flash of red inside her brain, and then nothing.

Something wet and cold was pushing against Ellen's left ear, accompanied by a high whine that cut into the ache in her brow like a hot blade. With a groan, Ellen rolled to one side and looked into a dark mass of curly hair with a sloppy, pink tongue lashing in and out of it. "Runt, get away," a man's voice ordered. The dog whined, gave a last lick, and sat back on his huge haunches. The face that replaced the dog's had wide gray eyes and was surrounded by the same shining black hair as Temerity's, only shorter. They were concerned eyes, and they were looking directly at her. Ellen jerked in alarm, causing pain to pound through her head like a piston, pumping the other fears from the chamber of her brain, and she clutched at her forehead.

"Don't sit up, not yet," the man said. Behind him, Temerity stood, leaning forward, offering him a pillow from the sofa. He took the pillow and slid it under Ellen's head. Using his hand to support her neck, he eased her down onto it. "Ice pack, Tem," he said.

Temerity hurried across the floor and Ellen heard the freezer door open and close. The man brushed his hand lightly over the tender spot on Ellen's forehead, making her shudder. "That was quite a stunt. How do you feel?"

"Clumsy," Ellen said, wincing.

"You're not seeing double, are you?"

Ellen tested it out, squinting through one eye and then the other. "No, it's fine." The scrutiny and his proximity were distressing her. She closed her eyes tightly to escape, pressing her hands over her face, but she could still hear breathing all around her, the quiet,

steady exhalations of Temerity's brother, and the unrestrained panting of the shaggy mutt, Runt.

Temerity came back with the ice pack and her brother took it,
holding it gingerly against the bruise.

Ellen fumbled to relieve him of it and risked a peek. He was
turned away, looking up at his sister. "I take it this is your knight in
shining armor?"

"Ain't she great?" Temerity asked with pride. "You freaked her out
when you came in. She wasn't expecting to see you, and she wasn't
expecting you to see her either."

The gray eyes turned back to Ellen. "I'm Justice," he said gently.
"Sorry I startled you." He looked her up and down as he tried to
decipher his sister's cryptic statement discreetly, but Ellen caught
it. He thought she was embarrassed by her clothes. Ellen hadn't
bothered to improve her appearance any more than usual, why
would she? Even if Temerity knew she was there, she was blind after
all. "Please." Justice waved a hand. "We're very casual here. You
should see some of the outfits my sister comes up with."

"Like I care." Temerity snorted. "But that's not what I meant, Just.
Usually, nobody sees Ellen. She's invisible."

Justice turned back to look at Ellen with genuine interest. "I see,"
he said.

"And he really can," Temerity told Ellen with a short bark of a
laugh. "He should have been a detective. He sees things other people
don't. I told you."

"Like me," Ellen said quietly, meaning both that she was one of
those things and that she too saw things other people didn't.

"Though I suppose crashing into the coffee table might have
drawn his attention even to someone less visually challenging,"
Temerity said wryly.

"Possibly." Justice was nodding.

"Just a stab in the dark," Temerity said. "As always for me."

"Uh, can I get up now?" Ellen asked.

The siblings rushed to lever her to a sitting position and then helped to heave her to the sofa, where Ellen held the ice pack to her head and wished for a duck blind.

"Do you feel nauseous at all?" Justice asked.

Ellen shook her head—a mistake—so she held it still and it didn't ache so bad. The ice was helping a great deal. Not only was she not sick to her stomach, the heavenly smell of the pasta sauce was opening a sinkhole in her gut. She was empty and unsteady. She needed food, something to weigh her down, to anchor her to the ground.

"I'm wondering if she should go to the hospital and get an X-ray. Concussions are no joke," Justice said to his sister.

"No!" Ellen cried out in alarm.

"Okay, okay, let's just keep an eye on you for a while."

"Do you want some Advil or something?" Temerity asked.

The smell of the simmering sauce was making Ellen's stomach bubble. "No, I'll be fine once I eat something."

Temerity twirled and headed for the kitchen. "Pasta's going in!" she called over her shoulder.

Runt, the large, mop-headed mutt, inched his way closer to Ellen until his huge head was resting on the sofa next to her thigh. Through the mass of curls, Ellen could make out brown, soulful eyes. Justice sat down on the other side of her. He reached out toward her hand, but she snatched it back out of his reach.

"I was just going to take your pulse," Justice said, moving more slowly. "I'm almost a doctor—of anthropology, it's true—but I started out premed."

"Oh." Ellen allowed him to rest his fingers on the inside of her wrist. His touch was light, but it was all she could do not to rip her hand away from the unfamiliar sensation, and her pulse began to race.

"Uh, what is anthru . . . that you're studying?"

"Anthropology? It's the study of human behavior, socially and culturally as well as individually."

"Oh, I do that," Ellen said without thinking, and then reddened and stared at her lap. She held the ice pack so that it shielded her face from his view. "I mean, not at school or anything, just . . . you know, watching."

"Cool." Justice looked down at his watch. From the corner of her eye, Ellen could see his lips moving silently as he counted. She forced herself to endure the conscious burn of his touch until he took his fingers away.

"Your heart is going a little fast."

Ellen could feel the pounding in her chest. She made a fist of the hand in her lap, pressing it hard into her yielding thigh. "I'm just . . . not used to . . . attention," she mumbled.

"Not much of a social butterfly?"

"Not much," she conceded. She had always wondered about this strange expression. She'd never noticed that butterflies were especially social creatures; of course, her experience of them was limited to the occasional park sighting.

"You live alone?"

"Yeah. Well, I have a cat. Usually people don't . . . see me."

Justice nodded. "So I understand. Even though my sister neglected to tell me that." He raised his voice and directed this reproach over his shoulder at Temerity.

"Like I would know!" she shot back.

Justice studied Ellen. "Why do you think *I* can see you?"

"What Temerity said, maybe," Ellen ventured.

"You know what I think?" He regarded her seriously and she couldn't detect any mockery in his voice. "I think I can see you because my sister told me about you, and so I knew you were here."

"I guess," Ellen agreed, feeling completely baffled by the strange night, the unusual people, the unaccustomed acceptance. Nothing was normal, and she was drifting. She needed mooring, the stabilizing ballast of carbohydrates and the hull of solitude.

"Does it make a difference if you want people to see you?" Justice asked. "Can you choose?"

Ellen looked up at him hesitantly with one eye. "Kind of," she said. "I mean, if I really make the effort, talk first, you know, like when I have to buy something. Then, people don't look at me much, but they respond, usually. Not always," she said, thinking of several situations at stores or markets where she had waited to be next, to be noticed, or just to pay, for so long that she had finally given up and left. "But not if I don't want them to."

"How does that work?" he asked simply.

Ellen shrugged. "I just, you know, go fuzzy, kind of."

"Do you feel fuzzy now?" Justice asked, his brow creased with concern.

"No," Ellen said, wishing fervently that she would.

"Good. And when you go invisible, or opposite, when you go visible, can you feel it?"

"Yes, to the second one. I . . . I'm sorry, I don't know how to describe it. It just sort of happened, you know, over years."

Justice nodded. "How's the bump?"

Ellen lowered the ice pack and tested the bruise. It wasn't so bad. She opened her mouth to say *Better*, but unfortunately her stomach chose that moment to growl so loudly that Runt raised his head and looked around for the source of the noise. Ellen wanted to melt into liquid and drip down into the dark space under the sofa.

But Justice sat forward, raising both hands in delighted agreement. "Exactly what I was thinking! I'm so hungry. C'mon, Tem!" he called. "How's that pasta coming?" He beamed at Ellen and she was so taken aback that she could only sit looking at him, wondering what that expression in his eyes was. "Thank you for helping Temerity last night," he whispered. "It means more to me than you know. I worry about her."

"She seems pretty tough," Ellen said, thinking that, compared to her, Temerity was Hercules.

"'Tough' doesn't mean you don't sometimes need help," Justice said. "We all need friends."

Before she could puzzle out his meaning, Temerity called out, "Pasta's up! Come sit down."

Justice walked with Ellen to the table, he didn't try to touch her again, but she suspected he was staying near enough to catch her if she stumbled or fell. Being seen was making her feel ridiculously enormous and ungainly. She tried to fold herself into a smaller shape as they sat at the table.

The whole time they ate, the delicious flavors and bulk of al dente pasta filling the hole in her middle with satisfying heft, Ellen thought about Justice's statement, *We all need friends*, and she wondered, so hard it made her dizzy, how those words could possibly be true and she could still exist. Maybe, she thought, friends made you more solid.

But her musing was interrupted by Temerity. "So, where do you live?"

"In a studio, Morningside."

"Tough neighborhood," Justice commented, taking a swig of beer.

"I don't go out that much. Just to work, so it's not bad."

"And what do you do for fun?"

Ellen was surprised at the question. She'd never really thought about it. What did she like to do? "I keep notebooks," she said.

"Oh, you write?" Justice looked approving. "Stories?"

"Not really, just record things that I see. I like to keep track, you know." It sounded lame.

But Justice was nodding. "I *do* know," he said. "You sound like me when I was a kid. I used to spend hours watching the neighbors, or my teachers at school, and writing down all the things they did all day. I actually had a map of the schoolyard and would write down which groups of kids spent how much time where. Of course, now I know I was documenting play patterns, but my family thought I was nuts." He laughed. "I can't tell you how relieved I was to find out that there was actually a science that suited my particular obsession."

Temerity skewered some pasta, raised the fork to her mouth, and sucked in a mouthful of spaghetti, getting sauce on her chin in the process. She left it there. "Lucky jerk," she said.

"Well, you didn't do too badly either," Justice said.

"Right. I don't need vision to play. . . . Jackpot!"

"Seriously, Tem, you are as good as you are because of your ear. It's remarkable."

"Tell it to Itzhak Perlman. He's got an ear, two actually, and two good eyes."

Justice grinned at Ellen. "But Itzhak doesn't have your good looks."

Ellen was curious who the hell Itzhak was, but she was used to being left out of a conversation, so it didn't occur to her to ask.

"He's the most famous violinist in the world," Temerity explained, as though Ellen had asked. "And he is not ugly."

"Okay, fine," Justice agreed. "Let's just say he won't be modeling swimwear anytime soon. And, anyway, how do you know?" her brother taunted.

"Because no one who plays that beautifully could possibly be an unappealing human being. It's only your dependence on vision that makes you so myopic."

"Ooh, that's a good one," Justice conceded, as though she'd scored off him.

"Besides, it would be lame of me to feel superior about my appearance when I can't see it."

"You're really pretty," Ellen stated, surprised that Temerity wouldn't know that.

"I know you mean that as a compliment, so thank you. And I know that physical appearance is important, though highly overrated, in the world of the seeing. It's just not a world I participate in. And besides . . ." She swung her wineglass precariously without spilling a drop. ". . . bitching about life's challenges would be like shouting at the sea for making waves, and I guess I like the slap of salt water."

Ellen had never felt salt water, or indeed seen the ocean. From what she'd seen on TV and read about it, it just seemed . . . too big. But not for Temerity. She could picture her rushing out into it, though the very thought made her shudder.

They finished the meal and Ellen checked the time on her men's Timex. Beneath its scratched crystal, it read 8:20. She said, "I wanted to ask you something before I leave, and I should go soon."

"Not yet," Temerity said, shaking her head firmly. "You said you don't have to be at work until ten, and I wanted to play you something. Do you mind?"

Not seeing a way out, Ellen said, "I guess not." She felt trapped.

Temerity pushed her plate toward her brother. "I cooked, you clean up," she said, then turned in Ellen's direction. "What did you want to ask me?"

Unable to adequately explain the situation, she produced the letter and slid it across to Justice. "This is my address, and what looks like my apartment number too, but I didn't recognize the name on the front. I thought, well, I didn't know what to think. So I opened it. Was that okay?"

Justice read the short letter out loud while Temerity listened eagerly. Then Ellen explained about Cindy's pregnancy and the meeting with the married legal team of Newland and Newland. She ended with a short description of how Cindy cried all the time and the fact that she didn't even have a job.

"Give her the letter," Temerity said after a short deliberation. "It's her decision."

"Hold on," Justice put in. "On the one hand, the letter was meant for her, but it's from someone she didn't even know existed and it will make her decision and her right to give the baby up more difficult, I would think. If it's true that the father's family has a claim to the baby, which is what the lawyers said, right?"

"Yeah," Ellen agreed.

"That's a serious complication. I think, if the letter wasn't delivered to Cindy and she never got it, there's no moral dilemma for her as far as the deceased father is concerned. It sounds to me like she's got enough to deal with and she's made her decision."

"But we don't have any right to mess with someone else's fate," his sister argued.

Justice rolled his eyes, for Ellen's benefit, obviously. "Oh please, it happens every day, every second of every day. Fate delivered the letter to Ellen instead of Cindy. Ellen is here tonight, and maybe so are you, because she 'messed with' your fate."

"Too true," Temerity said, and finished the last swallow of her wine. "Fine, negate my argument with a single rebuttal. Okay, so don't tell Cindy about the dead father's sister, then what?"

Ellen summarized. "She gives the baby to the rich couple and it'll be better off. Right?"

"First of all, you don't know that the lawyers are richer than the sister, or that the sister would want the baby. And second, it's not necessarily true, anthropologically speaking, that money creates happiness. Often the opposite," Justice reasoned. "Statistically, provided basic needs are met, the presence of money is not an indicator of proportionate happiness. In fact, worldwide, people with lower to average incomes tend to be happier, suffer less anxiety and illness, report more satisfaction with their children, and remain in marriages longer than their wealthier counterparts. It's interesting."

"But there's the dead boy's family to consider. How would you feel if I died and you didn't know I'd left you a niece or nephew?" Temerity asked her brother.

"I'd rather you left me money."

Temerity reached over and smacked his arm with unexpected accuracy.

"Ouch! Okay, I know. I would not like that, but I'm not the one pregnant who would be stuck with a baby that represents past debilitating loss and future hardship to me."

Temerity sat back and sighed. Then she stood up and pushed in her chair. "I still say give her the letter," she said. "It's her life," she added, though with less certainty. She walked a few feet, stopped and turned back as though a boardroom full of second thoughts were clearing their throats and coughing to get her attention. "It's not really our business," she insisted, but not very convincingly.

"So you're saying," Justice asked, as he stacked the dishes, "we should never interfere in someone else's business? Isn't that like saying that we should never help anyone no matter what? Because . . . why? If it's not our business, it's not our problem? Kind of blows the hell out of the entire institution of charity, not to mention kindness and compassion. And don't forget that if Ellen here had thought that you and your admirers were none of her business, I'd be eating out tonight."

Temerity's face twisted with a mischievous smile and she flung her arms out in surrender. "Okay, fine. Do whatever you think is best. And I don't care if it's our business or not, I want to hear what happens."

Leaving Ellen alone at the table, Justice started off to the kitchen area. "Do you want coffee?" he called out.

"Um, yes, please," Ellen said, hoping for dessert too. She'd finished off two large bowls of pasta to each of their single portions, and she'd tried to eat slowly, but it had only been half of what she would normally call a fulfilling dining experience.

"None for me, Just," Temerity called back.

"I wasn't asking you," Justice said.

"Nice." Temerity snorted. Then to Ellen, she added from the side of her mouth, "Brothers, such a pain in the ass." She swung a hand at the sofa area. "I'll get my instrument. Why don't you move over there, but be careful, the rug is slippery."

Picking up the ice pack from next to her plate, Ellen pressed it back to her tender forehead. "Thanks for the heads-up," she said.

Temerity twisted back. "Funny," she said approvingly. "That was very clever, Ellen." She gave a little grunt of amusement and then went on her way across the big room. "Be right back for a short performance."

Ellen had never had someone play an instrument for her before. There was a vague memory of an out-of-tune piano in a music room at school, but she'd always associated the instrument with acute fear that she would be called on to sing. As she stuffed herself into a corner of the sofa, she tried to steady herself to endure an uncomfortable affront.

When Temerity returned, she was holding a violin in one hand and a bow in the other. Justice came out from behind the kitchen counter and set a cup of coffee on the low table in front of Ellen. On the saucer were several fat cookies. She sipped the coffee. It was light with cream, sweet with sugar, and hot. Ellen smiled. Just how she liked it.

"That okay?" Justice asked.

"Good, thanks."

Meanwhile, Temerity had placed the instrument under her chin and was tuning it by plucking at the strings and adjusting the keys. This was all Chinese to Ellen.

And when Temerity raised the bow, Ellen grasped the sofa fabric and clenched, her fingers pressing into the cushions. Temerity held the bow, poised and ready, above the instrument, Ellen cringed inwardly, pursing her mouth tightly. Temerity drew the bow bravely across the strings, Ellen's mouth dropped open.

A strain of magnificence filled the space, followed by another and another until notes danced and sustained and flickered and pulled at every exhausted emotion in Ellen. The melody struck directly through her as though her body were an open chamber that resonated with each draw of the bow. She leaned forward, trembling, watching Temerity's face, alight with intense expression, and for the first time since she could remember, she felt something. For twenty-four years Ellen had watched, listened, and documented, but never, never, never had Ellen experienced such a thing. This wasn't the flat, recorded violin music she'd heard played on the single speaker of her cheap radio. This music moved all around her and changed, tinting everything with its moody pigment, like water-colors brushed in bold strokes through the air, softening as they faded, blending and shaping, dripping down into her, taking her from melancholy to elation to longing, and back again. It went on, telling its enchanted story with a long, sustained note, the vibrato shivering through Ellen so that she trembled with it—then it faded, lingering and haunting, from the air.

Ellen exhaled, spent.

"I like that one," Justice said. "That the new piece you've been working on?"

"The Mozart, yeah," Temerity said. "What'd you think, Ellen. Did I bore you?"

"What do I think?" Ellen repeated breathlessly. She was baffled, searching for the words that might begin to express the fireworks that had exploded inside and left her tingling: that if she didn't hear this music again, she would wither and die. What she said was, "I think that I was the opposite of bored." The words were sadly inad-equate; they were puny and wrong. She hung her head.

But both Justice and Temerity were smiling broadly. Justice said, "I believe, sis, that we have witnessed the birth of an aficionado."

Though she wasn't sure what that was, Ellen could tell from his tone that it must be a good thing. "I've never heard anything like that," Ellen breathed. "I mean, I've heard music on my portable radio and on TV, which is nice, but it's so much . . . smaller that way. That was . . . alive. It's a story, isn't it?"

Temerity agreed enthusiastically. "A journey, yes, the composers write them to take the audience through an experience, to make them feel something. The good ones anyway. Most people don't get that."

Oversaturated with feelings and overloaded with stimuli, Ellen desperately needed to get away, to think and absorb—or repel—what had happened. She said her awkward good-byes and made a hasty exit.

Out on the street, she breathed deeply, closed her eyes and swayed to the strains of remembered melody.

"I got it," she whispered, tingling and excited. *Most people don't,* Temerity had said. Suddenly everything was a little brighter and more frenetic, the buzzing light at the end of the alley had a living voice, the murmur of traffic was its own conversation. They were no longer indistinct noises, absent of meaning.

Though she didn't yet understand it, somewhere in the inner distance, submerged far away in her murky, sleeping consciousness, a bell was ringing, calling her to wake up.

6

rriving less than her usual hour early meant that the women's locker room was not empty when Ellen got to work, though, of course, none of the three women already there took any notice of her as she slid in and sat in the familiar, darkest corner. A more than usually despondent Irena was slumped on the end of a bench, staring down at her hands in her lap. Two of the other cleaners, whom Ellen had nicknamed "the Crows," were hovering over her. Ellen had assigned the name of the large black birds to these two because of their habit of poking their beaks into other people's business, and their arrogant disinclination to be shooed away from any scene of emotional carnage.

Though she'd never spoken to either of them, Ellen had learned many things from listening to their conversations. They both wore the sated expressions of women who had just partaken of their daily bread, several loaves of it.

Watching them, Ellen wondered what scraps they had pecked from Irena's bony hide that had left her so depleted. The Crows were both in their fifties. Kiki, an inappropriately youthful moniker in Ellen's opinion, was tall and pale with steel-gray hair and deep jowly lines that dragged her face down around her mouth. Her crony, Rosa, was short and stocky.

As Ellen watched, Kiki patted Irena on the shoulder smugly and said, "Now, don't you feel better? You can always talk to us, you know that." But the Russian woman, beyond caring, did not acknowledge the insincere sentiment. Exchanging a knowing glance with Rosa, Kiki cocked her head and the Crows moved away, around the far side of the lockers where Ellen could hear them whispering. Ellen slid along the bench until she could see down the other side of the square block of lockers and was within earshot.

". . . poor thing," Rosa intoned in the way that people do when they are disguising their invasive behavior as concern. "What bad luck. She comes with him to a new country and he deserts her with his baby and goes back to Russia."

"Well," Kiki contributed, "I'm sorry, but if you're going to run off with a married man, you can't expect him to treat you any better than he did the last one." She gave a superior sniff.

Rosa raised an admonishing finger. "She was desperate to get out of that horrible place. He must have seemed like the answer to all her prayers. And how would she know he'd leave her and the baby?"

"Oh please." The sardonic Kiki snorted. "I'm sure it was pretty clear what kind of person he was. I saw him talking to the Boss at the company picnic and the second he was ready to leave, he gave Irena a jerk of his head and she went all pale and sweaty. I don't think I've ever seen a woman look so frightened."

Caught up in the rush of gossip, Rosa added, "Because he beats her, I'm sure of it. I told you about those bruises I saw on her arms, and remember that black eye she had about a month ago, right before he took off? Ran into a shelf, my foot!" She made a sound like a raspberry.

Kiki pursed her mouth, deepening the lines around it. "Why would she keep the baby if it's not hers? That's suspicious."

Rosa exhaled impatiently. "Because he said he's coming back for it, and she's scared of him. And I think she has reason to be. I have a niece who married a Russian man who turned out to be a criminal. She divorced him and he sent her death threats from prison, saying he would take back his child, until she moved and changed her name. It'll be the same for Irena." She nodded and sighed. "It's a tough spot."

"Irena said the real mother died," Kiki said, earning a shushing from her friend, who glanced nervously toward the corner of the lockers, on the other side of which Irena sat. Kiki leaned in and whispered, "I'll bet he killed her!" Then, jerking a long bony thumb in Irena's general direction, she said, "She's lucky he took off."

"I wouldn't call her lucky. She's stuck with someone else's baby, no husband, and no friends in a strange country where she's not welcome."

Kiki sniffed again, more subdued this time. "If it's not her baby, then it's not her problem. She should hand it over to social services." She made this statement as though suggesting that Irena should return an ill-fitting skirt to a department store.

"He told Irena he's coming back for him," Rosa repeated. "You heard what she said. Plus, if there's a dad somewhere, they can't put the kid up for adoption. They have to wait for his permission, so it's foster care for that baby." Ellen shivered involuntarily at the mention of the black hole in her past. There were good foster parents, she had heard, but she had known none.

Kiki slammed her locker and, having exhausted her interest in Irena's problems, changed subjects as easily as flipping to a new article in *People* magazine. "Did you hear about the Boss's marriage?

Oh, you'll love this. I heard . . ." The Crows began to move away, their heads still close together, and the only thing Ellen caught as they passed her was ". . . apparently, she's fed up . . . don't mess with . . ."

Ellen waited until they were gone and then she went back to her locker, only three down from where Irena was still slumped despondently. The Russian woman, of course, did not acknowledge Ellen's existence, but that was nothing unusual. As she prepared for work, Ellen watched Irena and thought that she had never seen anyone who was still alive look so dead. There seemed to be almost no animation in the thin woman's body, no hope, no will. Ellen was tempted to poke her just to see if she would move, but she didn't. After a few moments, Irena roused herself almost without seeming to engage any muscles and sort of seeped out of the locker room.

It was then that Ellen noticed Irena had left her locker open a crack. Probably the latch hadn't caught when she closed it, or maybe she had just been too weary to push it home.

Sliding down the bench, Ellen slid one finger in behind the thin metal door and swung it outward.

The contents of the locker were sparse. Ellen was not surprised to see that, since being molested, Irena had left the beat-up CD player behind. In addition there was a bottle of water, refilled so many times that the lettering had worn off the plastic, a hairbrush with half of the bristles missing, and a cheap vinyl handbag with a frayed strap. Sticking out of the top of the purse was a worn piece of paper, folded and refolded neatly into three sections. Before she realized she'd reached out for it, the paper was in Ellen's hand.

The letterhead identified it as correspondence from the desk of some small-time immigration attorney. It stated in a few curt sentences that unless she paid him in advance in full, he would not file the final paperwork to complete her case. The amount she owed for the opportunity to remain in the country was four hundred dollars.

Ellen refolded the single sheet and left it where she'd found it, careful not to close the locker all the way. Then she made her way out to begin her shift.

Checking the assignment chart, Ellen saw that she had general cleaning in books and music first, followed by the staff restrooms. After collecting her cart, she headed out onto the vast floor, the enormity of which was offset for Ellen somewhat by the segmented aisles and the high-stacked racks that rose to the ceiling, creating the illusion of smaller spaces. Open areas of the floor were crowded with displays and stacks of product, making the monolithic warehouse bearable for Ellen. It was also mandatory to never, under any circumstances, look up.

Hugging the shelving, she pushed her cart to the music section and began to dust across the tops of the stacked CD cases. One of them caught her eye. Holding the fluffy duster over it, she slid it out of the stack with her back to the aisle's camera and pocketed the item, making a mental note of the price and computing it into the amount of unpaid overtime she would spend to pay for it, then continued working her way through the section.

The memory of Temerity's playing haunted Ellen, floating in and out of her conscious thoughts, and as the first two hours of her shift went by, she found she was tuned in to the sounds around her in a different way. They were no longer just background static to be ignored. In particular, the floor-buffing machine, driven by a tiny man who had to endure the nickname of "Squirt," imposed on him by his insensitive coworkers, passed her four times as she worked. It made a high-pitched, discordant whine that made Ellen wish Temerity was there to tune it.

Near the end of the CD section, she noticed a spill on the floor that spread up under the bottom shelf. Getting down on her hands and knees, she tested it with a dry cloth, but it had already solidified to a sticky, hard mass adhered to the floor. *Time to employ the industrial stuff,* she thought. Ellen pulled out a spray bottle of toxic green liquid and liberally saturated the mess, careful not to let any of the cleanser make contact with her skin. With a sense of power, she watched the oxidizer foam and bubble as it went to work on the mystery goo. She imagined that she was dispatching an enemy. *You will not escape your fate, vile spot. You have trespassed into my domain and I will destroy you,* she thought as she watched it froth and lather. Turning her head to escape the caustic fumes, she found herself looking through an open space between the boxes, all the way into the electronics section in the next aisle.

Standing against the far shelving was the Boss, which was weird, like seeing a shark fin cut through the surface of an urban pond. The Boss never came out onto the floor unless it was to work off his anxiety on some poor employee, or when there was a problem, such as a major spill or inventory loss, and procedure demanded it. Seeing the man here alone and without spittle flying from his furious mouth onto an underling's unprotected face was highly unusual. He had his back to the merchandise and was looking furtively around him. Intrigued, Ellen sat back on her butt and watched, keeping a clean rag against her nose to filter the evil vapors, which, even from a few feet away, made her eyes water.

The Boss was a bully, and bullies, Ellen had noted again and again, were not brave. He was transparent and he was up to something. Ellen had studied his habits well enough to see that. As she watched, he fidgeted nervously and licked his lips. His eyes darted constantly, glancing repeatedly around him, as he reached into his pocket and pulled out what looked like a store receipt. He read it, checked to see that he was alone again, and then studied the locked Plexiglas case of high-end cell phones until he located what he was looking for. Taking a key from his pocket, he unlocked the case, removed a package, slipped it into a shopping bag he took from his pocket, relocked the case, and slunk away.

Ellen looked down at the boiling mess on the floor; it could wait. Leaving her cart, she stayed level with the Boss until he came to the end of the parallel aisle, then she stopped, watching while he crossed to the registers. The general manager was there, a balding man with a horseshoe of thin red hair reaching from one ear to the other, checking the day's receipts against the register totals and pulling the cash for deposit in the safe. Two checkers were not yet counted out. One was a middle-aged man and the other, a young woman, recently hired. The Boss honed in on the newbie. He approached her and produced both the receipt and the box. The words ". . . wife didn't like it . . ." floated across to Ellen's position just at the corner of the aisles. The woman checked the receipt against the product and then counted out several hundred dollars in cash, handed the bills to the Boss and tossed the cell phone into a bin marked RETURNS. The Boss folded the money and slipped it into the inside pocket of his shiny jacket with a smarmy smile.

Interesting, Ellen thought. She pulled out her notebook and recorded the incident, then returned to her station and scrubbed up the stain. The harshness of the chemicals that had attacked it left a bleached spot on the flooring, a small island of lighter but still dull gray in a sea of grime-marinated, sealed cement.

Her break came at one a.m. Caffeine and sugar being mandatory, Ellen went to the break room a few minutes early and poured a cup of coffee, filling a third of her oversized thermal mug with artificial vanilla coffee creamer. She took it into the restroom and sat in a stall to drink it, washing down a packet of Twinkies and a chocolate PowerBar with the lukewarm beverage. The safety of the small, contained area and the stimulants revived her so that, at the end of her "lunch," she was fortified enough to return to work.

Still intrigued by the Boss's dubious return policy, she chose a route back to the floor that passed the lower-management offices. This took her down a long hallway, lined on her right side by a wall of glass, behind which were a series of small, fully visible cubicles allotted to the lesser administration. The general manager and the supervising floor manager used a more spacious office in the front of the store. Most of the lights were off at this hour, the occupants of these hamster cages being supervisors of the diurnal variety, and the dark glass reflected the blank wall on Ellen's left. But in the lone illuminated office, the Boss was seated at his desk, looking over paperwork that she recognized as time sheets. As she hurried past, he patted his jacket's bulging breast pocket as though to reassure himself.

At the end of the hallway, just inside the door, which opened into the freezer section in the back of the store, the thermostat for those offices was mounted on the wall. Ellen stopped in front of it and glanced back down the deserted hall.

Reaching out a tentative finger, she tested the electronic panel. It lit up when she touched the button. Ten seconds later, she was on the floor in frozen foods.

Irena, Rosa and Kiki were all busy scrubbing down the glass fronts of the wall of freezers. Ellen went back to work, but kept an eye on Irena's location. The droning floor buffer was still making its way through the aisles, Squirt at the wheel. After half an hour, Ellen went into the food section and located the fifty-gallon vats of cooking oil stacked three high. These large, impossible-to-steal items were always placed in the cameras' dead zones. She could hear the off-key whine of Squirt and his machine coming down the next aisle. With a grunting effort, she tipped the uppermost two vats onto their sides and popped off the tops. With a thick *glug-glug* the sickly yellow liquid began to run over the floor, spreading into a large, slippery pool. She could hear the buffer begin to make the wide turn into her lane, so she hurried off in the opposite direction and made her way back to the freezer section. Pulling a cloth from her apron pocket, she began to polish the glass doors, keeping an eye on the exit to the offices.

The shouts started within seconds. Accusations were made, walkie-talkies crackled, and then—as she had known he must be for a loss of over fifty dollars—the Boss was summoned.

He flew out of the door from the back, shouting obscenities, dispensing blame and vowing that heads would roll. He spotted Irena and Rosa and shouted, "You two, come with me! Bring your mops, hurry up!"

Red in the face, he was in his shirtsleeves, tieless, and his collar was unbuttoned. There were telltale half circles of dampness under his armpits.

Before the access door completely closed behind the Boss, Ellen slipped through it and hustled back along the row of offices, her inner thighs hot with the friction of rapid chafing. The Boss had left his own door ajar in his haste to verbally abuse his staff, and his jacket was hung on the back of his chair along with his tie.

It was muggy in the tiny room, not surprising, as Ellen had set the thermostat to eighty-nine. Feeling a sweat break on her back, she searched the jacket pockets and quickly came up with the wad of cash she had seen the Boss scam a few hours before. She stuffed it into her fanny pack, retraced her steps down the hallway, reset the thermostat to seventy-four and slipped back onto the floor. Squirt was emphatically denying the Boss's accusation of a collision with the vegetable oil, in profile to avoid the flying specks of spittle. Irena and Rosa mopped furiously. With a grunt of satisfaction, Ellen retrieved her cart and pushed it through the break room. She left it in there and took only what she needed to clean the staff restrooms.

She was scrubbing the stench of sticky urine off the base of a toilet in the men's stalls when she heard the door swing open. She stood stock-still. Heavy footsteps clumped in and then ceased. The Boss called out, "Anyone in here?" To which Ellen gave no reply. Then the Boss started swearing, a loud crash informed her that he had smashed his fist into the metal towel holder and it had most likely been permanently reshaped. A few more inventively profane expletives peppered the atmosphere, and then he left.

Unhurriedly, Ellen finished the stalls, rinsed the sinks and mopped the floor. She even polished the dented towel holder. Then she did the same in the ladies' restroom, though the towel holder was less concave there.

Shortly before the end of the shift, when she knew from experience it would still be empty, Ellen made her way to the locker room. Irena's locker was as she had left it. Opening it, Ellen took out her Tinkerbell pen and wrote a few words on the back of the lawyer's greedy letter, replaced it, and closed the locker, making sure that this time the catch was fast. Tired in a weird and completely unprecedented way, she went back to work.

When the shift ended at dawn, Irena Medvedkov dragged her exhausted body to her locker, knowing that her day would be almost as sleepless as her night after she retrieved the five-month-old boy from her resentful neighbor who kept him and gave him a bottle at midnight for twenty dollars cash but refused to change a diaper. She dialed the combination, lifted the latch on her locker and sat looking at the unexpected additional contents without comprehension.

Propped up against the battered CD player was a brand-new disc of Mozart, and leaned against her purse was the lawyer's letter. Inexplicably folded inside was over five hundred dollars in cash. Scrawled on the back third of the letter facing front were the words "Sometimes you can rely on the kindness of strangers, but most of them are bastards. Welcome to America."

7

The phone was ringing when Ellen reached her front door. Letting herself in, she stood gazing at it. It was still ringing, and she was mystified as to why that might be. Occasionally, she received sales calls from computers who didn't know her any better, but those usually came in the early evening. Ellen didn't have an answering machine, so she picked up the receiver and listened for the clicking static of a computer connecting to a prerecorded pitch. But all she heard was a muffled barking, and then, "Runt, hush! No bark, you shaggy mutt! Ellen? Ellen? I didn't hear a beep, was there a beep?"

"Temerity?" Ellen was dumbfounded. "How did you get this number?"

"It's on my phone, dummy. Welcome to the third millennium. Well, the third millennium if you count from when that guy got nailed to a board for suggesting that we should be nice to each other."

"Oh." Neither this highly technical information nor the historical reference computed to Ellen, but then an unfamiliar rush of pleasure at the unexpected call had left her slightly dizzy and she didn't care. "What's, uh . . . going on?"

"So, listen," Temerity said as though Ellen hadn't spoken, "I was thinking about that letter thing. Did you give it to the Cindy girl yet?"

"Um, no. I just got home from work."

"Right. Okay, here's what I think: we should definitely check out the sister before we decide whether or not to put it on Cindy's plate. Right? I mean, that was Justice's whole argument—we don't know if Auntie Janelle would make life better or worse for your buddy."

Ellen looked at the receiver and then held it back to her ear. Temerity had said "we" as though the pronoun were nothing unusual. And as for Cindy Carpenter being her buddy, or anyone . . . "Well," she said, for lack of a coherent thought.

"No, really. Justice might be right, fate put that letter in your hands for a reason, which gives you a responsibility to see it through. I mean, you've got the sister's address . . . what if she's some drug addict or psychopath? We don't want to dump some needy psycho on the pregnant one. But if she's cool, maybe she could help out Cindy chick, even if Cindy chick still chooses to give baby chicklet away. Given your particular, shall we say, *transparent* talent, I'd say it's a no-brainer."

Temerity's words were almost washed out by the resounding whoosh sweeping through Ellen's brain. It took her a moment to realize that the sound was caused by blood shooting through her body from her pounding heart. Fighting for time, she said, "Maybe, but what would we say?" On top of her initial panic, Ellen felt hysterical paralysis begin to set in at the idea of deliberately speaking to someone other than Temerity, who couldn't see her anyway.

"We won't say anything," Temerity said. "We're spying on her."

"Oh," said Ellen. That sounded more reasonable. Nobody would have to see her. Then she had a thought. "But you can't see."

"What?" Temerity shrieked. "Oh my God, I'm bl-i-i-ind!" She

drew out the word, giving it a strong, melodramatic vibrato. Ellen almost dropped the phone, and then Temerity said quite calmly, "Yeah, I know I can't see. You do the watching, you tell me what happens. I come along as a diversion, and for the sheer entertainment value for which I am well known. I can get close enough to listen. I mean, who the hell would suspect me of spying? It's really kind of great. We'll work it out. I'll find a way. That's a little something I've been doing since, well, since the day I was born, so I'm pretty decent at it." There was a muffled bump and a garbled curse, as though Temerity had dropped the phone. A few seconds of scrambling and then Temerity said, "Ouch. Stupid blindness."

"You're interested in other people's stories too, aren't you?" Ellen asked in all seriousness, hoping for confirmation that it wasn't only her.

"What else is there?" Temerity said with a rolling laugh. "I mean, when you get down to it, how we live our lives is really us writing our own stories about ourselves. Music is stories, lives are stories, hell, stories are stories. How soon can you get here? Or would you rather we started from your house?"

The possibility of Temerity coming to her house felt like a staple gun to her chest. To distract Temerity from that mortifying suggestion, Ellen asked, "What does Justice think about this idea?"

"Justice, smustice. We're going solo on this one. Well, duo, anyway. You up for it?"

Ellen thought about it. Spying might be okay; it was kind of what she did anyway, though with the variation that they would go looking for someone instead of just observing what came up. She wouldn't have to relate to anyone except for Temerity, and, so far anyway, that had been not so bad. Gritting her teeth, she forced herself to respond.

"Uh . . . okay. But I need to sleep first. How about if I come over at about three and we'll head out."

"Brilliant!" Temerity enthused. "Tell you what, I'll meet you at the bus stop. We'll go check her out at work. Hope she's there today. If not, maybe we'll just buy a couple of sofas. Until three!"

She hung up, and Ellen was left with the perplexed thought, *How would we get even one sofa home?* The very idea of it wore her out. Ellen decided that this outing would definitely require snacks.

Before she made breakfast, Ellen went to the back window to check on her pets. To her amazement, T-bone was seated on his back stoop. She wasn't sure she'd ever seen him up this early, but the more likely explanation was that he hadn't gone to bed yet. He had a cigarette in one hand and a large paper cup of coffee from the 7-Eleven in the other. He was beckoning to the small, suspicious dog belonging to the woman who lived below Ellen. The old dog would take a few wooden steps toward him, stop and bark a few yaps, then move a few steps closer, bark, repeat. Eventually, the ratty little thing came within arm's reach and T-bone propped the cigarette between his thin lips and stretched out a hand to scratch him behind the ears. The dog leaned into his hand with obvious pleasure, his stumpy tail wagging fast enough to propel him through shallow water. Ellen could hear T-bone talking to the ancient, bony little creature. Cooing with surprising affection in his smoke-roughened voice, he crooned, "Good little doggy. You're a handsome little guy. Good boy." Then the dog's mistress called him back, and reluctantly the tiny mutt turned for home. Left alone, T-bone too retreated inside.

Heidi—*no, Cindy,* Ellen corrected herself—was sitting in her kitchen, flipping through a magazine. She closed it and dropped it listlessly on the tiny table, then stared out at the dead gravel, one hand propping her head up, her face drawn and absent.

Pulling the binoculars from their hook, Ellen focused in on the periodical. Above a picture of a grinning, blue-eyed infant was printed the title of the magazine, *American Baby*. Ellen wrote down her observations, made herself a breakfast of three grape jelly sandwiches, and went to bed thinking that if Cindy were going to get through this adoption without it resulting in her suicide, she should switch to one of those, in Ellen's opinion, ridiculous girly magazines that flaunted Barbie-doll bodies and the application of makeup. Something like *Cosmopolitan*. Ellen fell asleep and dreamed of a fluffy baby chick with braids wearing little wooden shoes.

When she woke up, she went first to the kitchen window. Cindy was gone, but T-bone was back on his stoop, smoking a large joint this time, the herbal tang of the weed rising up through the courtyard. Ellen liked the earthy aroma of marijuana. Its exotic spice faded with a delicious whisper, unlike cigarette smoke, which left a rancid, stale stench on everything it touched and reminded Ellen of her unsavory past, houses and apartments saturated with tobacco stench and the inescapable, unceasing din of brain-dead television. Though it was chilly, the sun was shining and T-bone had his sleeves rolled up. Ellen could see the tattoos on his forearms, colorful, complicated images that she had studied through the binoculars many times. A snake encircled one arm, the fangs from its hissing open mouth reaching across the top of his hand, and the other was a hodgepodge of women with cartoon bodies, skulls, and motorcycles.

As she watched, two young men, who, if they weren't gang members, desperately wanted to be, came down the side alley and entered the tiny courtyard. T-bone stood up and a brief, wary greeting took place. T-bone received a small brown paper bag and took it inside.

While he was gone, the two young punks stood shifting and glancing sharply around, the classic demeanor assumed by the guilty trying to pretend they were neither nervous nor up to something they shouldn't be. They both had heads shaved to no more than shadow hairlines and multiple piercings that looked painful to Ellen through the binoculars' lenses. The taller of the Hispanic pair had a rod through his eyebrow, and even from this distance Ellen could see the raw red of the insertion point, as though it were done at home and had become infected. The second one, a little younger with paler skin and almost Asian features, had a pattern of scarring that circled his wrist: triangles burned into his skin. Obviously it had been done on purpose, a more brutal version of marking one's body than tattooing or piercing. Ellen wondered what would induce someone to willingly suffer that kind of pain. She'd given serious consideration as to why people did these things to themselves and had come to no conclusion. In a minute, T-bone returned with a larger brown paper sack and gave it to the two young men, who hurried away. A pretty run-of-the-mill transaction for the small-time dealer, who sometimes repeated this exchange or some version of it a dozen times in an evening. Ellen would have liked to stay and watch the parade, but she saw from a glance at the little clock that she needed to get going. Her nervousness about meeting Temerity again made her eat more enthusiastically than usual, and as she chewed, she watched her bed in the corner. She could get back in it, take a sandwich even, and pretend the blind girl had never happened. Comfort and sanctuary beckoned, but she felt oddly restless, too distracted to ignore Temerity's summons. So she dressed and hurried to the bus stop.

She prepared to get off at Temerity's stop by standing and moving to the double exit doors. But when the doors opened, she found herself blocked by the girl in person. Temerity felt for the opening,

was far more fearful of personal contact with cabdrivers. "No, it's okay."

Temerity smiled. "I wonder what she'll be like."

Automatically, Ellen shrugged, and this time, since their shoulders were lightly touching, it wasn't wasted on the blind girl.

"I know, right?" Temerity said. "We have no idea, that's why we're doing this. So, any news about Cindy?" Her voice was eager and interested, but it lacked the predatory lust of the Crows' intrusive meddling. Instead, there was real concern in it.

"Just that she was looking at a baby magazine this morning."

Temerity whistled a long, descending note. "So . . . she isn't quite as copacetic with this adoption as she might pretend."

Ellen wondered whether to ask what "copacetic" meant—she didn't remember coming across it in any of her reading but deduced that it must mean some form of "okay." "No. She cries all the time, and I mean *all* the time. And the other day, after the Newlands left, she made this sound." Ellen thought about how to describe the audible pain: "Like wind through dead tree branches. Really"—she searched for that word she'd read somewhere that seemed right and found it—"desolate."

"Keening," Temerity said with decision. "It's called keening, and it's something people usually only do when someone they really love dies." Her voice's resonance thinned as she said this, as though it were a sound to be envious of, instead of hard to hear.

"That's what I thought," Ellen said. Then, because there wasn't much more to say on the other subject, she asked a question because she'd been curious. "Why don't you take Runt with you when you go out?"

Temerity threw her head back and laughed so loudly that several heads turned, mouths tightened in skeptical suspicion, then, detecting no threat, the mouths relaxed and the heads dismissed the outburst. "Runt's a few paw lengths short of a service dog. Love him to death, but he's not the brightest canine in the kennel. A well-trained Labrador would help me find the right bus—Runt would drag me to my death chasing it."

"Why does he chase buses?" Ellen asked.

"I don't know. But Justice said he almost caught one once."

Ellen wondered what he would have done with it if he had. She had a momentary image of the huge black shaggy head with a bus hanging limp and wounded from its jaws. "What kind of dog is he?" Ellen asked. Not that she would know one type from another.

"Giant schnauzer. Or a big chunk of him is anyway. He came from the pound, so his heritage is a bit dubious."

Like me, thought Ellen. *Dubious heritage, and from a kind of pound.* She was surprised that it had never occurred to her before that the foster care system was similar to a no-kill animal shelter, unwanted pets hoping endlessly for an adoption that would likely never come. "Oh," was all she could think to say.

"And you have a cat, you said?" Temerity asked.

"Yeah, Mouse."

"Great name for a cat." Temerity grinned. "Why did you pick that?"

"Because he just came in my house through a broken window and started eating a plate of hash I had left on the counter, and when I tried to get rid of him, he kept coming back, like a rodent. So finally I just got him some food and a bowl, and now he won't leave. I almost named him Pest."

Temerity chuckled. "You're funny, Ellen. I like your sense of humor."

This gave Ellen pause because she'd never thought she had a sense of humor. She realized now, though, that even if she did, she hadn't really had the opportunity to find out. Humor for one has its limits. "Our transfer is coming up," she said, and then tested the new theory. "Next stop, ottomans and recliners."

"Listen to you!" Temerity said, jabbing her again in the ribs. "You're a regular stand-up comic. We should get you an agent."

"Oh, no, thank you," Ellen said gravely, and for some reason that made Temerity laugh harder.

They switched buses, and it was only a short ride to the mall. When they got out, Temerity reached out and took Ellen's arm. "Okay, let's go," she said, folding her stick.

The strangeness of not only walking with another but of having that person rely on her had Ellen in a sweat of anxiety, but it was so second nature to Temerity that by the time they had entered the warmth of the shopping megalith, Ellen wasn't exactly comfortable but she had gotten used to her discomfort. They found the store and made their way to the furniture department.

Then came the problem of identifying the sister. This was something they hadn't considered, and they hovered near the lamps discussing it.

"We can't ask for her by name," Temerity said. "I mean, how would that sound? 'Hi, are you Janelle? We intercepted a deeply personal letter you wrote to someone else, read it, and now we've come to intrude on your private life'?"

"Not good," Ellen agreed, more for her personal reasons than the dubious propriety of the thing.

"Downright stalker. But we could ask to speak to the manager, if we had a good excuse."

Ellen had never bought anything from a department store in her life. Just being there was as unfamiliar to her as space travel, and she could never have done it without Temerity beside her. The furniture she possessed had come with the sad apartment or been discarded on the street close enough to her house for her to carry it up herself. There was a secondhand store not far from her apartment where she had, on occasion, bought a necessary pot or lamp, but it was a depressed, crowded place and the people who worked there were so used up that there was nothing left for banter with the barely civilized clientele, so she could slink in and out unnoticed. Thinking of an excuse to speak to the manager in this fancy retail palace was beyond her realm of experience or courage.

"I know," Temerity said suddenly, startling Ellen out of her apprehensive stupor, "I'll say I'm in the market for a rug or some such, and I need someone to help me. Then I can ask for a handicapped discount and that's sure to bring the manager. Nobody wants to tell a blind chick she has to pay full price. I have no idea why. Thoughts on that?"

Not wanting to say that they probably felt sorry for her, because the entire idea of feeling sorry for this exceptional person was frankly asinine, Ellen just mumbled a negative.

"Just point me in the right direction." Temerity prepped for the mission by unfolding her stick. "You go sit down somewhere and watch carefully. I need you to tell me what you see. Okay?"

Ellen was fully amenable to any plan that removed her from the action at the front. There was one thing she knew about Sam's sister, but it wasn't something that would help Temerity, so she turned the girl in the direction of the sales desk and went to sit on the corner of a coffee table in the "as-is" discount section that was partially hidden by a support post.

Temerity clicked along until she came to the sales counter. There was no one there, but a man seated at a design desk noticed her and rose, coming forward with a big smile. When he spotted the stick, the smile sort of froze, drooped, and then seemed to give up, as if it were thinking, *What's the point?*

"May I help you?" he asked.

"Maybe," Temerity said brightly. "I'm looking for a rug, and as much as I'd like to pick it by softness, my brother, who lives with me, might be upset if I come home with something that jars his delicate sensibilities."

"I see," said the man, and then realized his faux pas. "I mean, of course I can help you." He repeatedly stole looks at Temerity's well-shaped chest. Then it apparently occurred to him that there was no need for subtlety, so he went ahead and leered. There was a smirk on his face that Ellen would like to have wiped off with a stout two-by-four. "What size rug are you looking for?"

"Big, really, really big." Temerity screwed up her face. "I live in a loft. And here's the thing"—she leaned in and stage-whispered—"I'll be needing the handicapped discount."

"The . . . what?" The salesman was so surprised that his eyes rebounded up from Temerity's breasts to her face.

"You know, I get most stuff for half off. That's not a problem, is it?" She assumed, quite suddenly, a vulnerable and lost expression. Ellen was impressed.

"I'm not sure we have that policy here at Macy's," he said, clearly flustered. "I'll have to ask my manager."

"Great, you do that, and if you could show me the rugs, I'll let my fingers do some walking."

The man touched her arm and directed her awkwardly to the rugs, then hurried away toward a door in the back.

Ellen shifted her position to get a better perspective. Temerity was now by a huge rack of suspended carpets that swung, fanlike, so that customers could consider each one with a minimum of effort. She was running her hands over each as she flipped through them like a vertical Rolodex.

From the back came a striking woman in her early thirties. *That's her,* Ellen thought, recognizing her immediately as Sam's sister. Ellen had watched Sam and Cindy together in Cindy's apartment for many long happy hours. Like her brother's, the sister's skin was black, luxuriously dark, rich and saturated. Her hair was plaited into tiny, long braids that had been twisted up on top of her head. She was tall, like the brother, and slim, but unlike him, she walked with a limp, a slight up-and-down addition to her forward gait, which was still remarkably smooth, and Ellen realized that one leg was shorter than the other. She wondered if the quirk was the result of an accident or an accident of birth. Either way, it added a rhythm to her stride that Ellen admired.

"Hello, I'm Janelle. May I help you?" she asked, looking directly at Temerity with the same respect Ellen felt sure she would give any person, seeing or non.

"Oh, hi." Temerity stuck out her hand. "Yes, I'm looking for a rug, but I need a little help, as you can see, because I can't." She laughed. "That just never gets old."

"My salesman told me you were asking for a discount?" Janelle said smoothly without even a paprika sprinkling of patronizing.

"Well, sometimes I get one. It seems only fair. You make this stuff so that it looks good, right? I mean, contemporary design and whatnot?"

"Contemporary and traditional. We keep a wide selection in stock."

"But I can't appreciate that aspect, so, it being lost on me, I don't really like to pay for it."

Janelle studied her for a moment and then broke into a grin. "I understand. That seems reasonable, but our rugs are also designed for function and comfort. I assume you can appreciate those things."

"Oh, heck yeah," Temerity agreed. "I'm all about cozy."

"Well, let's see if we can set you up with something that will work for you. Do you live in the area?"

"No, I live in midtown, but I heard you had good deals here."

"That we do. Maybe if you give me your price range, we can start there. I don't have a specific discount for what you are describing—maybe we should, I'll bring it up at the next corporate meeting—but in the meantime, we have several nice pieces on clearance that might suit the situation perfectly."

"You mean they're cheap because they're ugly and no one else wanted them?"

Janelle laughed out loud now. "Some of them *are* pretty ugly. Don't tell my boss I said that. But I wouldn't sell you one of those. There are several that are terrific, just been here long enough to have been discounted. Besides," she lowered her voice, "you'd be surprised what some people consider stylish. We'll get a piece in and I'll think, 'That's the tackiest thing I've ever seen.' And sure enough, it'll sell like hotcakes."

"I'm sure I would be horrified," Temerity agreed warmly. "Not that I know from tacky, unless it's the sticky kind, but I've heard a good bit about it. That's one of the advantages of being blind—ugliness doesn't offend." She sighed loudly. "I guess that's why my dreams of becoming a graffiti artist were never realized."

"A great loss to the metropolitan area, I'm sure," Janelle said, matching her humor.

"Fortunately, I've been luckier in my pursuit to become an air traffic controller."

Janelle laughed out loud at that.

"I like you," Temerity announced. "Listen, maybe it's better if I come back another day and bring my brother in with me. He's one of those seeing people, and sometimes he gets persnickety if I bring home some objet d'art that jars the functioning retinae. I just happened to be here and thought I would stop in. Would it be all right if I asked for you?"

"Please do," Janelle said. "Let me give you one of my cards. Sorry it's not in Braille—I'll bring that up to corporate as well—but it should work for your brother's retinae."

Temerity held her hand out flat and Janelle placed the card in it. "Thanks," Temerity said, pocketing the card. "You've been more helpful than you know, and I mean that. It's nice to meet someone who doesn't feel sorry for me." Ellen smiled. So Temerity did know why people acted differently around her, and that it was stupid.

Ellen watched Janelle's mouth twist slightly into a wry smile, but there was no mockery in it. "Why would I do that? You seem like you have more going for you than most. And remember, everyone has strong points and weaknesses."

"What are yours?" Temerity asked bluntly.

Janelle looked taken aback but recovered quickly and seemed to seriously consider the question before she answered. "For strengths, family and faith that good will prevail." Her eyes clouded and a shadow passed over her face, but it was quickly dismissed. "And for weakness, I'd have to say . . . mobility."

"So you're more the turtle than the hare."

"You know what they say, slow and steady wins the race."

"Good thing too!" Temerity exclaimed. "'Cause I can run like the wind, but solid objects happen." They both laughed, said good-bye, and Temerity reversed her way back toward Ellen, who slipped up beside her in the mattress section.

"How'd she look?" Temerity asked.

"Good, she seemed nice." Ellen paused and then added, "Strong, if you know what I mean."

"I do. You mean strong enough to lend strength to someone else." She sighed. "Not everyone is, you know. I like her," Temerity said with finality, and Ellen could not disagree. "I say we pass on the letter. How about you?"

Like a hamster in a clear ball, Ellen preferred to be protected and distanced from the world around her as she rolled steadily along, and she wasn't sure she wanted it to matter what she thought. But Temerity had been the kick that sent her spinning, and, even as dizzy as she was, Ellen knew that Temerity was right, and she instinctively liked Janelle.

"Okay," she breathed, and with an effort she started forward in her little plastic shell, only now, Temerity was along for the ride.

Or maybe, and Ellen suspected that this was more likely, it was the other way around.

8

Temerity insisted on coming along to give Cindy the letter. This was the equivalent of injecting a massive overdose of concentrated liquid panic directly into Ellen's aortic compound. Alarms sounded and defense teams rushed about, arming themselves with riot gear while heavy metal doors slammed shut, sealing off the perimeter, but the heart palpitations subsided somewhat when Ellen realized that Temerity wouldn't actually see her apartment. The thought of another human in the sanctity of her safe house required her to remain on high alert, but the security rating downgraded to code yellow. *Repeat, code yellow, this is not a drill.* Ellen gritted her teeth and told herself it wouldn't be long until the breach was closed and she could rearm the force fields.

As she opened the door, Ellen took a self-conscious look around, noticing acutely the musty odor of the closed-in space and the constant din from the nearby busy intersection. She squirmed, realizing that Temerity's heightened senses must certainly be experiencing a full-frontal assault verging on violation equal to her own. She barely noticed the noise or the smell anymore, but imagining the jarring decibels through Temerity's sensitive ears and the vague but persistent putrid smell of discarded garbage from the street made her cringe with shame.

"This it? I love what you've done with the place!" Temerity gushed as she crossed the threshold. "Fabulous!"

Ellen stopped and looked at her. "Really?"

"It's cozy, and you know me, I'm all about cozy."

"How do you know?"

"I can tell from the way my voice bounces that this first room is small."

Ellen blushed. "It's only one room. Well, and a sort of kitchen."

"And that's all anybody really needs," Temerity declared. "A girly den, I like it. So, show me where you watch the fun?"

After checking to make sure that the floor was clear through to the back window, Ellen told Temerity to just walk straight. She tapped her way to the back, felt the lay of the land and, finding the slatted window on the door, she cranked it open a bit and listened to the muffled music coming from across the small space.

"Is that Guns N' Roses coming from her apartment?" Temerity asked.

"No, that's music and marijuana," Ellen told her as she came up behind her. "It's coming from the guy who lives next to her." The man himself was sitting in his easy chair, a joint in one hand and a beer in the other. With his dirty, torn jeans and greasy hair falling into his gaunt face, he vaguely resembled a degenerate Raggedy Andy doll.

"He smokes some good weed," Temerity commented, sniffing at the aroma rising from below without apparent judgment. "Not that I'm an expert."

"He sells it," Ellen told her. "Have you . . . tried it?" she asked, curious.

"Oh yeah, couple of times. Well, a few times. Several. Okay, not more than once a week. Justice loves the stuff, but only when he's got nothing else to do. You should hear him go off about its cultural significance. It's great for relaxing, but I wouldn't want to have to function on it."

"I thought most musicians, uh, did drugs," Ellen said.

"Good lord, no," Temerity said. It's not mandatory, unless they play jazz and dubstep."

A large thump told them that Mouse had risen from his holding spot on the sofa and impacted the floor. He meowed loudly.

"Ah, the Mouse," Temerity said. Squatting down, she held out her hand and made a little kissing noise repeatedly. To Ellen's surprise, the cat trotted over, stomach fat flopping from side to side as he came. He thrust his giant head against Temerity's fingers and was soon purring loudly as she scratched the backs of his ear and a half.

Ellen watched this unlikely scene as though it were sideways. This was the first time she'd had another person in her apartment and it made the familiar seem foreign. In a moment of clarity she saw her cramped room as a larger version of the closets where she had taken refuge as a child, reading in the light coming from the crack under the door. Then she thought of Temerity's wide-open loft; it was a space big enough to hold the hugeness of the music she made and the life she lived. Temerity needed space to soar—some people did, she guessed. Then Ellen realized that she had just thought of someone as a friend, and all at once the space in which she lived seemed a size too small. Too tight to hold Temerity's bulging energy, so that Ellen, for the first time, wished it were larger.

There was a noise from the courtyard and Ellen sidled past Temerity and Mouse, a tight squeeze in the narrow kitchen space, to look out through the slats, down into the dark courtyard. Through

T-bone's window she could see him get up from his threadbare easy chair and stand swaying in the middle of the room. The sound came again, and Ellen could see the silhouette of a man standing in the dark outside his back door, knocking urgently. The fixture over the door, originally intended to light up the landing, had been knocked askew and the small, feeble circle of light it threw was like a dying flashlight beam focused on the door's small window. The man lifted his hand into the forty-watt glow to knock again, and Ellen clearly saw the diamond pattern of scars encircling the wrist where it extended from his jacket sleeve.

"Who is it?" she heard T-bone shout above the music, but she could not make out the response. He turned down the volume and moved slowly to the door, leaving Ellen's eyeline of him through the window.

"What going on?" Temerity asked. She had left off scratching Mouse, who now circled her ankles hopefully, and was standing just behind Ellen.

"It's the guy next to Cindy. I call him T-bone. Somebody is at his door," Ellen told her.

"Oh, company."

"More likely a customer."

Temerity shifted from side to side, swaying for what looked like the sheer pleasure of the movement. "You've got a good view of these people?"

"Well, there's not much else to look at from here." Ellen felt slightly embarrassed.

"Okay, give me the basic layout."

So Ellen explained. Five of the studio units had back doors that faced the courtyard of the U-shaped building. This central space might, in another, less paranoid age, have been meant as a small garden, but building and safety had nixed that long before Ellen's arrival, requiring its use as a fire escape access. The awkwardly placed wooden stairs to each back door had clearly not been part of the original design. A narrow alley ran the length of the block along the rear of the building where the courtyard's crumbling gravel spilled onto its cracked asphalt. The woman's door below her, in the apartment with matching curtains, she could not see. The upstairs apartment directly across from hers had blocked the windows. Ellen was the only one on her side on top. On what was the front of the building, to her right, only one apartment, the lower one, accessed the courtyard, and that was occupied by a shut-in who was visited by health-care workers twice a week. Ellen called him Badger. But other than "Badger gets a sponge bath from the nurse," she had very little to report about him in her chronicles. He never went out.

"Anyway," Ellen concluded, "it's hard not to see T-bone and Cindy, and it's not like I bother them. They don't even know I'm here. I don't interfere." She thought of the letter in her bag. "Well, I mean, I never have before, but you know, I mean, I didn't ask for that letter."

"Speaking of," Temerity said. "What are we going to do? Are you going to take it down there and give it to her?"

"Me?" The panic in Ellen's voice made it squeaky. "No, no, I was thinking I'd maybe leave it in her mailbox when she goes out or something."

Temerity shook her head ruefully. "I'm sorry, that won't do. You'll need to think again."

"What?"

"Ellen, seriously. Are we delivering dry cleaner flyers or possibly doing something that could help this woman change her life and her luck?" Temerity asked. "We want to see what happens when she reads it, right? Plus, you said she almost never goes out now. So, tell you what. How about if *we* take it down there? We can leave it on the stoop, then knock and run away." Her face screwed up thoughtfully. "Well, maybe not run exactly, but we could sort of speed walk."

Ellen was shaking her head forcefully, though it was another lost gesture. She said, "I can't do that."

"Go down there, speed walk, or knock on the door?"

"Both—I mean, uh, all of them."

"Why not?"

"I just . . . I could never."

"Like you could never stop a purse snatcher?" Temerity clicked her tongue impatiently. "You clocked that scumbag! Never could knock on a door, my butt. I'm not saying you should hang around after we do it, just ring and run."

Ellen said nothing.

Temerity hummed dubiously and seemed to be thinking it through. "Okay, fine. No running, no knocking. Let's compromise," she said. "Where is she now?"

Ellen checked. She couldn't see Cindy through the window, but the lights on the far side of the main room were on and she thought she saw the blue flicker of the television screen across the darker kitchen floor. "I think she's watching TV," Ellen said.

"Perfect. Okay, we go down, slip the envelope under her back door, maybe you write on it, something like, 'Sorry, this was delivered to the wrong apartment by mistake.' Then we come back up here and wait for her to get herself a snack and find it. It'll take, like, one minute."

"I guess we could do that," Ellen said, though without Temerity, it was a minute she wouldn't have considered in a thousand years. The word "snack" made Ellen's stomach clench and gurgle. To distract herself, she watched out the window. T-bone finally opened the door. The nervous man bumped fists with him, glanced back at the deserted courtyard, and was admitted.

"Is it all clear?" Temerity asked, having heard the door open and close.

"Yeah."

"Okay, get the letter."

Ellen did as Temerity directed her, in a kind of stupor. Her back door had never been opened, not as long as Ellen had been there anyway, and when they tried, it stuck so tightly that they decided to go out the front and around the building. In two minutes they were creeping slowly down her front stairs, Ellen leading and Temerity behind with one hand clamped onto Ellen's shoulder. To her mild surprise, the undertaking of what, to Ellen, was an inconceivable action, unfolded without the world bursting in a fiery apocalypse. In fact, it was disconcertingly chilly.

They had just reached the sidewalk and started toward the back alley when Temerity raised her head sharply and her fingers tightened. "What was that?" she asked.

Ellen looked around. It was rush hour and nothing but the sidewalk separated her building from the busy street. On the corner, several vagrants stood holding tallboys swathed in brown paper bags, and a confused argument was in progress. Random barking dogs, cars, shouts and stereos filled the air with a density of noise thicker than bad smells in an overstuffed laundry hamper.

"What was what?" Ellen asked. "Specifically?"

"I thought I heard a gunshot," she said. "Could have been a car backfire, I guess."

"Could have been a gunshot," Ellen said without emotion. "They're pretty common around here. People get drunk and fire weapons, in the air or at each other, a lot."

"Spunky neighborhood," Temerity said, urging Ellen on with a little push from the contact point of hand on shoulder. "I wonder if *Destinations* magazine has ever done a feature on it. The title could be something like 'Risk a trip to Morningside, where the days are dodgy and the nights are downright dangerous.' They could do a four-star taco-cart review and rate which corners sell the best crack."

Having never heard of this particular magazine and wondering who would read an article about crack, Ellen started forward again. They came to the end of the building and turned right, into the narrow alley, passing the windows of the apartment below Ellen's, the one with curtains. Ellen knew very little about its occupant, except that she was elderly and had that small, arthritic dog that she let out into the courtyard to relieve itself, its tiny excrements gradually drying to a hard white that disappeared into the bleached gravel.

They came to the opening of the courtyard and Ellen paused. From this angle she could see all five back doors, including her own. From the corner of her eye she detected movement in the curtain lady's back window, a shiver of the fabric being dropped back into place. Instinctively drawing back, she waited, shushing Temerity who made to speak. The curtain did not move again.

She realized that she had never looked at this familiar scene from this perspective before, and she found it disorienting. It was peculiar, like the eerie, unnatural darkness of a daytime eclipse or hearing a familiar movie scene dubbed into an unfamiliar, more aggressive, language. She shuddered slightly.

"You okay?" Temerity asked, feeling the shiver. "Are we there?"

"We are in the opening to the back," Ellen told her in a whisper. "Okay, stay here, I'll slip the letter under her door."

Clutching the missive tightly, Ellen started across the gravel to the low landing, painfully aware that she had all the silent stealth of a hippo walking on bags of extra-crispy potato chips. As she placed her weight on the first of the two wooden stairs, it objected with a loud creak. Wincing, she leaned forward across the shallow landing and slid the letter easily through the wide gap under the door.

All at once, on her immediate right, the door to T-bone's apartment opened partway, and Ellen had a clear view of his visitor as the man peered out past her. Ellen, crouching in the darkness, could also see past him into the apartment. T-bone was slumped in his chair, staring straight ahead. *Stoned out of his mind,* Ellen thought. The man in the doorway, not much more than a teenager, was holding two parcels: a large grocery bag tucked under one arm and a smaller brown paper bag under the other. Looking right over Ellen's crouching bulk, he spotted Temerity standing in the dim light at the edge of the building and retreated back inside, closing the door with a muffled slam.

Straightening up, Ellen hurried back to Temerity. They retraced their steps and went immediately through to her kitchen, eager to see what would happen next. It was only a few moments until something did. Not Ellen's anticipated apocalypse, but something equally alarming.

T-bone's door opened again, just a crack this time. Ellen could still see T-bone in his chair through the window, and so assumed it was the young man, checking to make sure the way was clear before he exited with his contraband. Everything was relatively quiet now that T-bone's music had stopped. There was no light, except the TV, in the apartment and all Ellen could make out was the shape of the man as he came out and closed the door behind him. He took two cautious steps to the edge of the landing and paused.

As though from the ether, a police car flew down the alley and screeched to a stop, its searchlight exposing the courtyard with sudden and chaotic clarity. The man froze like a trapped rabbit, then spun back toward the door, but it had locked behind him. The siren beeped a sharp warning, ricocheting the glaring sound against the walls, and the officers began to get out of the car. "Stop right there!" one of them shouted. "Hands in the air, stay where you are."

The man spun in place, scanning desperately for an escape route, but he was hemmed in on three sides by the building and the cops blocked the only exit.

"What's going on?" Temerity whispered. "Tell me!"

Ellen tried to follow the action as best she could. "The police are after the guy who went to T-bone's. He just bought drugs, I think. He's . . . he's coming this way!" To her horror, in two gazelle-like leaps, the young man was at the base of her stairs—in four, he was up them and at her back door. His face loomed large in her window, inches away, and Ellen launched herself backward, knocking Temerity to the floor as she fell. The door rattled as he shook the knob and threw his weight against it, trying to force it open.

9

From the floor, Ellen watched the man's head swivel as he desperately looked around for escape. Then the police shouted from below, and she heard a furious scrambling. As best she could tell from within the limitations of the tiny window and in her near hysterical state, he was climbing. His silhouette moved, blocking the window, as he climbed up onto the stair railing, and she could hear the complaint of the aging metal as he grabbed on to the gutter and heaved himself up. The toe of one sneaker smacked hard against the bars over her window as he pushed off, and his body disappeared from sight.

Before she could recover, Ellen heard a high-pitched wheezing voice from beneath her. "Ahhck . . . squished," it said.

Mortified, she rolled off of Temerity, who took two deep breaths and sat up.

"Where did he go?" she asked, scrambling easily to her feet, apparently fully recovered and unconcerned that she had been slammed to the ground and rolled over like biscuit dough.

Ellen was so startled by the man's direct charge that she felt as though the breath had been knocked out of her as well, but she tried to explain. "He's . . ." She wasn't sure. She paused, listening.

But Temerity was better at that than she was. "He's on the roof!" she exclaimed. "He's running around to the other side."

It was true. Even as Ellen collected her scattered wits, she could see the man rounding the center section of the building and then stooping low, making his way across the flat roof on the far side. He took refuge behind one of the many protrusions jutting from the tarred roof, an air vent, Ellen thought. He was apparently listening to the commotion below. The cops were shouting, their guns were drawn, but they could not see the young man from their grounded positions.

"He's hiding," Ellen whispered. "On the roof across from us. No, wait." She pulled the binoculars from the hook and focused in on the shadowy silhouette. As she watched, he ducked down and his shape twisted strangely. Then, with a run and a leap, arms waving for balance, he flew off the roof, leaping to the one-story building next door. "He jumped! He's on the next building." They waited as the cops circled the building, but within a few minutes, they had returned to their patrol car.

The two women listened, both of them with their ears pressed to the screen. One of the cops said, "He's gone, over the roof. I'll put out an alert." The radio sputtered and then they heard the door to the apartment downstairs open.

"Did you get him?" The elderly voice was like glass riddled with spidery cracks, but plenty loud, and Ellen recognized it as the woman who owned the little dog. "I heard the shot. I'm the one who called. That man is trouble. I knew it, the people who show up here, day and night, I knew there'd be trouble."

So curtain lady had called the police, probably when she'd heard the same shot as Temerity, who punched a fist in the air triumphantly, then winced and rubbed her rib cage as she said, "I told you I heard gunfire."

"I know," Ellen said, massaging her backside and hoping Temerity hadn't been hurt too badly when she'd landed on her, "but that guy was running because he just bought a big bag of drugs, he had it when he climbed up."

As if the gates had been opened to admit the general public, a crowd was venturing down the alley to see the attraction, gathering in little cliques. They expressed resentment when the police tried to deter them. This street was their theater, and they were not going to leave without seeing the finale. Cindy's face appeared at her window, roused by the commotion, but she did not come out.

"All right, everyone stay back." The cops, arms extended, restrained the rowdy audience, who booed and shouted insults to express how they felt about their fun being interrupted by anything as petty as law or civilized behavior. Once the small crowd was contained, the officers returned to the old woman, who was standing on her landing, directly below Ellen and Temerity. Out of sight, but they could hear the conversation perfectly. "You said the shots came from that apartment? We'll check it out."

"It won't be good," the quavering voice said from below. "I told him he'd come to a bad end. But would he listen? No."

"Yes, ma'am, we've run across that same problem," one of the officers said dryly. "It might be better if you wait inside."

"Like that's gonna happen." Temerity snorted under her breath. "Snoop lady is jonesing for an action fix."

The cops approached T-bone's door with practiced stealth and knocked. There was no answer. "Police," they called out loudly, standing to either side of the door, guns drawn. No reply. Ellen could see T-bone in his chair through the window. "He's not getting up," she whispered to Temerity.

One of the officers turned and peeked cautiously around the edge of the windowsill. From that viewpoint, he could see the man inside at a profile, slumped in the chair. He motioned to his partner, who risked a glance as well. "Sir?" The first officer tapped on the glass with the muzzle of the gun. "Sir!" he shouted.

No response. "We have a possible casualty," one officer said into his radio. "We are going in." Stepping back to the door, the officer smashed two slats of the door and reached in to turn the lock while the other one kept watch on the inert figure through the window.

They both entered with their guns raised. Searching the small apartment was the work of a few seconds, then they went to T-bone.

Within a minute Ellen heard the static of a radio and heard the words "We have a victim down with a gunshot to the chest," but she couldn't make out what else was said because one of the impatient crowd yelled, "There's a dead body in there! This is scary!" This observation was greeted with a rousing, if somewhat slurred, flurry of enthusiastic comments from his fellow penny-ticket holders.

"Oh my God," Temerity said. "He's been shot!"

Ellen couldn't respond. She felt like her insides had been vacuumed of everything familiar. Her personal menagerie had just become a very public zoo, and that was *not* okay.

Backing away from the window, she slumped down on the kitchen's only stool. "They'll come here," she said, horrified by the certainty. "They'll ask questions."

"Probably," Temerity said, her voice tentative, as though she detected Ellen's panic and was trying to decide how best to keep her calm. "A man has been shot. Are you afraid?"

"Yes," Ellen whispered. "I don't want . . . I can't talk to them."

"But they're the police, and someone's been shot."

"I can't! Don't ask me to, please. I . . . just . . . can't." A strange, fuzzy blank spot in her past threatened to take shape, and she shoved it away. Though she couldn't have recalled the incident specifically to save her life, the memory still cast a wavering shadow. In one of her early foster "homes," the father, an alcoholic police officer, had amused himself by tying a six-year-old Ellen to a chair and scratching her arm with a sharp pin to see how long she could go without crying out. When a teacher had asked how she had acquired the network of long, scabbed scratches, Ellen had covered the wounds and shaken her head, pressing her lips together. As a matter of routine, Ellen was taken to the school office and visited by a police officer. At the sight of the uniform, Ellen had retreated into a corner, sobbing, choking back the sounds, rocking and refusing to speak. She'd effectively blocked those memories, but the shadow lingered, making her skin crawl whenever she ventured too close to a dark blue uniform.

The thought of anyone staring at her, that look on their face that too closely resembled nausea, was enough to stop her breathing, but that memory she'd packed away stung Ellen from the inside. Partial images of a uniform and a sharp implement dive-bombed her consciousness, then retreated into darkness. A small whimper escaped her as she brushed at her upper arm as though to wipe away a wasp.

"Okay, okay. Tell you what. Tell me what you saw, everything. I'll pretend to be you and answer their questions."

Stunned at the grasp and generosity of this woman, Ellen gasped. "You would do that?"

Temerity's face twisted into a scowl, as if she were impatient with Ellen's doubt. "Of course I will. You can't, because . . . well, because you can't. How are they supposed to talk to someone they can't see? That would freak them out, don't you think? And besides, I heard most of it. That's almost as good."

"We could pretend we weren't here," Ellen suggested weakly.

"Yeah, I don't think that's going to work." Temerity frowned, thinking. "What's happening now?"

Ellen twisted so that she could see out her kitchen window. "One of the cops is trying to help T-bone, the other one is keeping people from getting too close. Wait!" She noticed something. In the window next door, Cindy had spotted the envelope and was stooping down to pick it up. She turned it over in her hand, reading the handwritten line on the outside before letting it drop again as though it had burned her.

"Cindy found the letter," Ellen whispered, breathless.

"What's she doing?"

"She looked at it and then dropped it, and now she's picking it up again. She turned on the light and she's opening it. She's reading it."

"How does she look?"

Ellen studied what she could make out of the girl's face. She fumbled the binoculars up to her eyes and the face leapt toward her, startling in its intimate detail. "She looks really scared," Ellen said. "She put one hand over her mouth, tight, like she doesn't want to scream. She's staring at it—her hands are shaking."

Confusion was heaped on commotion as an ambulance and two more patrol cars raced into the alley, bringing with them a demented carnival atmosphere of spinning lights and discordant sirens. The paramedics were directed into the apartment with their trauma kits, and after a hurried conference with the original officers on the scene, the other uniforms took over crowd control and began questioning everyone in it. One of the officers knocked on Cindy's door. She started, as though it were her first indication of the hubbub outside, clutching the letter to her chest. "Police. We'd like to ask you a few questions."

"The police are going to talk to her," Ellen said, her fingers itching to reach for her notebook, but she didn't. Temerity drew in a quick breath. It came to Ellen that what two days ago she would have written in her journal, she was now orally chronicling for Temerity. Instead of simply recording facts, she was communicating a story and getting a response. Her ledger had come alive.

"She's right next door," Temerity said softly, leaning in to listen, but the ambient noise from the radios and the gathering crowd was blocking out individual voices. "She must have heard the shot. There's only a wall between them, right?"

"True," Ellen said. "But maybe she thought it was the TV or something, or like me, that it was just another drunk firing off a round for fun. I don't really pay much attention to them anymore."

"Could be. Did she know him?" Temerity asked. "I hope she's not too upset."

Ellen thought about it. She'd seen them exchange a few words, but never anything more, so she doubted there would be much personal trauma over his injury or demise. "Kind of. I mean, they said hello and stuff like that, but I think she was a little afraid of him, of everyone really. Mostly she avoided him."

"Can't say I blame her. The guy's a drug dealer who must have some dubious visitors. She probably just wanted to steer clear of him. What else?"

Ellen dutifully narrated what she could see of the action below. The police officer went into Cindy's kitchen and stood with his notepad open, taking a statement, no doubt. Cindy did look somewhat horrified, but then, as Ellen told Temerity, that had pretty much been her expression for the past eight months or so.

"Does she still have the letter?"

"Yes. But she put it back in the envelope. Now she's kind of doubling over. The cop has pulled a chair over for her. He is leaning over her, he put his hand on her shoulder, I think she might be upset, no, wait . . ."

Ellen pressed the binoculars to the screen, watching as best she could as Cindy folded forward as if trying to see over her stomach to between her legs. She could hear Temerity's quick breaths near her ear. And then Ellen saw it too, a dark, wet stain spreading between Cindy's legs on her light-colored sweatpants. She related this with alarm, confusion, and embarrassment to Temerity, who simply patted her shoulder and summed it up in three words.

"Her water broke."

10

Temerity explained to Ellen that, unlike on TV, there was no mad rush to get to the hospital just because the amniotic fluid sac had burst. The doctors did like the mother to deliver the baby within twenty-four hours so as not to put it through undue stress, but Cindy might not even be feeling the labor yet. She also said something about the girl's pelvic bones having to rotate so that she would "dilate" and the baby's head could get through, but the image of pain that summoned was too medieval for Ellen to even consider.

While they planned what to tell the police, who would certainly come knocking soon, they kept an eye below. T-bone was put on a stretcher and half wheeled, half carried across the uneven surface of the courtyard. Cindy changed, packed a small bag, and made a phone call. But the call coincided with a round of hooting and cheering from the delighted vagrants as the ambulance, now loaded with T-bone, pulled out, siren wailing, making it impossible to hear any of it. All Ellen could report was that Cindy had read the phone number off of a business card. The letter was left, forgotten, on the counter.

"So she probably called the legal pair," Temerity surmised as Cindy was helped into one of the police cars, which left with her in it, presumably to take her to the hospital. "What was their name, the baby buyers?"

"The Newlands."

"So they'll meet her at the hospital." Temerity sighed. "Now I feel bad for Janelle. I mean, she's not even going to know her brother had a son or daughter." She pressed one hand against her mouth, then let it drop. "How sad. If it was Justice's, and I'd lost him, I'd really want to know that kid. I'd feel better about it if Cindy had had at least a couple of minutes to think it over." She sighed again. "But we did our part. She read Janelle's letter. Now it's up to the pregnant one." Temerity stood listening to the hubbub, considering. And then she said, "Did they seem nice? The Newlands? Like they'd be good parents?"

Ellen thought about the way the man had casually bullied Cindy to agree to their terms. "No," she said. "Not that I know anything about good parents."

Temerity reached up for Ellen's shoulder. She missed slightly and her fingers accidentally brushed Ellen's left cheek. The contact made Ellen jerk away. Temerity's hand hovered uncertainly for a moment, then found its goal. She squeezed Ellen's shoulder gently. "I'm really sorry you had to grow up without anyone to support you. That must be very painful and very lonely."

For a second, Ellen was confused. Her life had been hard sometimes, that's just the way it was. This was the first time anyone had said they were sorry for what she'd been through, and Ellen couldn't make sense of it. The concept that Temerity felt pain for her, or that she should feel badly for herself, floored Ellen. Deep in the moldy basement of her subconscious, something else stirred and struggled to find breath and express itself, to escape the bonds that Ellen had unknowingly imposed.

"I'm really sorry," Temerity repeated softly. Ellen heard the click of some internal latch being released, and suddenly she was floundering. Overwhelmed by a force that instantly engulfed her with sensations she could not even comprehend, she shut her eyes in a desperate bid to avoid it.

But she couldn't stop it from hurling her backward. She was five, on the day her mother walked out. The door closed behind the woman, and Ellen, tiny and malnourished, pressed her ear to the door. When the footsteps blended into the chaotic noise that was the building's constant soundtrack, Ellen went to the pile of blankets where she slept and wound into a ball. She lay there wondering if her mother would ever return, and what she would do if she didn't. A search of the room turned up nothing more than cigarette butts and empty liquor bottles. The gnawing hunger in her stomach grew over the next hours until she was weeping with emptiness, but she muffled the sounds. Tears, she had learned, brought only retribution. Ellen moved her blankets to the floor by the door and lay with her back curled against it, listening to people come and go, babies wailing, voices raised in drunken argument, sirens, and the occasional gunshot. Finally, the pain in her stomach grew stronger than her fear, and the next time she heard footsteps, she cracked open the door to see a wheezing man on the stairs, cigarette dangling from his mouth. He turned to look at her, grimacing at the sight of the scabs covering part of her face. She had whispered, "I'm hungry." Muttering in disgust, he reached into a bag he was carrying and pulled out a packaged cinnamon bun. He threw it to her like she was a dog, shook his head, and shuffled on.

Ellen wiped her face angrily to wring out the memory. She was bewildered to find Temerity's image blurring before her as tears squeezed from her eyes. She knew, of course, that her life had been hard, bad, lonely, but she'd known nothing else and she'd been kept busy surviving it. But now Temerity had identified the pain, named it, and all at once the buried effects of her past began to pulse, the sides of the locked compartment that held it bulging as it strained to escape its containment. Ellen gritted her teeth. "No big deal," she muttered.

Temerity squeezed harder. "Really? Because I think it is a big deal. I think it sucks. But we can talk about that some other time." She removed her hand.

"We don't need to," Ellen said, swallowing hard and trying to still the tremor inside. "I'm okay with it, really."

"Right." Temerity raised her hand again but held it tentatively in the space between them. "I don't want to take a liberty, but . . ." She reached out, quickly brushed her fingers down Ellen's left cheek. ". . . what is this?"

"It's a scar." Ellen had jerked back convulsively at the touch, and she could feel her face flushing. She raised one hand and placed it firmly over the ravaged skin that began at her eye and extended in a wide swath to her jaw.

"From?"

"Something that happened a long time ago. Never mind. I'm glad you don't have to see it, that most people don't. I'm sorry that Justice did." She whispered the last sentence, burning with shame that her disfigurement had been revealed.

"Justice wouldn't care," Temerity said with a dismissive wave. "And if you think he does, you're not giving him enough credit. Ellen, my new friend, you have to have a little bit more confidence in people."

"Like strangers?" Ellen asked, knowing that Temerity would pick up on the attempted humor in her voice.

"Strangers? Hell no! But there are people worth letting in, a few anyway." She paused and then said, "Speaking of which, thanks for sharing this with me. It's been quite an adventure. Honestly, T-bone's physical assault excluded, it's the most fun I've had in a long time. I just hope that he's okay."

There was a knock on the door, and they both jumped, then giggled behind their hands. "Cops," Temerity whispered. "Let's do this."

She fixed her sunglasses on her face and went confidently to answer the door. Ellen stayed in the kitchen, smushed in behind the refrigerator.

"About time!" Temerity said as she opened the door to the stocky man in blue. "How's T-bone?"

"Excuse me?" The officer was taken aback.

"My neighbor who was shot. I don't know his name, so I call him T-bone."

"I see. And you are?"

"Ellen Homes. Nice to meet you, Officer—"

"Ricco. Officer Ricco. Can you tell me if you saw or heard anything?"

"Sure. I thought I heard a gunshot, but that's not unusual around this place. You should be here on Cinco de Mayo, it's like the O.K. Corral. Then I saw a guy at T-bone's back door. You guys rode up, guns blazing, and he freaked. He ran up my back stairs and climbed onto the roof. He ran around to the far side, then jumped down onto the next building."

"Did you get a look at him?"

"Well, I'll tell you." In an attempt at what she must have assumed would be a casual stance, Temerity crossed one foot over the other and reached a hand out to lean against the doorjamb. She miscalculated its location by a couple of inches, lost her balance, but recovered and propped herself up, attaining an awkward, unnatural pose. Between the sunglasses at night and the unsteady movements, the officer probably thought she was drunk, at least. "It's dark, and I wasn't really paying attention at first. But, best guess, he was young, I'd say about seventeen, eighteen, shortish, about my height, shaved head, jeans and a white T-shirt, white sneakers, light gray jacket, oh, and scars, a bracelet of burn scars around his right wrist."

The cop had been fiddling with his pad, listening with skeptical disinterest, but now he looked up sharply. "Scars?"

"Yep, a bracelet, in a pattern, you know, like connected triangles, diamonds. Here." She pulled a paper from her pocket, a small sketch that Ellen had made, and held it out, slightly off to one side. "I drew it for you, so you'd have it." Ellen saw the officer narrow his eyes at the paper, but he took it and studied it. "That's about it. I'm afraid I didn't get a good look at his face, so . . ." She threw her hands out to illustrate their emptiness, smacking her knuckles against the door with the gesture. "Ouch, I have *got* to switch to light beer." She smiled angelically in Officer Ricco's general direction.

The officer grumbled and glared down at the sketch. "We've seen this before; it's a kind of gang marking." His deep sigh said all he could have about what their chances were of catching the guy. He pulled a card from his pocket and held it out. "If you think of anything else, can you give us a call? This is the supervising detective's number."

Temerity hesitated, and Ellen realized she had no idea where the card might be floating in front of her. Pawing repeatedly at thin air would be a definite giveaway. But showing her capacity to *find a way*, as she had put it, she stuck her hand out, palm up, the way she had with Janelle, and the officer placed the card in it. "Sure thing. You didn't say if my neighbor is going to be all right," she pushed.

"I'm afraid I don't have that information," he evaded.

"And how about Cindy?" The cop looked slightly confused and didn't answer. "You know, the pregnant one. She okay?"

"She's fine. One of our officers took her to Saint Vincent's."

"Oh, great. Good hospital. I'll have to drop in on her, maybe tomorrow, take her a basket of baby . . . uh . . . stuff, you know. Blankies and diapies and whatnot."

"Sure." The officer was ready to go now. Ellen could see him close his pad and shift impatiently. "Well, thank you. Good night."

"You take care now!" Temerity called after him as he went down the stairs. It took her three tries to find the door and shut it, but fortunately Officer Ricco did not look back.

Ellen came out. "That was awesome!" she said.

"I was good, wasn't I?" Temerity seemed surprised and proud as well: she was trembling from the excitement. "Whew, thought we were toast there for a minute when he offered me that card. It could have been a bad Marco Polo moment."

Ellen thought back. She had heard of this Marco Polo guy as some kind of trader, but maybe he was also blind or had trouble finding things. Before Ellen had time to ask why this moment would have anything to do with him, Temerity went on.

"And guess what else?" Temerity said, doing a little dance in place. She sang the answer to her own question in a playground taunt that Ellen had to disassociate from her own torturous memories. "We know where they took Cin-dy. We can go check out the New-lands."

"Oh no." Ellen's heart sank, and she followed it onto the sofa with the rest of her body. "We're going to the hospital?"

"You bet we are. But not tonight, she'll need some time to have that baby. I'm guessing we can meet there tomorrow morning. No, darn it! I have rehearsal at eleven."

"Then let's go at nine." Ellen was shocked by the finality of the decision, and even more stunned to realize it had come from her own mouth.

She walked Temerity to the bus stop and waited with her. It would have been insanity to leave her. The drunks, deprived of their diverting drama by police barricades, were staggering about in wobbly, circular patterns of increasing radius looking for something new to occupy their polluted double vision. She wasn't sure how it had happened, but Ellen felt a strange sense of protectiveness for this woman who had meant nothing to her two days ago.

She got back to her apartment, watched the police team taping off doorways and collecting evidence, and wrote furiously in her notebook until she was groggy enough to try to sleep.

Though Ellen wasn't aware that she was doing it, she replayed what had happened outside to distract from the festering poison that had bubbled up within. And in that rushing montage of everything she had witnessed, one image kept on repeating itself in her mind's eye, a picture stuck on instant replay.

The young man's silhouette as he jumped from her roof. His bare arms waving for balance.

She forcibly turned her thoughts to the next day, and somewhere among the jumbled pile of emotions, trepidations and fears lurking in the near future, a new sensation was emerging.

Because of its unfamiliarity, it took her a while to identify it, and even when she gave it a tentative label, she was uncertain and untrusting of her conclusion.

It couldn't be anticipation, could it?

She was actually looking forward to tomorrow.

11

Her life being largely nocturnal, her nights off were always fitful, and Ellen slept only a few hours. When she woke, a confusing combination of dreams and memories sparred in her brain, sending her rushing to the back window, half expecting it to be as barren as every other morning. But the bright-yellow police tape across the courtyard and T-bone's door, with its smashed window, confirmed the reality of last night. She stood watching for answers, feeling a vacant space where the information was lacking. What had happened to T-bone? Was he even still alive?

Left alone, Ellen would eventually have been able to put these questions aside like an unfinished novella left on a park bench, but knowing that she would see Temerity, who shared her interest, fortified her curiosity. A fresh, unfamiliar enthusiasm prodded Ellen to action. She dressed quickly, then crept down her stairs and turned left on the sidewalk. At the corner, she went left again, past the front of the building, took a third left down the narrow access between her apartment and the neighboring one, and came to T-bone's front door, which was crisscrossed with more yellow tape. Next to the door was his mailbox. The painted 1A had faded to a mere suggestion.

Opening the flap top, she pulled out a magazine, and on the label was a name—J. B. Tunney.

She put it back into the box and let the lid fall, its squeaky hinge objecting to its rude dismissal. *J.B.*, she thought. *J. B. Tunney, T-bone.*

The hospital, Saint Vincent's, was only a few blocks away, and she and Temerity had agreed to meet out front. After breakfast, Ellen walked the short distance, eating two Snickers bars as she went, to keep her strength up. The peanuts and caramel fortified her nerves, padding her still new but emerging courage with plump, stiffening insulation. She waited outside until a cab pulled up and Temerity got out.

"Did you go in yet?" Temerity asked as Ellen approached her.

"How did you know it was me?" Ellen was startled.

"I heard you." Temerity smiled. "Everyone has a pretty distinct footstep, and you also have a floppy rubber sole."

Ellen looked ruefully down at her left shoe and sure enough the silver tape had worn through and a larger section of sole had pulled away from the canvas so that it made a soft, flapping sound with each step. She'd have to get some more tape until she could get to the thrift store.

"There's a guard," Ellen told her. "You have to sign in."

"Do you see a gift shop?" Temerity asked.

Ellen looked through the glass doors into the lobby of the hospital. The guard sat at a security desk in front of the elevator banks, and tucked into a corner of the lobby on the left was a small shop selling flowers and cards. "Yes," she said.

"Good, I'll go in and buy some balloons or something and then we'll head right up to see our friend's new baby. Common enough. I don't think anyone would question that."

Ellen thought it sounded risky, but it was the best idea they had, so she took Temerity to the door of the gift shop and left her to negotiate the transaction. In a few minutes, she tapped her way out, holding three silver balloons tied to a small teddy bear. Temerity inquired from the security guard where Maternity might be and was told to take the second elevator bank to the fifth floor. When he asked her to sign in, she smiled and said that might be difficult but gave him Cindy's name. He checked for it on the hospital roster, then told her to go on up. Ellen, her eyes fixed firmly on the back of Temerity's shoes, just followed along like a dinghy on a towrope in her powerful wake.

In the elevator, Ellen told Temerity about finding T-bone's actual name. Temerity clutched at her arm in excitement. "They must have brought him here," she said. "It's the closest trauma center. Okay, first Cindy, then J.C."

"J.B."

"Right."

"What are you planning to do?" Ellen asked nervously as the elevator doors slid open. "Maybe I should just wait here for you."

"You're coming," Temerity said, grabbing a fistful of Ellen's shirt-sleeve. "We're not going to talk to anyone, just listen—that's me—and watch—that's you. Now, where is the nursery?"

Ellen read the signs, and they headed off down a slick hallway dotted with framed children's art until they came to the nursery. A window looked in on a large room with clear plastic cribs filled with babies bundled in blue or pink blankets. Each crib was marked with a large, handwritten sign declaring the baby's family name. Ellen searched but did not see any label that said either Newland or Cindy's last name, Carpenter. "I don't see it," Ellen said.

"It's only been about, what? Fourteen hours? Maybe she hasn't had it yet." Temerity stuck out her bottom lip thoughtfully.

The sound of vaguely familiar voices caught Ellen's attention. Standing a little ways down the hall were the Newlands. They were involved in a heated discussion, and Ellen couldn't quite make out what was being said. She leaned toward Temerity and whispered, "It's them."

Temerity cocked her head to listen and then motioned that they should move a little closer. There were a few chairs in a small waiting area close to where the Newlands were arguing in restrained, tired voices, and Ellen steered Temerity toward those. They sat down and listened.

"This is outrageous. I'm just stunned. I can't believe she didn't tell us," Edward Newland was saying.

"But she's a beautiful baby," Susan countered. "I know we said that it's not what we wanted, but it's been so long and . . ."

"You aren't seriously considering this," her husband said. He looked at her searchingly. "I thought we wanted a child that people would think was ours. We discussed this in depth. Nothing against mixed families, but we didn't want to put a child through that."

"Would it be so bad?" Susan asked, and Ellen heard in her voice a human pleading that hadn't been there before.

"Yes!" her husband insisted. "She should have told us the father was black!" He shook his head. "Unbelievable," he half moaned.

"Ed, please." Susan put a hand on his arm. "I want a family. I've wanted a family for so long. What difference does it make if this baby's skin is a different color from ours? We would love her just the same." She burst into tears, and instead of comforting her, her husband took a step back as though she were contagious.

"What *difference* does it make?" Incredulous, Edward leaned toward his wife. "Why are you acting like we never talked about this and both decided against it? We might as well run up a flag that says 'Adopted, we weren't capable of having our own child.'"

"What a dick," Temerity whispered under her breath.

But Ellen was watching Susan Newland. A nurse was coming down the hallway from a double door marked DELIVERY, pushing one of the plastic cribs. Susan's eyes, tear-filled, followed the crib as the nurse pushed it through the nursery door.

"Let's go," Edward Newland said wearily to his wife, grasping her arm. "We're done here. You've been through enough, we both have."

But Susan pulled roughly away. "I'm not going." She said it with so much conviction that even Temerity sat up and looked impressed. "A black child might not have been our first choice, but maybe that child has come into our life for a reason."

"What reason?" Edward licked his lips as though his mouth had gone dry. "So that we can be the desperate, infertile parents with the ethnic kid? So the kid will have to explain to everyone in her life why her parents are white and she's not? I thought we agreed that wouldn't be fair to the child." He was pleading, but Susan looked so affronted that he stepped in closer to her, lowering his voice. "Listen, honey. I know how you're feeling right now. I know you're disappointed, but there will be other babies."

"Better ones? Whiter ones?" she asked, and there was steel in her voice.

Edward began to plead in earnest. "That's not fair. I'm not a racist, and I want us to have a family too. You know that! We agreed. Why are you making me the bad guy? Do you want a child to be ridiculed and scoffed at? Kids can be ruthless!" He stopped to take a couple of deep, calming breaths.

Well, I can't disagree with that, Ellen thought.

"It doesn't have to be like that!" Susan said, softening and clutching at his arm. "People don't think that way anymore, things have changed."

He snapped. "The partners at the firm think that way and you know it! We show up at the company Christmas party with that little bundle and I can say good-bye to ever making partner. It might not be fair, it might even be sad and pathetic, I'm not arguing with that. But it's the unfair, sad, pathetic reality."

The door to the nursery opened and the maternity nurse stuck her head out. "Mr. and Mrs. Newland? Would you like to come in while we bathe the baby? Then you can feed her if you like."

Susan kept her eyes fixed on her husband's face. Edward shuffled his feet uncomfortably and mumbled something inaudible. Watching his eyes intently as though tracking a target, Susan said very clearly, "I'll be right with you." She waited for the door to close before she spoke. "I'm making a choice, Edward. You have to do the same. You go home with me and that child, or you go home alone."

"Susan, please, you're not thinking rationally." His eyes were wide with fear.

"On the contrary, I've never felt so lucid," Susan said to him. With tears streaming down her face, tears that Ellen was sure Temerity could hear clearly in her voice, she said, "I'll be here. Let me know what you decide."

She turned toward the door, but before she'd gone two steps, Edward said in a tortured voice, "We can't do this, and you know why."

Susan stopped, took a deep breath, and turned back. "I'm sorry that I had a relationship with Jeff. But you were the one who wanted a separation, not me. I know he's black. I know that you think everyone will assume it's Jeff's child, but I just don't give a damn anymore what everyone else thinks. I'm sick to death of it." She leaned forward and touched his arm. He flinched and wouldn't look at her. "I guess if you don't understand that, then we feel differently and there's nothing more to say."

She smiled with heartbreaking sadness, and then turned and went through the nursery door.

Edward Newland leaned against the wall and watched, his face a twisted mask of pain, as the nurse picked up the tiny baby and placed her in his wife's arms. Then, with a bitter exhale, he turned and strode away down the hall.

"Do you want me to tell you what happened?" Ellen asked Temerity.

"I got most of it. Just tell me one thing," she said. "How did he look?"

After a moment's thought, Ellen said, "Like he was really devastated."

Temerity made a thoughtful noise in the back of her throat. "Okay. I want to hate him, but it's been a hard day for him too, so I'll wait. Let's go see how T-bone's getting on." She put her right hand on Ellen's left shoulder.

They started down the open hallway at a good pace but had only gone a short distance when Ellen stopped short. Given no warning, Temerity collided into the back left half of her and sort of bounced back a step.

"There it is," Ellen whispered. "There's that sound."

From behind a closed door to their left, a muted, extended wail was seeping through.

"Keening," Temerity whispered. Releasing Ellen's shoulder, she followed the sound to the door and pushed it open.

12

N o!" Ellen said, but Temerity held up one finger and then went on into the room, leaving the door ajar. Moving to the edge of it, Ellen listened. The wailing was muffled suddenly as though someone had made an effort to contain it by holding a pillow to their face, then it turned to short, gasping sobs.

"Are you all right?" Temerity asked in a voice soft enough to calm a frightened rabbit.

"Wh-who . . . are . . . y-you?" Cindy gasped.

"My name is Temerity. I heard you crying. Is everything okay?"

Cindy gasped a few more times, then a long groaning hum came through clenched lips. Ellen leaned around the doorjamb until she could see them. Temerity had gone to the far side of the bed, and she could only see Cindy in profile, but she looked exhausted and horrible. Her face was puffy, her eyes were reddened slits, and her hair was plastered to her head with dried sweat.

"No, it's n-not okay," she said. "But you d-don't need . . . to worry ab-about it."

"But I am," Temerity said. "Worried. I'm not sure if anyone could hear someone crying like that and not be concerned." Ellen felt a sting across her face as sharp as an openhanded slap. She'd heard that sound and not been affected. But no, that wasn't quite right; she had cared, at least, she hadn't liked it at all, but it had never occurred to her that she might be able to do anything about it. It was the recognition of her self-drawn safety zone that left the imaginary burning finger marks on her cheek. Temerity said gently, "It sounds like you might need someone to talk to. Do you have someone who can come and see you?"

A quick snort of hopeless disgust, then, "No."

"No family?"

Cindy shook her head violently.

"What about your baby's daddy? Does he have family that might want to help?" Ellen drew in her breath and leaned farther into the room.

After a series of quick, moist inhalations, "I wouldn't know" came thickly through.

"You might not have noticed, but I'm blind," Temerity said, feeling for a chair or somewhere to settle herself. "But I'm not *blind*, if you know what I mean. May I sit down?" She went ahead and did without waiting for a reply. "There, that's better. Now, tell me all about it. I can't see what's going on here, but I can tell that you need someone to talk to. We all do."

"I d-don't know . . . you."

Temerity reached out a hand until she found the end of the bed, then slid it across the rumpled sheets until she came to a lump. She patted Cindy's foot. "And I don't know you, so there's no reason not to tell me. I have to rely on people I don't know all the time. You can do it this once." She smiled softly, gently, and Cindy broke down utterly, weeping without the capacity for speech for several minutes.

"That's a good start, actually," Temerity said when the sobs subsided a bit. "Now tell me what it means."

"I met . . . this guy," Cindy began haltingly. "He was really nice and I liked him. He was in the service, and his unit was called up for deployment in Afghanistan. He was going to be gone a year, but we agreed to try to stick it out. We said we would write and get together when he got back."

She stopped and turned to look out the window, which faced a depressing concrete wall. Tears ran steadily down her face.

When she spoke again, the words rushed out in a gush of breath. "I really thought he was the one. About a month after he left, I found out I was pregnant."

Temerity said nothing, but the tilt of her head and the way she leaned in, shoulders curled forward, said that she was listening to every word and hearing much more.

"But he was kill—" Cindy's voice choked off and it was a minute before she could continue. "I found out when my own letter was re-turned to me unopened, with a note from one of his buddies, who let me know. By then . . . it was too late for . . . I didn't have any choice, but I was so sad. It's like I was paralyzed, couldn't do anything.

"Then these people got in contact with me through the clinic where I was going for free care, you know. They wanted to adopt the baby, so I said yes, 'cause I don't have any money and I didn't want to raise a kid totally alone."

"Of course you didn't," Temerity said matter-of-factly. "No one should have to."

"But now"—Cindy gasped for breath as though her pain threat-ened to overwhelm her again—"I just don't know. I mean, I don't have Sam." The emotion throttled her temporarily and she struggled to continue. "But it was like, while I was pregnant, he was still there, or a part of him anyway. And now he's . . . gone. I didn't know until I lost him that I was so in love with him, and now he's gone."

"That's a tough situation," Temerity empathized, her voice offering both sympathy and strength on loan. "But you shouldn't be trying to deal with this alone. Don't you have any friends who might be able to help you through this?"

The girl shrugged, and Ellen could have told her how useful that was. "Not really . . . I mean, I know people, but not well enough for . . . this." She sighed and her head lolled back on the pillow. "Most of the people I've met in this town are kind of busy just surviving their own stuff."

Temerity got up and felt her way to the edge of the bed, then perched on it. "I'll tell you something, Cindy. Life is tough, and not always fair, I know something about that, but you never know what's just around the corner. Take me for example. A couple of days ago, some bad guys tried to rob me. They cut the strap of my bag with a knife, and I stood there thinking the knife was going to cut me next, that I was a goner. Then out of nowhere comes this girl who saves my butt. I didn't expect it, but there she was. It made me want to save someone else, you know what I mean?"

Cindy wiped her face on the sheet and said she guessed so.

"That might happen for you too."

There was another hopeless snort from Cindy, who stared flatly at the wall with unfocused eyes. "Things like that don't happen to me."

Temerity held her hand out and Cindy wiped her own on the sheet and tentatively took it. "I have a funny feeling things might change for you. There are so many people out there, other people who are hurting, who have no extra strength to give, but they relate, you know what I mean? Sometimes it helps just to know that you're not the only one who's hurting. And then there are other people who have strength to spare. I honestly believe that you will find one of them, maybe more than one. Thank you for talking to me. Now, if you'll excuse me, I have to go visit someone else."

Temerity stood up and made her way around the foot of the bed.

"Wait a minute," Cindy said, stopping her. Her face was scrunched, not with tears, but with suspicion. Very slowly, she asked, "How did you know my name?"

Temerity stood, frozen to the spot, and then she turned back. "It's on your door."

"But you're . . . blind."

With a dawning, contented smile, Temerity said, "Blind—with friends." And then she walked away.

"Gosh," Ellen said when they were on their way, "thought she had you there."

"Me too," Temerity told her. "Okay, next. Find me a nurses' station and stay out of sight." She laughed loudly. "Get it? Out of sight. Works on two levels for us." She was still cackling at her own joke when Ellen found the nurses' workstation. She hung back while Temerity approached it.

"Hi, excuse me, could you help me?"

A frazzled nurse looked up in annoyance from her endless computer busywork, but when she saw the dark glasses pointed toward the empty space between herself and the next nurse, she softened. "Of course, what can I do for you?"

"I'm a little lost, go figure," Temerity joked. "I was looking for my friend J. B. Tunney. He was brought in last night with a gunshot wound. I'm not sure I'm in the right place, to judge from the sound of sucking and the smell of talcum powder."

The nurse smiled, obviously relieved by the humor and the simplicity of the request.

"You're in the maternity ward."

"Ah, that would explain it."

"What was the name?"

Temerity repeated it and the nurse typed on her computer, then her smile tightened to a grimace. She glanced up at Temerity with concern. "Are you family?"

"No, six degrees," Temerity said, avoiding explanation.

"Okay, you need to turn to your left, go to the elevator banks at the end of the hallway, go up to six, and check with the nurse in ICU." Before Temerity could thank her, she added, "But I'm not sure they'll let you see him."

"Well, at least he'll know I tried." She bounced the teddy bear, and the silver balloons danced a bit.

"I'm sure he'll appreciate it."

Temerity made her way back to the hallway where Ellen was waiting. "You heard?" she asked.

"Yeah," Ellen said.

They made their way up to the sixth floor, but instead of finding a nurse, they sat in the crowded ICU waiting room to scope it out. There was a set of double doors, the top halves of which were large panes of safety glass, no doubt to lessen the chance of a collision of gurneys, with a code lock and a sign that read RESTRICTED ENTRY. Ellen positioned herself so that she could see through the glass, down the long narrow hall cluttered on both sides with ICU cubicles and portable medical equipment.

About halfway down that hall, outside one of the glassed and curtained rooms, a police officer was sitting in a folding chair. He had a cup of coffee and the paper. It looked like he'd been there for a while. Ellen explained the layout to Temerity. "You think that's his room?" she asked. "Why would he have a police officer outside?"

"Don't know," Ellen said. "Maybe they think somebody will try to kill him again." She thought about it. "So they're protecting him because he can ID the guy."

"Or maybe," Temerity said, tightening her mouth into a thoughtful pout, "they found out he's a dealer and they have him under arrest. Would they put a policeman here for that, you think? I mean, it's not like he's going anywhere."

Ellen said she didn't know. "Wait, there's someone coming out."

It was actually two people: a pear-shaped man with slim shoulders and a wide backside in a telltale white jacket and a taller man in a brown suit. As the suit held the door open for the doctor, a badge flashed on his belt. "It's a doctor and a detective," Ellen told Temerity.

The two men paused outside the room, heads together in consultation. An orderly pushing a patient on a gurney came from the far end of the cramped hallway and tried to make the turn to get into the ICU cubicle across the hall from J.B.'s, forcing the pair to vacate. They began a slow walk toward the waiting area. At the exit, the doctor reached out and hit a panel. The pneumatic double doors swooshed open.

". . . and if he can be stabilized?" the detective was asking.

The doctor spoke matter-of-factly. "This guy is not the healthiest, but he is tough. If he can make it through the next couple of days, I'd say there's a good chance of recovery—if infection doesn't get him. I'm afraid that's common with chest wounds, especially for smokers. Have you been able to locate any family?"

"No, we had a lead on a son, but he's a trucker and moves around a lot. We're hoping to hear from him eventually."

"What was the shooting about? Robbery? Argument?"

"Drug related, most likely. His neighbor said he gets all kinds of strange visitors, 'lowlifes,' she called them, who pop in for a couple of minutes, no more."

The doctor checked the clipboard in his hand and nodded. "Yeah, he had enough THC in his system to make a horse hallucinate, and a high blood alcohol level. He's really lucky he didn't bleed out. Your guys did a good job."

The detective puffed out his cheeks and exhaled hard. "If he dies, I've got nobody but the old lady to ID the shooter. She did give us a positive ID in a lineup, but it was dark when she saw him come out of Tunney's apartment, and her eyeglasses are thicker than the glass in Shamu's tank at SeaWorld. Any hack of an attorney could challenge her testimony."

"So you have the guy who shot him?"

"If it's him. We picked him up a few blocks away. The problem is there are about a thousand other guys who fit that same description. And the old lady said the guy had on a jacket and was carrying a brown paper bag, I'm guessing something he stole from Mr. Tunney. But this kid had neither."

A harsh wake-up alarm went off in Ellen's head as she flashed on her last image of the shooter.

"He could have hidden them somewhere," the doctor said.

"Or ditched them in the river, either way." The detective rubbed his eyes. "We ran his prints. He has a juvenile record, but nothing since he turned eighteen. There were no print matches at the scene and no gun. We checked his hands for residual gunpowder, but they had been scrubbed and then rubbed with vegetable oil, so the results were compromised."

"That's weird."

"Not really. Gangs are savvy these days. And most of these guys have spent their lives figuring out how to get away with shit. They're good at it, and they always have an alibi. He claims he was helping his grandmother make tamales. A real model citizen."

"And she backed up his story." It wasn't a question. As an urban doctor, he seemed to know the drill. Through the glass, in the hall behind them, Ellen saw the orderly with the gurney, empty now, emerge from a room and start toward them.

The detective heaved a long sigh and then said, "They always do. Unless we can find some other way to tie him to the shooting, he'll walk. In fact, I'll have to let him go tomorrow."

The doctor shook his head, as though to rid it of disgust. "All I can tell you is that we'll know more tomorrow, day after by the latest." The orderly reached the double doors, a whack, a swoosh, and he started to push the gurney through, only to be stopped and quizzed by a nurse. They stood there comparing notes, the doors automatically remaining open. The noise from the frantic activity in the ICU wiped out any further eavesdropping.

A young man with the hood of his sweatshirt pulled up was seated with his back to them. As the detective and doctor drifted closer to him, he stood up and glanced around furtively. Ellen recognized it as the action of someone who did not want to be noticed, which caught her attention. As she watched, the young man glanced first toward the detective, tugging his hood farther down as he did, and then he turned in her direction, his eyes sweeping the room as if checking for danger.

He was Hispanic, like half the people in the hospital, so that was not exceptional, but in the split second he was facing Ellen, she saw that his eyebrow was pierced and the point of entry was red and swollen, as though it had been done at home and was infected. She took in a sharp breath. But he was already moving quickly away down the hall.

Ellen watched as the detective and the doctor shook hands, turned in opposite directions, and went back to serve and protect a largely ungrateful public, leaving only the muffled beeps of a hundred monitors blended into a wall of background sound, like the falling of electronic raindrops.

Temerity was the first to speak. "Poor guy," she said. "I don't suppose we can do anything to help him, not now."

Ellen wasn't so sure. But her newfound courage, still a small and shaky thing, had spent itself and needed to retreat for the time being, so she said nothing. Maybe T-bone would be okay, maybe he could ID the shooter, maybe the teenager was not the same one who had been with T-bone's attacker. Ellen could not recall him as well as the shooter, whose face, inches away from hers in her kitchen-door window, she would never forget, but the very idea of making that known sent the tiny bit of fluff that was her bravery scuttling back into its dark hole.

13

On the way out of the hospital, Temerity pressed a button on her watch and it told her the time. "Oh my gosh, I've got to get to rehearsal!"

She pulled a cell phone from a zippered pocket. "Justice? Hey, can you drive me to rehearsal? Great. Pick me up in front of Saint Vincent's on Seventh, see you in fifteen? I'll tell you when I see you. By the way, I've got Ellen with me. Okay. I'll tell her. Perfect."

As soon as Ellen heard Temerity include her in the conversation, she had instinctively tried to retreat, but Temerity had anticipated this and, after only a slight flail, snatched her sleeve, holding on tight. When she ended the call, she said, "I want you to come with me. Justice said he'll hang out with you while I'm rehearsing. I won't be long. It's a run-through for a performance."

"I don't think that's a very good idea."

Temerity smiled. "That would be an accurate assessment of absolutely everything we've done in the last couple of days, but we did it anyway and I don't see any reason to quit now. Besides, Justice has been asking about you. You can fill him in on all our adventures. There's a nice park in front of the music hall and you guys can have a picnic or something."

Food sounded good, crucial in fact after the last strenuous hour, but she didn't think that Temerity had any idea of how much, and she certainly wasn't going to let Justice watch her eat the amount she required. That kind of commitment called for privacy. The Snickers bars' protective effect had worn off, and she felt drained and raw.

Ellen's knees wobbled at the thought of the lunch Temerity and Justice would consider a good meal. Probably salad. She shuddered. The strangely emotional morning had left her light-headed and shaky. Her interior fortifications craved caloric sustenance to thicken their worn walls, and a lot of it.

Normally, by this time in the a.m., she would have consumed several times the recommended daily allowance of carbohydrates as determined by the, in her opinion, far too fervent Food and Drug Administration, whose tidings of gloom were constantly being broadcast on her little radio. She'd listened with lukewarm interest to their warnings about calories per day, fat percentages, and fiber intake and had been left with a sense of indifferent futility. Those limitations seemed more fantastical than the thrift-store paperbacks with the long-haired, half-naked supermodel pirates on the cover. Neither the novels nor the labels on her food interested her, and they struck her as equally absurd. Who could adhere to those calorie counts? Who wanted to do the math? For that matter, who could sail a ship through a storm without a shirt or a hair tie? Sure, it looked good, but the windburn would sting like the dickens and it would be next to impossible to get the tangles out, was the way she saw it.

"I . . . need to go home first," Ellen fumbled. "I have to, uh, feed Mouse."

"And we don't want the fragile little darling to waste away, so okay. We'll run you by there. Good?"

"I don't want Justice to see—" Ellen could hear the panic in her own voice, and Temerity's exceptional hearing had certainly not missed it. Hell, that girl's ears could probably pick up her inner monologue.

She was right. "We won't go up. We'll wait in the car." Temerity sat down, signifying that it was a done deal.

So Ellen sat with Temerity, restraining her preferred impulse to flee into the nearby planters, dig a hole and cover herself with compost. As she waited, she repeatedly reached up and finger-combed her hair down over the left side of her face. Not that it would hide her ravaged cheek from Justice's perceptive gray eyes. But she consoled herself with the memory of how indifferent he'd been to her appearance the first time he had been able to see her. For a brief moment, she indulged herself by imagining that, if she tried, she might be able to not only be invisible, but to control her appearance when she chose to be seen. The fantasy didn't last. Double the miracles seemed highly improbable.

Every time her fingers accidentally brushed against the rutted, poreless scar tissue, she flinched. Not from pain, but from the hated images it recalled to her mind—flashes of her early life with the woman who, impossibly, had been her mother, the constant hungry burn in her stomach, sleeping on the cold floor at night, curling into a ball until the hitting stopped. And, worst of all, she could feel her mother's fist twisting her hair, holding her while she struggled, see the red glow of the electric hot plate coming closer and closer, the heat searing even before her skin reached it. The smell of . . . no. Ellen snorted to clear her nose of the phantom stench of liquor and burnt meat. She would not think of it. It was over, gone, dead, and she would not resurrect it, or her. It didn't matter anymore, anyway, no one could see the mutilation. She was spared the dull stab of seeing the revulsion in their eyes before they could avert their gaze, or worse, the staring and jeering that had been her youth. The relief of invisibility was profound.

"Here he comes," Temerity said, rousing Ellen from her murky thoughts. She looked up in surprise to see a black BMW rounding the drop-off circle of the hospital, engine purring so softly that Ellen's inferior ears could barely hear it when it stopped right in front of them.

The driver's door opened and Justice got out. He was dressed in a corduroy jacket and jeans, more formal than the first time she'd seen him, and Ellen looked down, humiliated by her worn clothes. But once again, Justice didn't even seem to notice as he rounded the front of the expensive auto.

"Your carriage awaits, ladies," he said with a smile and little comic bow. "Hey, Ellen," he added in a secretive undertone as he opened the back door for her.

"Yeah, hi," mumbled Ellen, keeping her face down. It was a bit of a squeeze, but once inside, Ellen sat in awe. She was afraid to touch anything in the cream leather interior at first, but she could not stop her fingers from running back and forth on the supple seat cushion. She had seen this kind of car by the thousands, but she had never imagined that she would be granted access to such a luxurious ride. In spite of her fear and embarrassment, she couldn't keep one side of her mouth from grinning.

She told him which way to go and blushed profusely when they pulled up in front of the run-down building. She had never looked at it as anything but a hiding place before, but seeing it through his eyes made her burn with shame when she thought of their beautiful, stylish apartment.

But Justice turned to her with a smile and jerked a finger toward his sister. "We'll wait for you. Hurry back. We've got to get Ms. Mole here to her rehearsal."

"I wish you wouldn't call me that," Temerity said. "It makes me feel like an informant."

"I'm so sorry," Justice chided her in a baby voice. "I meant the furry little blind rodent."

"Oh, that's much better," Temerity said with droll sarcasm. She crossed her arms and withdrew, pouting.

Ellen got out and hurried as best she could up the rickety wooden stairs to her front door. She went straight to the kitchen, pulled out a loaf of white bread and ate four slices by rolling them into doughy, chewy balls and eating them whole. She followed this with several large handfuls of dry Cap'n Crunch cereal and a few cookies.

Still chewing, she turned to look out the back window, though she didn't expect to see much with both of her pets in the hospital.

But she was wrong. An initial sweeping glance of the courtyard revealed nothing but police tape and the balding toy poodle squatting arthritically in the gravel. As he eased his backside stiffly into position, he tilted his little head upward. Then suddenly, he began to bark in a high-pitched, furious stream, his original business forgotten.

Ellen looked up to the roof across the courtyard to see what was upsetting the little canine, and spotted him. A boy was looking down from the flat roof, crouching low. Ellen leaned forward and stared, but she knew immediately it was not the same young man as the night before. This was little more than a child, maybe twelve years old, and the skin on his wrists was clean and unscarred. He hissed at the dog to shut up, and then searched around him. He picked up a small rock and threw it at the animal, hitting him on the rump, which sent him into a spasm of spinning and indignant yapping.

Then the kid froze, dropping his body to the rough tarred surface below the two-foot raised edging. But too late.

"I see you, you!" Ellen heard the dog's mistress shout in her crackly voice, outraged that he had attacked her beloved dog. She must have been standing directly below Ellen, because she couldn't see her, but the volume of the old woman's voice was every bit as strong as before, and Ellen could hear her perfectly. "I've already called the police, you little shit! They'll be here in one minute. You leave my dog alone!"

But the kid was gone before she'd finished the sentence, running and dropping off the far side of the roof like Spider-Man's scrawny, brown, inner-city nephew.

Ellen exhaled, unaware that she had been holding her breath. She felt a huge wave of relief. It was not the first time she'd seen kids on the roof. Because only three apartments were on the second story, the flat roofs of the lower story gave perfect access to the exposed walls, and the local gangs had pissed their marks there for more than a decade. The window over Ellen's kitchen sink, striped with wrought-iron bars, led onto this roof; it was from the broken slat at the bottom of that window that Mouse had first crept into her life. She had to wonder if the boy was a coincidence or a messenger. It was unusual for one of these kids to be up there in broad daylight, but in view of the onslaught of strange events in the last few days, this rated low on the list.

Because on that list was the strangest thing of all: Ellen had a friend. Well, an acquaintance with mutual interests, and she supposed, having no point of reference, that it amounted to the same thing. That was the most peculiar thing that had ever happened to her, even considering that the last few days had been some of the oddest ever.

Back in the car, Justice glanced back at her before asking, "So, you want to tell me what you two have been up to?"

Ellen couldn't see Temerity's face in the front seat, but her shoulders did a little dance of anticipation. She had a story to tell. "Visiting neighbors of Ellen's. There was a little incident at her apartment building last night. You want to tell him?"

She didn't, but Temerity had offered like it was some kind of treat. "Some guy got shot."

"Oh good," Justice said dryly. "Glad to know you girls are staying out of trouble."

"*We* didn't shoot him!" Temerity said. "But Ellen saw the guy who did."

"Not really, it was dark," Ellen filled in hastily.

"And," Temerity rushed on, "Cindy went into labor, so we went to the hospital, just to check up on how they were doing."

In the rearview mirror, Ellen could see Justice's brow furrow as he shook his head with resigned acceptance. "I knew I should have come home last night," he said.

"Oh, that reminds me, how was your date?" his sister asked.

He grinned. "I didn't come home last night."

"Excellent," Temerity said, and held up one hand to be slapped by her brother. "So you like her?"

"She's pretty cool, actually. Smart. But back to you two meddlers."

"Meddlers?" Temerity turned her body toward him so that Ellen could see the determined set of her mouth in profile. "I seem to remember you talking about 'fate' and 'charity.' You said we should help."

"Help does not include gunfire or any other exchange of deadly force. How is the guy doing?"

Temerity sighed. "Not great. It'll be a couple of days before they can even say if he'll make it."

"How about the girl . . . Cindy? Did she have the baby?"

"Healthy baby girl. Not quite the color the would-be adoptive parents had ordered, apparently. There was a good bit of discussion about returning it to sender."

Justice glanced back at Ellen and asked, "And how, exactly, do you know all of this?"

Temerity held up one fist. "I'm blind and she's invisible. It's a powerful combination when it comes to gathering information."

A long, tortured sigh came from Justice. "Great," he said, but it came out more like *Blast*.

"And anyway, Mr. Anthropologist, you're the one who's always saying that gathering is an important part of our human history and development, especially for women. Men were the hunters, women were the gatherers, that's what you said."

"Gatherers of nuts and berries, not other people's business. I was talking about traits that affected certain evolutionary changes in society and physiology. And that's Dr. Anthropologist to you."

"Some doctor. Everybody likes to gather information, in other words, 'other people's business.' Hell, in some places it's hard currency, just ask the CIA or the folks at JPMorgan Chase. Oh, and I talked to Cindy."

"You did what?" He braked hard for no apparent reason and Ellen felt the seat belt, already maxed out, tighten across her chest.

Temerity used one of her fingers to respond before she spoke. "If you would have heard the sound she was making, there's no way you would have walked away, so don't even."

They were pulling up to the artists' entrance at the music center and Justice reached over the back of the seat to get the violin case from the floor. His fingers brushed Ellen's knee. "Sorry," he said, as though it were nothing, and found the case. He lifted it over the seat and set it in his sister's lap. "You're probably right. I have to admit the whole situation with the girl is culturally pretty fascinating. Sad but fascinating. How did she react when you told her about the letter?"

Temerity didn't answer, so as they came to a stop, Justice turned to Ellen for an explanation.

"We didn't tell her," Ellen muttered. "I mean, we gave her the letter, but she didn't know it was us, and then she went into labor, so, well . . . I mean, it's not like she had any time to think, or, you know, do anything about it, uh, you know . . ." She trailed off.

"And she's not adjusting very well, I take it? Emotionally, I mean." Justice sounded resigned, as if it were a foregone conclusion.

Temerity said brightly, "Let's review. She's all alone, doesn't talk to her family, if she even has one, she met a guy, fell in love, allowed herself to hope, he left to go to war, she found out she was pregnant, he died, she has nobody to help her, and no way to take care of a baby in a harsh world."

"So . . . not great."

"Not great," Temerity agreed, dropping the false cheer and unfolding her stick. "Okay, I've got to get in there. Pick me up in an hour and a half?"

They watched until she was through the door. The second she disappeared, Ellen became hyperconscious of the fact that she was now alone with Justice in a car. Every nerve in her body was on high alert, and her brain was screaming, *Get out! Run!* But before she had time to act, Justice thumped the steering wheel and asked jovially, "Hungry?"

He couldn't have said anything else better designed to put Ellen's fears back to their "standby" position. *Always,* she thought, but what she said was, "Sort of."

"Cool. You like Italian sausage, with pasta anyway, I know. There's this amazing food truck that parks nearby that makes the best sausage subs on warm Italian loaf. I say we pick up a couple of foot-longs with onions, peppers, cheese—the works—a couple of iced teas, eat until we can't, and soak up some sunshine."

She wasn't sure about the sunshine part, but the rest of the plan sounded like something perched on billowing clouds behind pearly gates. "Sure," she said. And then she added two words she couldn't remember ever using as a stand-alone pair before. "Why not?"

14

It was hard for Ellen to believe that someone as slim as Justice could actually finish a sandwich that was larger than his own head, but he did. Ellen savored hers, finishing it, but only just. When they'd balled up the white paper wrappings and crushed the iced tea cans, they lay back on the grass and made satisfied noises.

The early-spring wind was still refreshingly cool and the feel of the sun heating the dark clothes she always wore was actually welcome, nothing like the usual sweltering broiler heat she usually associated with a sunny day. The pleasant fullness of a satisfying meal and the fact that Justice was with her in the middle of a large field of grass insulated Ellen from her usual state of high alert when she had to be outside in any kind of sunlight. The novelty made her sleepy and contented.

"Mmm." She made the noise without realizing she'd done it. It came from her chest, like a purr.

"My sentiment, precisely," said Justice. They lay there for a few minutes, sluglike, until Justice rolled up on one elbow with a groan of effort. Immediately self-conscious, Ellen sat up, crossing her legs and flattening her hair down over her cheek.

But he wasn't looking at her. He was watching the people enjoying the sunshine and the fountain in the plaza in front of the music hall. "Aren't they fascinating?" he asked.

Ellen followed his gaze and noticed several vignettes: a family with small children who had "accidentally" gotten wet in the fountain and were now sporting their parents' jackets and shivering in the light wind, a young couple making out against the ticket booth wall, an elderly group of men playing chess. "Who?" Ellen asked him.

Raising the hand not supporting his head, he waved it grandly. "All of them! I mean, look at them. Look at what we've built: high-rises and electronics and space rockets. The things we can choose to do every day: music, art, sports. We even have leisure time! We can eat tacos or spaghetti or hamburgers or sushi for lunch and something else for dinner. It's unprecedented, what humans can do in our age, yet so many of us are still so unhappy."

She watched the men at the chess table argue about a move, but the altercation passed quickly. She'd never really thought about people on the whole as being unhappy, though she had seen and recorded hundreds of individual moments. Come to think of it, she never thought of people as a whole, except possibly as the faceless mass outside of her safety zone. "Why do you think that?" she ventured to ask.

"Me?" He puffed out his cheeks and let out an audible breath. "I think it's because we've forgotten the important things."

Ellen snuck a peek at his serious face. Unused as she was to pursuing a conversation of any kind, she found that she really wanted to know what he thought. "Like . . . what things?"

He turned as though remembering to whom he was speaking and sat up. "Our place in the world, for starters. By that I mean humans as part of a living organism, the planet. Think about it. We're part of a huge, balanced biology that's being messed up. That's the first thing. The second thing we've forgotten about is the human need to connect. We were meant to function together to be whole; without that, we feel fundamentally incomplete."

Ellen must have looked as lost as she felt, because he clapped his hands together and said, "Okay, look at it this way. Human beings developed as tribes, each member had his or her role and was necessary for the survival and well-being of the whole. That is how we managed to evolve so far. But we don't give much thought to the common good anymore. It's every man for himself, and on a really basic survival level, that's unnatural. Therefore, people feel unfulfilled, but they don't know why."

Ellen knew that last part, about every man for himself, was mostly true from her years of observing people's behavior toward each other. She wasn't sure she understood the rest of what he was talking about—"common good" was a phrase that escaped her—but she liked listening to Justice talk. She liked the way his eyes got brighter and his face lit up when he was explaining. "But we *are* alone," she said to keep him going. "I mean, aren't we?"

Justice smiled. "We are individuals," he said, "unique even, but that's not the same thing as what I'm talking about. It's an occupational hazard. Anthropologists see people, and their behavior, not just as individuals, but as part of a larger whole."

"But most people just live their lives and don't see past their own . . . you know . . . stuff."

Justice's eyebrows went up and he nodded approvingly. "Exactly." Then he laughed and added, "That's why there are anthropologists. It's our job to point out to everyone else on the planet where they went wrong. It's very big of us." He waved like a prince in a parade.

For Ellen, who was not comfortable having an exchange with

a single human, the state of the planet and all its occupants was beyond contemplation. A gust of wind lifted the hair veiling her face, and her hand flew up to cover her rutted cheek. She shifted her eyes and knew that Justice had seen it, but there was no trace of repulsion in his expression.

"It's just different," Justice said softly. "Everyone is unique. You know, there are societies where they deliberately scar their faces for beauty."

Ellen bit her lip. It sounded unlikely. "Not here," she whispered.

He shook his head. "The truth is, the standard of beauty is variable. Americans, as a social group, pride themselves on being individual, yet most of us are so isolated inside"—he pointed to his chest—"that we try to bond through uniformity outside." He gestured to a group of four teenage girls, each of them wearing tight jeans, tank tops of similar colors, and those slipper boots that were so popular. They wore the same makeup and hairstyles, but for all their efforts at uniformity, they were each distinctly different.

Ellen thought of the young man with the bracelet of scars and the officer saying, *It's a kind of gang marking.* So that too was a bid to connect, if she understood Justice correctly. It was all very weird and it took so much effort to try and make sense of it. Ellen's brain felt full of dust, but dust with rays of sunlight streaming in through a small, grimy window.

"And you can't agree that something is more attractive without also agreeing that something is less attractive. To make themselves feel better, an unfulfilled person puts other people down." He shrugged. "The human ego is a greedy beast." Justice laughed and shook his head. "I'm sorry. I get carried away, but I know you like to study the way people act too, so I hope you don't mind." He gri-

maced apologetically, which bewildered Ellen. She might not understand everything he was saying, but she loved listening to it.

"Come on," he said, looking at his watch. "I've got a treat for you."
He stood up and offered his hand. Ellen pretended not to see it. Talking was one thing, touching, another. Also, she was afraid her larger
weight might pull him to the ground instead of being helped up, so
she kept her eyes down and pushed herself awkwardly to her feet
instead. They threw away their trash and walked across the field to
the music hall. At the artists' door, Justice stuck his head in. "Okay,
all clear. Come on." He beckoned to her with smiling eyes.

Ellen followed him down a long hall, past dressing rooms and
rehearsal spaces, through piles of cables and light fixtures neatly
stacked, walls of switches and tied-off cables, until they came to
a stop.

They were standing in the wings of the stage. To Ellen's right
the thick velvet of a massive curtain rose until it disappeared into
the darkness above. Only a few work lights illuminated the stage
ahead of them. Ellen could see the backs of a row of musicians, some
seated, some standing near percussion instruments, all of them
focused forward on a man she could not see but whom she could
hear.

Justice tilted his head and moved around the very edge of the
curtain. She followed, pushing aside the voluminous fabric, and
found herself facing the empty house. Rows of upholstered seats rose
in a graceful swoop up to the first balcony, and above that, another
level, perched in the dim heights. She caught her breath at the scope
of it, both awed and frightened, but Justice took her arm and led her
down a short flight of black steps and then up the long, carpeted
aisle along the wall, ascending until they reached the very back row
of the first level. The exit doors were closed and it was dark. Turning

sideways, they moved along the last row until they were almost at the center aisle and then Justice motioned that they should sit.

On the stage below them, bathed in soft light, the orchestra members sat in an expanding semicircle on the polished wood of the wide stage. Far above them, a massive chandelier hung. Its bulbs were dark, but its crystals reflected the lights from the stage far below, the thousands of tiny glints hinting at its grandeur. Ellen had never been in such a splendid place in her life. But what fascinated her most was the fact that, even from this distance, with his back to them, she could hear everything the man on the stage said as though he were standing just in front of her.

Justice smiled at her obvious amazement. "Acoustics," he whispered. "Amazing, huh?"

The man, who must, of course, be the conductor, was saying, ". . . allegretto beginning in the fourth bar of the second movement, and building until the crescendo. The first movement, with the duet, must be piano, piano. We do not want to overwhelm the cello and the violin. They must play softly for this piece. Okay? Here we go." He tapped a long, narrow stick on the stand in front of him and raised both arms.

Now Ellen noticed that two chairs had been placed out in front of the others and in one of them was the unmistakable form of Temerity. Next to her was a red-faced man not one iota less circular than Ellen herself, and wedged between his thick thighs was a cello. The idea that someone as big as her could be sitting up there, in front of this many people when the hall was filled, was hard for Ellen to even assimilate, much less accept.

". . . three, four . . . and . . ." The stick swished and, like the sun rising, the violin and the cello began to play.

The two instruments combined in this space had a quality of

sound that she had never heard but that she instinctively recognized. It had the same timbre as something she'd felt inside herself all her life but never named. The music pulled at that part of her with an ebb and flow that called it out, and she had to put both hands over her mouth to keep from sobbing out loud.

She clamped back her tears and tried to shush the voices inside as the sound outside multiplied, the orchestra coming in, blending and mixing, until something entirely new was created. *Just like the tribes Justice was talking about,* Ellen thought. Each member was unique, but they all needed one another to make this. She felt oddly proud of the comparison, which only strengthened the tide inside her until her shoulders shook with the effort of containing it.

When it ended, Ellen realized that Justice's arm was resting softly across her shoulders, and she did not move away.

"Very nice." The conductor's voice broke through the ringing stillness. "See you all tomorrow."

There was the rustle of sheet music and a murmur of activity, starting low and then breaking out into laughter and conversation. But still Ellen cradled her face in her hands and would not look up.

"I'll go get Tem," Justice whispered. "Wait here."

Ellen was happy to do so. She stayed, inert, feeling *deconstructed,* as though she'd been sucked down through a sieve into a muddy bog. This thing, this having experiences, was every bit as exhausting as she had always feared it would be; that didn't surprise her. What she had not anticipated was the inexplicable combination of fatigue *and* exhilaration. The thing she hadn't known, had never dreamt, was that she was capable of feeling so much, and, far more astounding than that, that it could be worth it.

Then she heard the tapping of Temerity's approach, felt her arm slide around her shoulders and squeeze, felt her seat rock as Justice sat down on the other side of her.

Still hiding from everything, Ellen mumbled, "I'm sorry."

Temerity's hand patted Ellen's hair as she whispered, "Don't be. Are you sad?"

Nodding her face and hands as a unit, Ellen said, "And happy. I'm not used to these . . . feelings. It's like a . . . one of those . . . horrible carnival rides I've seen, that go up and down and spin and jerk, and, well, usually I'm so . . . on the ground. I'm not sure I can take it."

"You're just a little overwhelmed," Temerity said, "and that happens to everyone sometimes. You know what helps? Thinking about someone else. That takes the pressure off of you. Trust me."

The suggestion was like a light in a distant window, a path through the fog that Ellen could follow out of this mire. *Someone else,* she thought vaguely. Yes, it would be a relief to look away. She raised her face slowly from her hands, took a deep breath, looked from sister to brother, and said, "Then I think I know what to do."

It wasn't far to the downtown Macy's. Justice drove while the two women sat in the back and decided what to say. Actually, Temerity decided, and Ellen wrote, but she felt that they were her words too. When they'd finished their note, Ellen read it back.

Janelle,

You don't know us, but who we are is not important. There is someone who needs you very much, and maybe someone else who can help you as well. Your brother, Sam, is a father. He had a little girl, not even a day old. She is at Saint Vincent's hospital. Her mother, Cindy, is desperately in need of a friend. She cannot

take care of the baby, so she has decided to give it up for
adoption. She did not know of your existence either until
last night, just before she went into labor. She is confused
and alone, and she misses Sam very much. Perhaps you
can help each other.

It was signed simply, "Two friends." Ellen wanted to make it "three friends" but Justice begged off. "This is *your* good deed," he said.

"Okay, we're here. How do you want to do this?" Justice asked as he slipped the car into an available parking space.

"I kind of thought you'd take it in," his sister said.

He sighed. "Of course you did. Okay, what does she look like?"

After a brief pause, Ellen realized that she would have to answer that.

"She's tall, slim, dark skinned, with pale gold, almost greenish eyes, very beautiful, and one leg is shorter than the other," Ellen said.

Justice frowned. "Can you be more specific?"

"I don't remember anything el—" Ellen began, but Temerity cut her off with a smack to Justice's arm.

"He's joking. Go on," she told her brother. "Just give it to her and leave. Tell her you're the messenger, or something like that."

"Don't they always shoot the messenger?" Justice asked, switching off the engine and unbuckling his seat belt.

"That's only when it's bad news," Temerity said brightly, earning herself a look that only Ellen could appreciate. He got out of the car. They sat in silence for exactly three seconds and then Temerity blurted out, "What do you think she'll do?"

"What do *you* think she'll do?"

Temerity hummed for a second and then said, "She'll go, right away. Of course she will. And I think we should be there."

"Wh . . . wha . . . what?" Ellen stuttered.

"Don't you want to see what happens? How she reacts?" Then before Ellen could answer, she said, "I do! And that means you're coming, since, you know, I don't have the ability to process light and whatnot."

Justice returned within five minutes and told them that he'd handed over the note and gotten the heck out of there.

"Great, to Saint Vincent's," Temerity said.

But Justice protested. "Okay, now you're crossing the line into creepiness. It's one thing to find out someone needs help and make a connection for them to get that need met, but it's another to spy on the event." Temerity opened her mouth to object, but he went on. "No, I won't. I'll tell you what I will do. You know my friend Amanda?"

"Sure, the one who finished premed and actually became a doctor?"

"Yes, her, smart-ass. Guess where she works."

"Tell me it's Saint Vincent's," Temerity begged. "Say the words."

"The words." Justice snickered.

"Give me strength." Temerity clasped her hands and raised them to the sunroof. "Don't make me kill my brother. He doesn't mean to be so stupid, he just can't help himself."

"It's Saint Vincent's." Justice smiled broadly.

"Thank you." She dropped her hands and turned toward Justice. "You may now sleep without immediate fear of reprisal," Temerity said.

Justice rolled his eyes at Ellen. "And she's interning in obstetrics, so guess *where* Amanda works at Saint Vincent's."

"Ellen, you want to take this one?" Temerity turned in Ellen's general direction.

"Um. The baby place?" she suggested.

"The baby place," Justice agreed. "Exactly. I will call her and ask her to check in and let me know what the status is of both of your adopted characters. Okay?"

Ellen couldn't have been more relieved. As much as she wanted to see the outcome of their machinations, she didn't think she could take one more moment of being out in the world. Besides, she had to get to work in a few hours, and she needed a nap first.

"Fine." Temerity crossed her arms and stuck out her lower lip. "Typical. I miss all the fun."

Justice shook his head. "You've been having more fun than even monkeys should be allowed to have," he said. "Ellen, can we drop you off somewhere?"

"Home, if it's not too much trouble."

"You don't have to be at work for a few hours. We could go do something," Temerity suggested.

But Ellen felt so twisted and wrung out that the only "something" she wanted right now was semidarkness, four walls and her bed. Justice seemed to understand. "Home it is," he said.

Ellen climbed the stairs to her apartment feeling spent but softer, more pliable, as though if someone poked her, it would leave an indent. She went to the back window and looked out. The scene hadn't changed and the courtyard was deserted. Ellen didn't even get anything to eat before she took off her shoes, curled up in her bed, set her clock radio alarm to ring in two hours, and dropped off to sleep.

15

When the jangle of the phone woke her, Ellen picked it up automatically, as though she'd been doing it all her life, and murmured a sleepy, "Yeah?"

Temerity's voice was eager. "It's me." Even half-asleep, Ellen smiled at the irony of the pronouncement. Who else would it be? But Temerity was already on a roll. She was saying, "Okay, so here's the deal. Janelle went to meet Cindy. I guess that went pretty well, because according to Justice's friend Dr. Amanda, Janelle has now taken charge of Cindy's care, and the baby's." Trying to clear the fog in her head, Ellen sat up and asked, "Is that good?"

"Have you ever seen someone who needed taking care of more than Cindy?"

The question was a difficult one for Ellen. She hadn't ever evaluated the level of "need to be taken care of" in anyone before, much less compared one to another. So she just made a noise she hoped sounded like she agreed with whatever Temerity thought.

"What about those other people?" she asked.

"The Newlands? Not sure."

"Oh." Ellen was undecided if she felt anything about that, though the memory of Susan Newland's face streaming with tears left a rough spot just under her collarbone. Having an opinion was more of a nuisance than she'd expected.

"And while we're making our rounds through the hospital wards, T-bone, I mean J.B., is not as sprightly as we would wish. In fact, he's pretty much spright-less. I wish there was something we could do to help him."

"Like what?" Ellen asked.

"Give blood, or, I don't know . . . catch the guy who shot him might be good."

Ellen had a brief image of the man in the hooded sweatshirt with the pierced eyebrow in the ICU waiting room, but she kept it to herself. Both of Temerity's suggestions sounded substantially more demanding than slipping someone a note, and Ellen was doubtful that she was capable of any undertaking that involved either the gathering of clues or the giving of bodily fluids.

"You going to work?" Temerity asked.

"Yeah, I have to get ready now."

"Okay, call me in the morning, I'll let you know if I hear anything else."

Ellen stumbled to the shower, wondering how her life could possibly have changed so much in seventy-some-odd hours. But while the tepid water splashed over her, the answer came so clearly that she spoke the words out loud. "Because I got involved." Something she'd arduously avoided, with truly remarkable results. She'd done one thing, tripped one guy, and it had snowballed into expecting phone calls and visiting people at hospitals and being ambushed by music that made her weep. That last one she really hadn't seen coming. She almost—not quite, but almost—longed for the numbness of the good old three days ago.

Instead, as she dried herself with a thin, practically nonabsorbent towel, lifting her breasts and stomach to dry beneath the overlapping skin, she found herself thinking curiously about Irena. She felt . . . she searched for the right word . . . invested in the woman. And there was something, something reassuring, in a very uncertain way, about the fact that she would speak to Temerity tomorrow. She ran the sentence through her brain again to try to interpret it. She would speak to Temerity tomorrow, and she found it impossible to decipher accurately without any point of reference. She'd never, as far as she could remember, been committed to "speaking to someone tomorrow" just to exchange ideas or information. That deceptively simple sentence could mean, or bring, anything, because it meant plunging into the sea of unknown, especially with Temerity, and the unfamiliarity felt like a thrown rock that sent up a disruptive splash.

From standing back and watching it, she'd always known it was a crazy world, but it was a whole different crazy when you wandered out into its churning eddies. Persuading herself that she could retreat at any time, Ellen got dressed.

When she headed out to work, it was dark and the sky overhead had filled with clouds that bounced back the light from the city, casting a pewter sheen on the streets. It was like slipping into an illustrated world, and Ellen felt more than usually unnerved.

Trucks were stacked up three deep at the loading dock, and it was swarming with drivers and loaders, hindering her sneak entry. She was early as usual, so Ellen walked along in the shadow of the building to wait for a lull in the activity. Several large Dumpsters were lined up against the wall, green for garbage and blue for recycling, filled to overflowing with broken-down boxes. The excess cardboard was stacked in neat piles in between them. Ellen sat down on a comfortable pile and took out her notebook.

In the light from the gargantuan parking lot fixtures, she read back what she'd written on the bus ride over.

One line read, "A woman with an expensive handbag slapped her child for playing with it. The child did not understand. The woman should have explained, or given him something else to occupy his time." And another, "Scowling, mean man is rude to a woman with groceries. She asks him if he's having a bad day, and he says yes. They talk for a while, then he helps her carry her groceries off the bus. Both are smiling." There were several others, all of them supplemented with comments.

They were different from the lists of misdemeanors and petty behavioral crimes that were only a page or two back in the notebook. Leaning her head against the brick, she thought about this. What she was recording wasn't different. They were still just small observations, written snapshots of moments; what was different was how she was documenting them. She wasn't sure if it was because she was looking at people more closely or that she had taken a step back and was slightly farther away, but the result was that she could see more of the picture. She smiled. Imagining what caused people to behave the way they did was growing on her, it added to the story. Because, Ellen saw now, there was always more to the story. She thought about the woman with the grocery bags. Instead of immediately taking offense at the man's frustration, the way most people would, and snapping back at him, she had made the unusual choice to ask gently if there was a reason for the man's mood. Of course, the man could have chosen to continue being impolite and mired in his misery, but something as simple as a question instead of a retort had drawn him out and paid off for both of them.

Her musing was interrupted by the sound of footsteps. Someone was walking toward her hidden nook with deliberate, heavy steps. Instinctively, Ellen leaned into the shadows.

But whoever it was had stopped on the other side of the recycling container. She heard the flick of an old-fashioned lighter and smelled the taint of unusually harsh cigarette smoke. A low, tubercular cough, from deep in a tortured chest, accompanied the odor.

After a short wait, more footsteps approached. These were quicker and clicked along at a pace that said their maker was in a hurry.

Someone barked, "Get out of sight of the dock."

Ellen tensed, recognizing the Boss's oily voice.

"Nobody will see me," said a husky voice, definitely the smoker's voice, she thought. It had the rasp of a Slavic accent, though his English seemed confident. "Okay, I'm here. You got my money?"

"There's going to be a delay on that." The Boss sounded nervous. He quickly added, "And anyway, I have a proposition that will make your half of a cell phone chump change."

"I'm listening." The fruity cough was followed by the sound of spitting. *Gross*, thought Ellen. "I'm interested," the smoker said, and then he coughed again. It sounded like infected thunder, rumbling and soggy in the distance.

"I have to know you're in. I'm not telling you the plan unless you're in."

The smoker laughed. "How much?"

"Fifty thousand, at least." The Boss boasted like a kid who'd cheated on a geography test and gotten away with it.

"Tasty. What do I have to do?"

"Create a diversion, enough to distract everyone there, take care of one security guard, if necessary."

"You want me to kill somebody? That's extra."

"No, I don't want you to kill the damn security guard. Just . . . distract him. Jesus, try not to maim anybody. That's all I need. One of the guards is my wife's uncle. He's seventy, for God's sake."

"Relax. When?"

"Saturday evening, that's our biggest day, and we empty the cash from the registers right after ten p.m." The Boss laughed nervously. "I'll take care of that side. You need to make a big noise at exactly ten fifteen, and when the guard comes to investigate, I need him occupied for maybe five minutes, then I'll meet you at the usual place and you'll have more cash than you can fit in your saddlebags."

Saddlebags? Ellen looked around for a horse, not that she really expected to see one. She didn't, but she did see a motorcycle, parked in a shadowy corner at the far end of the huge, mostly deserted, side lot.

The scratchy voice said, "No problem. I'll let you know when I'm ready."

Ellen could imagine the Boss puffing up. She'd seen it a thousand times when one of his employees dared to presume to be his equal. "Remember, I'm in charge here," he said.

The laugh came again, triggering a coughing fit. When he recovered, the man said, "You're the boss. Oh, and just in case you were thinking of showing up next time without the cash . . ."

A paper rustled, and the Boss said, "What is this?" There was a frightened intake of breath as he answered his own question. "This is the route my kids walk to school."

"Yeah, I know. Cute kids."

"How do you kno—? You stay away from my children." The Boss's voice rose to a squeak from the real fear in it. *So,* Ellen thought, *he does care about something.*

"Up to you." There was the sound of footsteps, retreating this time, and Ellen watched the back of a huge man in a black leather jacket and boots as he crossed a football field of asphalt toward the bike, lighting another cigarette and hacking as he inhaled.

A few seconds later, the Boss made his way back toward the docks. Ellen waited for a full five minutes, spending the first two of them recording what she had heard, before heading in after him.

It was 9:45, so Ellen quickly changed and then did something she had never dared before. She went out onto the sales floor before the store was closed. The lines at the checkout were long, and the checkers were working furiously to get out on time. Ellen found a spot near the registers, a camping display, where she could sit on a foldable chair between large, stacked boxes of portable barbecues and watch.

As the last of the customers were herded through the wide lanes, the cashiers began to count out the drawers, making bundles of the various bills and writing the totals on a daily record. Then the manager came to collect it into a heavy canvas bag. It was the tall, balding manager with the sparse half circle of thin red hair. He carried the bag to the front office, opened the door with a key card he wore on a retractable extender attached to his belt, and went in. The door closed behind him, locking securely. One of the cashiers, who was lagging behind the others with her totals, knocked on the closed door, and it opened. They began a casual conversation, the checker leaning a hip against the office door to hold it ajar. Through it, Ellen watched the manager add her rubber-banded cash to the canvas bag and then drop the bag into the safe as he chatted with her. Then he began to record the totals from the cashiers' slips, and the cashier said good night and let the door fall closed. The bag was never reopened and the cash never recounted between the cashiers and the safe.

Interesting, Ellen thought.

The single security guard who had stood near the office door for the transfer of the money now left that post, and he and the rest of the security staff made their evening pass through the store, starting at the back and sweeping toward the front to make sure that the customers had all found their way out. Ellen sat very still, and the elderly man in the gray uniform walked past the boxes without any recognition that she was seated between them. As soon as he was gone, she got up and went back to collect her supplies.

As she opened the door, cautiously as usual, to the acrid atmosphere of the storeroom, she heard the sound of singing in a strange language from among the shelving. Ellen fetched her cart, topped off her cleaning fluids, and waited. In a minute, Irena came from around the back. Her earbuds were around her neck but not in her ears. *Good choice,* Ellen thought. Out on the floor, it would be safe to wear them, but not here, where someone could slip up behind you, as Irena had learned the hard way. Ellen turned her back and the woman walked past her, stopping at the door to peer out, checking, no doubt, for the lascivious Boss. The hallway was empty, so she crossed herself, muttered something in Russian, and went on her way, humming.

So, Ellen thought, things were looking up for the battered cleaner. Ellen felt a warm sensation in her chest and laid a hand flat on it. She didn't feel sick, but she wondered if the heat meant she was coming down with something. She'd check for a fever when she got home. She gathered the last of her things and was out on the floor working before she realized that she had forgotten to eat dinner.

The realization panicked her with a sensation that the floor had dropped out from below her, but a quick check told her that, though she was hungry, she was neither on the brink of death nor in

immediate danger of starvation. In fact, she felt better rather than
worse. Stranger and stranger, this changing of routine.

The work-task sheet told her that tonight she'd been assigned to
the fresh food section first, and then the dry goods. As she wiped
down the signs and cleaned up the free fruit samples smashed into
the floor, some still skewered with toothpicks, Ellen eyed the piles of
red and green apples. She'd never found fruit very appealing—it
just wasn't substantial enough—but she pushed a few from the edge
of the pile into her dusting rag and slipped them into her apron
pocket, and when her break came, she took them, along with a family pack of fried chocolate pies, into the bathroom.

The first bite of the red apple was crisp and chewy and crunched
satisfyingly. The juice dripped down one side of her mouth and Ellen
felt the fresh, sweet taste explode on her tongue. Once, long ago,
she'd been given half an apple by a school nurse and she remembered
its firm, sugary snap now. But the apples she'd received at school
lunches or at the group home had been tasteless mush in comparison. She devoured four apples, liking the sour tang of the green
almost as much as the sweetness of the red, and then found she
could eat only one of the single-serving pies. To her surprise, she
drank less than a third of the large coffee with the hazelnut creamer
she had brought in from the break room. It tasted . . . fake with the
apples. The artificial flavoring coated her mouth and clashed with
the authentic sweetness of the fruit. *I must be coming down with
something,* Ellen thought. *Possibly the stomach flu.*

She was back on the floor when she heard an announcement over
the PA. "Irena, please come to the office."

That couldn't be good. The only encouraging sign was that the
voice was not that of the Boss but of Thelma, one of the stock managers. Ellen wasn't sure but she thought Thelma was Produce; at any

rate, she always saw the woman counting boxes filled with leaves of unidentified plant life.

Three minutes went by before the PA clicked on again. "Irena Medvedkov, you have an emergency phone call. Come to the office."

Ellen looked around. She did not know where Irena was working tonight, but she had a good idea why the woman wasn't responding. Taking a duster, Ellen started along the row of aisles. She spotted the American hopeful in the toy section.

Her ears were plugged with the tiny speakers that led by a twisted cord to the scratched and dented portable CD player on her cart. She was humming as she pulled down packs of toys, scrubbed off the shelves, and then replaced them.

The problem was how to pass on the message without having to reveal herself, but Ellen needn't have worried. She'd forgotten the Crows. A public announcement of some kind of personal emergency ruffled their black feathers like a strong wind rich with the scent of sloppy picnickers. Within seconds the two women, one tall and scrawny, the other short and thick, came hurrying around the end of the aisle. Kiki's long strides providing a slower backbeat to the rapid pattering of Rosa's hurried, short, clipped steps.

"Irena!" Kiki shouted, tugging at the woman's sleeve so that she spun in alarm. "Take those off!"

"There is problem?" Irena asked, the fear making her voice quaver.

"The office has been paging you," Rosa said, more gently. "There's an emergency phone call for you."

"I don't want to go," Irena said, physically cringing.

Kiki sniffed and squared her bony shoulders. "I'll go with you. I don't want you to be alone if this is bad news."

Ellen snorted. The Crow meant, of course, that she didn't want to miss being the bearer of Irena's private misfortune to the masses. She'd be back to broadcast the bad news quicker than live TV. Rosa looked disappointed. "I'll come too," she said, but Kiki wouldn't hear of it, and Rosa, a sour scowl puckering her already pickled countenance, was relegated to waiting.

So as Kiki got a talon gripped on Irena's wrist and propelled her toward the back offices, Ellen decided her best bet was to stay near Rosa, who sulked her way to the frozen foods and pretended to dust while she kept one eye fixed on the doorway that led to the management offices.

It was only a matter of minutes before the door opened again and Kiki rushed out. Rosa met her halfway across the floor. "The baby is sick," she reported breathlessly. "Thelma is going to take Irena to the hospital. The kid is there already."

"What's wrong with it?"

Kiki shrugged. "I couldn't find out, something about a cough and a fever. She was yammering in Russian and that's all I could get out of her. We'll go in the morning, take some flowers to the poor girl. We'll find out the rest then."

"Yes. She must be frightened. Poor girl," Rosa echoed. "What hospital?"

"Saint Vincent's, of course. You don't think they'd take an immigrant with no insurance to a private hospital."

Rosa crinkled her nose. "Rough place."

"I offered to go with her," Kiki said grandly, "but the Boss said no, only Irena and Thelma could go. He looked pretty satisfied with himself about it."

Rosa's eyes glittered. "Getting back at her for not putting out?"

"Of course." She sniffed. "Men. Can't live with 'em, can't shoot 'em."

Rosa ignored the comment and said, "I hate Saint Vincent's, so run-down and depressing. They took my nephew there when he was accidentally shot by a drunken friend."

"Well, that's just not fair."

"I know, he spent two weeks in the hospital and has a hell of a scar."

Kiki's beady eyes narrowed with happy malice. "I don't mean it's not fair that he was shot. I mean it's not fair that they can shoot each other. We should get a turn too."

The two women laughed and moved away, bellyaching ferociously, all their "concern" for Irena easily relegated to the back of their minds.

Ellen returned to work. Was Irena's life, she wondered, a journey over stormy seas that she had to successfully negotiate before eventually winning through? Or was she doomed to spend her life bailing seawater out of a leaky boat?

Now that Temerity had pointed out certain things on the horizon, Ellen was finding it hard to pretend she didn't see the woman drowning.

Ellen Homes wouldn't have put it this way, but Temerity's promptings had roused her, stirred her to lift her head so that maybe she could see just a little bit farther out into that uncertain ocean. And she found that she wasn't as eager to turn away as she had been.

Because she had a feeling that, far out, past the storms and waves, the sunlight on the water must be lovely.

16

J.B. is no spunkier, so we're giving blood," Temerity said instead of "hello" when Ellen woke up and dialed her number before even getting out of bed. Ellen looked at the receiver. It was unnerving the way she knew it was her, even if there was a supposedly logical explanation. But the girl went on without waiting for a response. "Or, *I* am anyway, and you're going with me. We'll tell the hospital it's for J.B. from an anonymous donor."

This confused Ellen. How would Temerity know J.B.'s blood—what was that word? Kind? Sort? Her drowsy brain wouldn't let it through. It was funny how you could forget a simple word sometimes. She knew, of course, that not all blood was the same, she'd read about it in at least two books. One was a medical thriller, and the other was a book that claimed vampires were real, which she hadn't finished. Ellen thought that vampires were silly things to believe in, because she'd never seen one and she worked nights.

"Why? Does he need your blood . . . uh, kind?" Ellen asked.

"Don't know what kind he has, but mine's that flavor lots of people like."

Cautiously, Ellen's lips twitched at a thought. She decided to go for it. "Vanilla?" she dared.

There was a barking laugh that made Ellen feel practically plucky. "More like tutti-frutti. Meet me there? My appointment is at four."

Ellen looked at the alarm clock. Three. That meant she'd had about eight hours of sleep, not her usual twelve to fourteen, which typically used up most of her nonworking time. But she had something else to occupy her today. As well as possibly meeting Temerity, she could no longer put off going to the thrift store, because her left shoe was not of much use for anything other than throwing at spiders. Not that she would; she quite liked spiders, as long as they stayed in their corner. "Okay."

"Great, see you outside."

The thought of meeting up left Ellen humming a few notes of the music Temerity had played for her. She opened her refrigerator and stood looking in. After some consideration, she took out a loaf of bread, cheese, bologna, mayonnaise and a jar of pickles. She made a triple-decker sandwich, opting out of the mayonnaise, which, when she opened it and gazed in, made her stop humming. Her stomach vetoed the gunky white goo and she put it back, wishing she had brought home more of the apples. It had come as a complete revelation that she'd forgotten the taste of a good apple, outside of fried dough, and the compact orbs would be far easier to stash in a duffel bag than a ten-inch pie and nowhere near as sticky. She'd get some tonight.

Another layer of tape resurrected her mostly dead shoe enough to take her the three blocks to the thrift store. Ellen slipped in behind an unruly family. Their half dozen or so young boys jerked and hopped and burst out like microwave popcorn around their parents, who, though not much older than midtwenties, looked worn-out and completely done. The activity was frenetic and dizzying to watch, so Ellen edged her way carefully around the frenzy and went to the shoes, which were an equally confusing, but less mobile, mess on rickety racks. After several minutes of searching, she found first the left and then the right of a slightly worn pair of black Converse that fit well enough. Now she had two shoes, but only one lace between them. Situating herself on a pile of rolled-up carpets, Ellen pulled the lace out of her old shoe and began to thread it into the new one. She had almost completed the task when she heard a cough, a sickly one, deep and grumbling.

The producer of the unhealthy reflex, whose size and symptoms fit the general description of the man she'd seen walking away from his meeting with the Boss last night, was standing near a large cardboard box. He was rooting through a tangled heap of hats, scarves and other miscellaneous accessories, holding a black leather glove in one hand and trying to locate its mate.

Ellen studied his face. What she could see of his skin had the yellowed and rutted pallor of a lifelong smoker who spent a lot of time in harsh weather. Most of his face was hidden behind a severely trimmed black beard. A woman stood next to him, fidgeting and tapping one foot compulsively. She looked forty but was probably in her late twenties. She was meth-addict thin and wearing so much makeup that it gave her skin the same cracked, rough appearance as her leather jacket. She was antsy and jumpy, her eyes constantly cutting to the door. She reached impatiently into the box and pulled out a different pair.

"How about these?" she asked.

"No good," he muttered.

"Come on, let's go, Georgi. What's wrong with these?"

With an obvious effort at patience, he said, "No fingers, Loretta. We'll go when I'm ready. Go look around."

Without taking offense, Loretta threw the gloves back into the box and pulled a pack of cigarettes from her jacket. She dug in it with shaking fingers until she extracted one of the bent white cylinders and stuck it in her mouth. "Maybe I should look for a wedding dress," she mumbled.

The man, Georgi, smiled and shook his head. "You don't need a dress to get married at the courthouse."

"I want one," she whined.

"If you want, my sweet. Go outside and you can smoke."

She began to wander toward the door, searching her pockets for a light. "Hurry up. I need a bump."

When she was out of earshot, Georgi mumbled what sounded like a profanity in what Ellen assumed was Russian and continued rooting through the box.

Ellen took her shoes to the front and paid. The man behind the register, his back twisted into a cruel, unnatural angle, did not trouble his tortured spine to look up as he slid the change across the counter. Grateful, Ellen took the shoes and fled the store.

The wiry Loretta woman was standing just outside the door, smoking next to a sign that read NO SMOKING WITHIN TWENTY FEET OF DOORWAY. Every deep drag on the cigarette pursed her mouth into an ugly pucker. A woman entering with two young children gave her a reprimanding look and waved a hand in front of her face. "Do you really have to smoke right here?" she asked, gesturing to the children.

"Yeah, I do," Loretta said and exhaled a cloud of tar and nicotine in the woman's direction. For a moment Ellen thought that the mother, whose nostrils actually flared, would launch into Loretta, but after an assessment of the brittle drug addict, the fire in the mother's eyes faded to quiet disgust and she hustled her kids through the door.

Ellen wondered what would have happened if the mother had asked Loretta if she was having a bad day, like the woman on the bus with the groceries. She knew that it would probably have unfolded differently, most likely ending in physical assault. Loretta was the kind of person who had long ago replaced any kind of decency with a switchblade. She'd seen Loretta's type before—"type," that was the word, "blood type"—angry, miserable and violently self-destructive. The only way to deal with someone that mean and unstable was to walk away, or better yet, run, so that they didn't have time to hit you in the back of the head with a convenient brick.

This Loretta woman struck an old, ominous chord in Ellen, launching another unwelcome flashback. A clear picture smacked on Ellen's mental windshield of a chain-smoking drunk, her mother, arriving home with a shopping bag. Afraid to hope, Ellen watched eagerly as her mother reached in, handed her a small pack of peanut butter crackers, then took out a carton of cigarettes and a gallon bottle of vodka. Even after she greedily consumed the snack food, Ellen cried with hunger until her mother slapped her and sent her to her blanket on the floor.

Banishing the memory, Ellen turned her gaze through the plate-glass front of the thrift store to watch the young mother with her kids. The kids seemed well fed and happy. The woman leaned down and kissed the taller one on the head. Ellen thought, *I'll bet that's nice.* She would have been happy for her mother not to beat her.

Long years of experience made it easier to shake off the longing and the repulsion when the thankfully sparse recollections unleashed a sneak assault on her, though even the suggestion of hunger still panicked her. To distract herself, Ellen turned her focus back on Loretta, pulling out her notebook and writing the details of the vulgar couple and their exchange. It did the trick. It wasn't long before the man Loretta had called Georgi came out.

Loretta took a last long, hard drag, then flicked her still-burning cigarette onto the sidewalk. She rubbed her hands together compulsively. "About time. Let's go."

He pulled the new gloves from the front of his pants with a smug glance back at the store. Stolen. Ellen wrote that down. Without bothering to hurry, he said, "I'll drop you at the Clown, then I've got business."

Loretta started to whine. "You promised me a fix."

Ellen wrote, "The Clown." It was a bar, not far away, that seemed to cater to the Russian populace around it, judging from the language of the altercations outside. She'd passed it many times. Its windowless front was a constant backdrop for drunken fights and its back parking lot for the occasional unsolved stabbing.

"You'll get it, baby, but business comes first," Georgi said. Before she could respond, he started up the bike that Ellen had seen last night. The engine's earsplitting volume shattered the relative quiet of the storefront, and Ellen's hands flew up to cover her ears protectively. She could see Loretta's mouth moving, but the discordant roar blocked out all other sound and interrupted everyone and everything around it. As the pair rode off, taking the onslaught with them, and Ellen was capable of thought, her first was why anyone would choose such a noisy vehicle, but then it occurred to her that anyone who had a brain would most likely want to be able to use it, so maybe only stupid people wanted to ride those things. She wrote that down too.

In the deafness of the thumping reverb in her eardrums, Ellen switched her shoes, throwing the old pair into the trash can, and started out for the hospital.

The "new" shoes were a good find, only slightly worn with plenty of squishiness left in the soles, and Ellen enjoyed the cushioning, the bouncy effect. The bottoms of her old ones had been compressed and worn until they were leaf thin, with all the spring of a sheet of aluminum foil. She found herself walking a bit faster and enjoying the separation between feet and concrete.

The spring in her step got her to the hospital in half the time. She positioned herself between two of the large planters at the very edge of the entrance plaza, waiting for Temerity, feeling winded but oddly energized. When she did arrive, the blind girl found her way to the same bench they'd occupied while they waited for Justice, and sat listening.

After a glance down at her shoes, Ellen crept slowly up behind Temerity, leaned down and was just about to whisper *Boo*, when Temerity jumped up and said, "Oh good, you're here. Let's go in."

"What . . . how? I got new shoes."

"I can tell. Nice, by the way. But you also have a distinctive smell. Everybody does. Yours is very homey, like"—she paused with a concentrated, dreamy look—"breakfast cooking, something like that."

"Breakfast?" Ellen asked, her mouth starting to water. "Like bacon?"

Temerity smiled. "Yes, but combined with cinnamon rolls in the oven. One of my very favorite smells."

"Mine too!" Ellen said.

Temerity reached out a hand and Ellen automatically turned so that she was facing the same direction and her friend could lay it on her shoulder. "Between you and me," Temerity whispered, "it's always mystified me that some people get up and have just coffee. Really?"

"I know, right?" Ellen said. It had always befuddled her that anyone could skip breakfast, especially bacon.

Temerity got a pass to the blood donor suite. Once there, she sat with a volunteer who filled in her paperwork for her. Ellen took up a position in a chair by the door and stared listlessly at the TV in the waiting room. A soap opera was on and it grated on her nerves. Did people really say, *He's a shadow of his former self*? or *You will be mine. Oh yes, you will be mine*? She'd never heard a real person say either of those phrases, and she listened to a lot. The theater of real life was so much more intense and interesting, which was why it was her un-contested favorite diversion. Second to that, Ellen liked books—at least you could pick and picture your own show, and the paperbacks were only a quarter at the thrift store.

After a half hour or so, Temerity was led into a different room. She was back in about fifteen minutes, with a cotton ball taped on her arm and a box of juice in one hand. She found Ellen and sat down next to her. Ellen stared at the cotton where a small, dark red dot showed through the clear tape that covered it. The spot of blood made her feel queasy and she had to look away.

"I'm not supposed to go anywhere for a few minutes. They're afraid I'll black out and then they'll have to admit me. I tried to explain that I'd faint if I saw something *besides* nothing. Blackout is my norm. Alas, to no avail, so we have to wait."

"Did it hurt?" Ellen asked.

Temerity rocked once. "No, not really. I mean, there's a little prick at the beginning, but then you don't really notice it. Are you afraid of needles?"

"I don't know." Ellen considered her answer and then decided that was wrong, so she changed it. "Yes. I mean, it's weird, having some-thing metal go into your skin." The very thought made her dizzy and the room teetered a bit. A flash of standing in a line at school, a cold swab on her arm, and a stinging prick. Waking on the floor, the other kids laughing at her, her face burning. She shuddered and pushed the thoughts away.

A frown creased Temerity's pretty face. "You know nobody *likes* needles, don't you?" When Ellen didn't answer, she seemed to take it as a yes. "All you have to do is think about how the medicine will make you better, protect you, if you're getting a shot, or how much worse it is for the person who needs the blood you're giving, if that's the reason, and that puts it all in perspective."

Perspective, Ellen thought, meant so many things. She didn't like to think about it.

17

They waited for fifteen minutes, during which time they shared a small pack of cheese crackers that Temerity had selected from the mandatory after-donation snack foods. It was a tiny snack, but Ellen enjoyed the salty crunch. While they ate, Ellen told Temerity about Irena and the phone call the night before.

"So now she has a sick baby to care for that isn't even hers that she got saddled with in the first place?" Temerity summed up.

"Pretty much, yeah."

"And people feel sorry for *me*. Jesus, how does someone like Irena, and so many others, get along in the world?" Temerity asked sadly. Ellen thought, *Some do, some don't*, but she didn't say it out loud. "And you said they came here last night? We should see if we can find out what's wrong."

"You could just ask Justice's friend Dr. Amanda," Ellen said.

"No. She can't really tell us about patients' medical details. What she told Justice about the other two was either general knowledge or outside the hospital's legal domain. Think about it. Janelle met Cindy, and a shooting victim wasn't doing well. No medical details. Next idea."

"Um . . ." Ellen didn't have any other ideas, and then she remembered the Crows. "There are these two women who work with her. They said they were going to come down here today to see her."

"Oh." Temerity softened. "I'm glad she has friends."

"She doesn't." Ellen explained, briefly, about the Crows' insatiable appetite for gossip and the real reason for their visit—information. "So, I'm likely to hear whatever there is to know at work."

"Okay, I guess we'll have to count on that. We've been sitting here long enough." She stood up. "I want to go and see if we can find out anything about J.B."

Ellen didn't even try to talk her out of it. The force that was Temerity just drew her along. They snaked their way through the passages again until they were seated in the intensive care unit's waiting room. Ellen searched around, but there were no suspicious-looking young men this time. Looking through the glass down the hallway, Ellen did not see the police officer who had been posted outside J.B.'s room on their previous visit.

"I'm not sure if that's good or bad," Temerity said when Ellen told her. "I mean, on the one hand, he could have stabilized so they moved him to a regular room. On the other hand . . ." She let it hang.

"He could be dead," Ellen finished.

Temerity sighed and patted Ellen's arm. "Yes, that was implied," she said.

They waited for half an hour. Ellen occupied the time by watching some of life's other vignettes around her: a young woman crying in the corner who was being comforted by a young man who might be her boyfriend; a cold-faced older man engrossed in a thick spy novel, whose exterior calm was betrayed by the anxious twitching of his eyes to the ICU door each time it swung open; a family of four who was joined by a man exiting one of the units. They huddled together to hear the news of a loved one. The outlook was uncertain and the reactions of the four were evenly tied. Two took the news as hopeful, the other two despaired.

Perspective, Ellen thought again. *It's all in the perspective.* Losing patience, Temerity tried to get information from the nurses' station but, unable to claim being a family member, she found herself denied.

"But he doesn't have any family," Temerity pleaded. "I'm his neighbor."

There was such pathos in her voice, which Ellen thought was probably mostly legitimate, that the nurse relented and told her that the patient had been moved, but that was all she could say.

"So, that's good news, right?" Temerity pressed.

The nurse glanced around. "He's been moved from intensive care. I'm afraid I can't tell you anything else." The phone on her desk buzzed and the nurse answered it, effectively ending any further exchange.

"So," Temerity said as they walked away, "he's probably somewhere else in the hospital. I think we should seek."

Though Ellen was as intrigued as ever by many of the stories she was seeing about the hospital, the new addition of seeing the characters in these scenes as people who were suffering was beginning to leech strength from her. Empathy, something Ellen had only a sketchy understanding of, and still, for her, in its infantile stage, was draining. But she was aware enough to understand that maybe if the stories were positive, she would feel somewhat restored.

"Let's go back to the baby floor," she suggested. It was mostly happy there.

"J.B. won't be there, and Cindy won't still be there either, I don't think," Temerity told her. "As long as she had a normal delivery, which she did, with no insurance and the Newlands most likely out of the picture, they would boot her out as soon as possible, two days max."

This threw Ellen. "She's not back at the apartment," she said.

Temerity smiled. "I think I know where she might be." Ellen waited. "Where did Janelle say she lived?"

"Something Estates," Ellen told her. "I'd have to look it up."

"You know, that Newland woman's voice . . . What was her name?"

"Susan."

"Right. It kind of stuck with me. She really cared about that baby, and I think she must have been truly disappointed—it makes me sad. But the way her husband talked, I'm still glad we did what we did. Imagine having a father who resented you from the start."

Not being able to imagine having a father, Ellen had no response. But she too had thought about Susan Newland and her strong insistence that they keep the baby. She hadn't cared that the child was a different race. It probably took that kind of determination to be a good mother. Ellen remembered the mother kissing her child's head in the thrift store.

"Okay, let's make like the Jews and wander out into the desert," Temerity said, taking hold of Ellen's shoulder.

Having never been outside the city, Ellen wondered why Jews would want to go out into the desert. Was it nice there? Did Christians like the desert too? Did Muslims? Maybe it was fun. It was probably sunny all the time, and some people liked that. They decided to go floor by floor, working their way down. They made their way through the fifth floor fairly quickly. No police occupied folding chairs outside any of the closed doors, and the ones that were open and occupied contained the elderly in various stages of dementia. It was depressing. Floor four was busier—there were casts and doctors studying charts and families bringing flowers—but other than dodging the crowd, it too was proving uneventful until Ellen saw the detective coming down the hall toward them.

He walked purposefully, his face screwed into what might have been a perpetual, preoccupied scowl.

Ellen stopped and turned to face Temerity. "It's the detective," she whispered. "He's coming this way. What should we do?"

Temerity tilted her head so far to one side that it almost touched her shoulder. "Really? Let's see, what are our options? We could . . . ignore him and traipse aimlessly through these antiseptic halls for hours, or . . ."

"We could follow him," Ellen finished.

"Great minds," Temerity said, and tapped her skull with her folded stick. Half of it swung free of her grasp on its fanlike hinge and smacked her harder than she had intended. "Ouch," she said. "Well, moderately competent minds anyway."

They huddled together until the detective passed, and then trailed a few yards behind him. They didn't have far to go until he went into a room, closing the door again behind him. There was no police officer posted outside the door, which, when Ellen asked Temerity if she thought that was good or bad, caused her to comment that it could go either way.

The room was near the end of the hallway, not far from the elevator banks and an area that included a few random chairs, so they took up their positions and waited.

"I wish we could hear what he's saying," Temerity bemoaned. "You don't think you could slip into the room and listen, do you?"

"I'm not much of a slipper," Ellen said, glancing down at her thighs overlapping the folding chair. "Those rooms are small, and I'm not."

"Which increases the odds of being bumped into," Temerity observed.

Ellen didn't say it, but it also increased the already strong possibility of her knocking over some outrageously expensive and fragile piece of medical equipment, causing the immediate demise of some unwitting patient as well as exposing herself. All she said was, "And I'm not really the most nimble person, as you may have noticed."

"Why?" Temerity said. "Because you slid across my living room floor and tried to take out my coffee table? Personally, I think you were acting in self-defense. I've had my suspicions about that table's intentions for quite a while. It's attacked my shins on several occasions when I wasn't looking." She snorted with laughter and Ellen found herself smiling at the image. "I refuse to believe it had anything to do with your nimbility factor."

Ellen frowned. "Is 'nimbility' even a word?"

"It is now!" Temerity told her. "You are present at the birth of a noun. Nimbility factor must be computed against sneak attacks of all ornamental furniture."

"Shhh, he's coming out." Ellen squeezed Temerity's arm and they sat quietly as the detective strode to the elevators, dialing on his cell phone. He held it to his ear.

"Morton here. Yeah, he's not much help. He says he knows the kid by sight, but not by name. . . . Yeah, I do believe him . . . because most of these guys go by tags. He confirms that he let him in, but won't say why, for obvious reasons." He listened as he pressed the down button for the elevator, then continued. "No, the place was clean except for a small bag of weed—personal stash, I'm betting. If he had quantity, the kid took it. . . . I have no idea, sold or smoked by now. It looks like a dead end." The elevator doors opened with a chime and the detective stepped in. The last thing they heard him say was, "Seems like a nice enough drug dealer. Small-time. Too bad he'll probably be dead soon. . . . No, he'll survive this, doctor says, but there's not a chance in hell the Germenes will let him stay alive if he can finger one of them."

The doors slid closed and Ellen watched Temerity think. "Germenes," she said thoughtfully. "I heard a radio news report about them. They're a relatively new gang who consider themselves sort of an elite group, very organized. Kind of like the Mafia, but meaner."

"Do you think that, you know, bracelet-scar thing on his wrist meant something?"

"The cop said it did. It's like their mark or something."

Ellen rubbed her wrist unconsciously, then touched her face, feeling the remembered, searing, haunting pain of her own wound. The prolonged throbbing ache and the infection that lasted for months, aggravating the scarring. She could not fathom any reason why someone would willingly take on that kind of pain. It had been horrible. Her face twitched at the thought, so she shoved the disquieting memory aside with a great mental thrust.

"I'm going in," Temerity announced, standing suddenly. "Point me in the right direction."

"What are you going to say?" Even as she asked it, Ellen realized that she couldn't fathom Temerity at a loss for words. "Never mind, stupid question, just leave the door open so I can hear you."

"You can come in too, if you like."

"I don't think so." She walked Temerity to the right door and pushed it open. Though it was a double room, only one bed was occupied and Ellen could see her neighbor in it, closer than ever before except through the lenses of her binoculars.

He was awake, she could tell that at a glance. His left arm was bare, and his shoulder was covered in a large bandage. The various tubes that she assumed were dripping medicine into him snaked under the blanket, which covered the rest of his thin body. He turned his head to look at Temerity, and, for a split second, Ellen thought his eyes registered her as well. Then Temerity spoke, drawing his gaze again.

"Excuse me, I'm looking for a friend. Is this room 5023?"

"Don't really know, but it's just me in here," he said. "It's awful boring."

"I've got a minute, if you want to chat." She advanced into the room. "My name is Temerity. Sorry I can't see you; it's a curse."

"And a blessing sometimes, I'll bet. It would be if you had to look out this window." J.B. laughed, but it turned quickly into a painful-sounding cough.

"Are you all right?" Temerity asked, concerned. "Do you want me to call a nurse?"

He waved away the idea with a hand that only rose a few inches. "No, no. I'm okay. I have some congestion in my chest. Took a bullet in the shoulder and I smoke too much. You wouldn't have any cigarettes on you?"

Temerity smiled. "No, sorry. I'm not sure they'd let you smoke in here anyway." She found a chair and sat down.

"At this point, I'd climb onto the window ledge for a nicotine fix." He smiled. "Who's your friend?"

Shocked, Ellen drew her face back around the doorjamb, her heart beating wildly, before she realized he was asking who Temerity had come to visit.

"Oh, a girlfriend—minor thing, no big deal, but like you said, it's boring to lie around all day. You were shot? That's exciting. Not fun, I'm sure, but it's more interesting than an appendectomy."

"No, it was not fun," he said. Ellen risked leaning around the door again. He was turned away now, toward Temerity on the far side of the bed. "I'm J.B., by the way."

"Nice to meet you, J.B. You live around here?"

"Not far, apartment over in Morningside."

"Oh, I have a friend who lives in Morningside."

"I'm sorry for them. You?"

"Midtown. I'm a musician, so I have to commute to the music center, and with my particular affliction"—she pointed to her eyes—"public transportation is a must."

He grinned with a wry amusement. "Must be interesting, seeing the world through your eyes, if you know what I mean, no offense intended."

"None taken," Temerity said cheerfully. "I know what you mean. I always think it must be interesting to see the world from anyone else's point of view. I think it might be a better place if we all tried it more often." There was a quiet moment while they both considered this and then Temerity asked, "What do you see?"

J.B. seemed taken aback by the question. "Oh, good things, bad, lots of things that could be better than they are. Some people give up, some people go on trying."

"It's about the same from here," Temerity said. "Are you going to be in here for long?"

"A few more days, at least."

"Then back to your Morningside mansion?"

J.B. gave a short laugh, but then stopped himself as a cough mustered. "No. Then I'll be leaving town, pretty quick."

"Why is that?"

"Let's just say the bullet they took out of me has owners, and they'll come looking for it." Ellen saw his face darken, and he fixed his stare flatly on the wall.

"I'm guessing that means they didn't catch the person who did this?"

He shook his head and grimaced from the movement. The hand under the blanket came out to gingerly touch the bandage. "No such luck. And I've had a sudden loss of income, loss of merchandise, and an inability to finance future business endeavors."

"I'm sorry to hear that. Do you have somewhere to go?"

"Got a son. He's in Flagstaff, Arizona. Talked to him this morning. He said I can crash with him for a few weeks, but he didn't sound too happy about it. Can't say I blame him."

"Kids today," Temerity said.

J.B. managed a weak laugh. "Yeah." He yawned; his eyelids seemed to be getting heavy.

"So, not to pry, but I am curious. Did you know who shot you?"

"I knew him, not well, he was a kid, a . . . customer who decided it would be a better deal if he cut out the middleman. Me."

"He robbed you. Do you think you'll be able to recover your . . . stuff?"

"Not damn likely. The guy who did this isn't exactly the kind of person who thinks things over and has a change of heart. In fact, I'm not sure he has a heart." He snorted softly and then winced. "Most likely any heart he had was ripped out of him when he was little. No hope after that. Probably a good time for me to get out of the business anyway. Time to start over."

"That sounds like a healthy attitude," Temerity said.

"Yeah, it would to me too if I weren't so tired." His lids came to half-mast as he said it. "Morphine's kickin' in. Sorry if I get slurry, but . . ." He licked his lips and tried to straighten his head.

"I'll let you sleep," Temerity said. "That's the best thing you can do right now." She stood.

"Thank you, young lady," J.B. said, closing one eye to prop the other open. "Not many people would take the time to talk to somebody they don't even know."

"I like talking to people I don't know. Breaks up the monotony, you know, same old voices, over and over. I'd like to come back, maybe tomorrow?"

"That would be nice, to have something to look forward to." The words connected to each other as he lost control of his speech.

"You feel better," Temerity said softly. "You never know, maybe the police will catch the guy while you're napping."

The response was a soft snore. J.B. was already out. Temerity turned and felt her way out of the room.

She took Ellen's shoulder and they walked down the hall in silence until they reached the elevators, then Temerity said, "He seems like a kind soul, actually."

"He likes dogs," Ellen said, remembering how gentle he'd always been with the mangy old poodle. She wouldn't have wanted to touch it.

"That's always a good sign."

Ellen made a mental note to try petting Mouse more often. He certainly seemed to seek her out, but she'd always thought that was for warmth. "Can we go now?" she asked.

"Don't you want to see if we can find out anything about Irena's baby?" Temerity asked. "I mean, we're here."

Ellen did want to find out. So they went to the pediatric wing and walked slowly through the halls. This was much more difficult for Ellen. For some reason, seeing children sick was much harder to reconcile than the elderly. And the parents all seemed so lost. Ellen was grateful that it wasn't long until she spotted Irena.

Through an open door, she saw the Russian woman asleep in a

chair near a sterile crib draped with plastic sheeting, her head crooked at an awkward angle. It was difficult to see inside the sheeting for the humidity. Ellen explained the scenario to Temerity, who whispered, "Sounds like pneumonia. Or some kind of bronchitis maybe."

"Will the kid die?" Ellen asked, watching the exhausted figure of Irena and debating whether or not the demise of the child would be a relief for her, though a sad one.

"Probably not," Temerity said. "I had it when I was a kid. As long as the baby gets the right antibiotics and care, which it sounds like he is, he should be okay. Do you want to talk to her?"

"What?" Ellen drew back, a knee-jerk reaction.

"I didn't think so. We'll stop by tomorrow when we come to see J.B." They began their stroll to the exit. "So nobody at work sees you either?"

"Not for a long time. I mean, I had to be interviewed and stuff when I first got the job." She gritted her teeth at the thought. "They didn't say so, but I know that my . . . how I look . . . is why they put me on the graveyard shift, so no one would have to see me." Her cheeks burned as she recalled for Temerity the experience of the human resources woman who had physically recoiled when Ellen had come into her office, and then, embarrassed, nervously kept her focus on her paperwork and never looked directly at her again. She found it easier to tell Temerity the story than she thought, because Temerity would never see the face that had made the woman in human resources stare, horrified, her mouth an unguarded grimace, her eyes wide and bulging.

"I'm sorry," Temerity said softly.

"Don't be," Ellen told her sincerely. "It's been great for me. I can work on my own and I never have to deal with, you know, people."

"I think I do know." Temerity patted her arm. "You haven't had many people to trust, have you?"

This irrefutable fact was a punch in the gut, but, much the same way a fighter learns to tense his muscles to take the hit, Ellen automatically deflected the blow off of emotional calluses developed from long practice. "Not many," she muttered, trying to think of even one. She hadn't trusted anyone, at first out of necessity, but then it had become habit. All her life she had watched attentively and seen that some people were good, loving, caring, giving. It had been enough for her that those people and relationships existed. Allowing herself to hope for it personally would have been begging for a beating, so she'd not permitted herself that luxury. *That was okay*, she told herself, as she did every single day. *It doesn't have to happen to me, it doesn't happen for lots of people, as long as it's out there, as long as it could be true.*

Ellen turned to gaze at Temerity's face, and felt a wash of relief.

Proof.

18

"Tell me more about Irena," Temerity said as they made their way through the hospital's maze of hallways.

So Ellen did. She told her the whole story as she knew it. Starting with Irena's fear-filled existence, she moved on to how the immigrant's misery had been compounded by the Boss's sexual harassment. Then Ellen told the saga of discovering the Boss's fake-receipt ruse, how she had stolen the conned money from him and passed it on to Irena anonymously with the note. She could not remember ever talking so much in her life, but explaining the world she saw to Temerity had become like writing the story in her notebook, and the words just flowed out of her until her mouth felt dusty and her throat was dry.

And still she talked, about Irena's cautious new optimism and how it was cut short by the emergency phone call. She finally concluded with the Crows' attempts to entertain themselves with information from the hapless Irena.

At some point, they had stopped walking, and Ellen was surprised, when she looked around, to find that they had exited the hospital and were standing off to the front of the entrance.

Ellen cleared her scratchy throat. "So what do you think?"

Temerity held out both arms, stepped forward and hugged a confused, and suddenly rigid, Ellen.

"I think that you are an amazing person, and I'm really glad you coldcocked your way into my life. Now can I tell *you* something?"

"I'm pretty sure it's your turn." Ellen grimaced at her own joke.

Temerity laughed out loud. "Who knew you could be so loquacious?"

Encouraged, Ellen admitted, "Not me. But that's because I don't know what 'loquacious' means." She made a mental note to check her worn dictionary.

"Talkative," Temerity told her through her bubbling amusement. "The only reason I know what it means is because Justice told me that's what I was, among other things. Okay, here's my story: I don't have many friends. Lots of acquaintances, but the reality is that most seeing people aren't comfortable being friends with a blind chick. It's not their fault. I mean, I have a few girlfriends, other musicians mostly, who I can talk to about music and other stuff too, when we take the time, but I know it's not comfortable for them to meet me out somewhere, for lunch say, much less go see a movie or visit a museum. What would be the point?" She sighed and turned her head toward a light, moist breeze that promised rain. The resulting clouds made the late afternoon darker than usual. Not that Temerity would know that. "I understand, of course, but the unavoidable result is that, more often than not, I'm on my own. That's definitely been a factor in my becoming a competent musician. I had lots of spare time to practice when I was a kid. Not too many blind kids my age at the Braille Institute. Which, I like to remind myself, is a good thing overall. If it weren't for Justice, I think I'd just give up on people and play violin by myself all day long."

It was Ellen's turn to sigh. "Heaven," she half sang.

Temerity laughed so hard she doubled over and held her stomach. When she had wiped the tears from her eyes, she said, "Oh, I'm so glad I met you. You want to get something to eat?"

Of course Ellen wanted to get something to eat. After only one sandwich and a few crackers, she was stunned to still be standing. "I don't go to restaurants," she reminded.

"Fine. Let's pick something up and go to your house since it's closest. Okay?"

Resistance was futile. So Ellen found herself standing outside a restaurant while Temerity went in and ordered something she called "taco salads." Though Ellen was concerned about the use of the word "salad," she was reassured by the weight of the brown paper bag as she carried it back to her house. When they arrived, she was presented with a new problem. There was no table, and only the one stool that pulled up to the kitchen counter. When she mentioned this, Temerity said, "Fine. I'll sit on the counter—it's safer for me to eat sloppy food over the sink anyway—and you can have the stool. That way, you can watch outside. Anything interesting?"

Ellen took up her usual post, but everything was quiet, so they devoted themselves to eating. Much to Ellen's relief, the "salad" was a hearty pile of beans, beef, cheese, guacamole, sour cream, fresh tomatoes and lettuce piled into a huge crispy shell. It was delicious, and Ellen enthusiastically consumed even the greens and the fresh tomato, which, before, she would have pushed aside. Temerity too, ate with relish, and Ellen watched her system. Using her fingers to feel the food, she broke off a piece of the shell, piled it with the other ingredients, and ate it like a chip and dip. "Yummy!" she said with her mouth full.

The heaped pile of nourishment was so filling, in fact, that Ellen couldn't finish it all. She knew if she'd been alone with no other distractions, she probably would have polished it off just for something to do, but today, after eating only half, a glance out the window drew her interest.

"Someone is in Cindy's apartment," she said.

Temerity paused with a section of the shell loaded with refried beans and sour cream halfway to her face. "Is it her?"

Ellen watched as first Cindy and then Janelle came into Cindy's kitchen. The tall, elegant black woman stood at the window for a moment, gazing out at the dead courtyard, its morbid appearance now replete with the addition of police tape. Then she shook her head sadly and turned away.

She was reporting all of this to Temerity when the blind girl asked, "And who's that?"

Ellen heard the crunch of gravel, and shifted her eyes to the alley to see Edward Newland and a younger man in a suit with a face as interesting as dry white toast making their way toward Cindy's back door.

"That," said Ellen, "is a pissed-off lawyer."

Newland did indeed look aggressively angry. His companion just seemed slightly annoyed to be there, glancing around with obvious disgust. As they approached the landing, Ellen heard Edward say, "We'll try this side first. She won't be expecting us to show up at the back."

He went up the two steps and knocked smartly. In a moment, Janelle's face appeared, first in the window, and then she opened the door but held it firmly and blocked the opening with her body.

"What do you want?" she asked in a steady voice.

"Is Ms. Carpenter at home?"

"Yes, but what do you want?"

"I have something to give her," Edward growled like a mean, wounded dog. It was easy to hear, even from across the tiny courtyard.

"Give it to me."

"No can do. It needs to go straight to her."

Janelle put one hand on the jamb and looked Edward straight in the eye. "Listen. I know we had some hard words at the hospital, and I'm really sorry for your wife, but this is not necessary. We'll pay you back for the doctor and hospital fees. I'm already talking to my insurance company about the adoption—it will probably all be covered. If not, we'll pay it out of our own pockets. I told you that."

Though Ellen couldn't see his face, she could well imagine Edward Newland sneering as he said, "Oh, this is a different issue. I'm suing her."

Janelle put one hand to her forehead and took a deep breath. "And what," she asked in an exhausted voice, "do you hope to get out of suing someone who has nothing? Look around, what could you possibly expect you would get?"

"That doesn't concern you," he said, and the sharpness of his voice was so full of himself that it sliced clearly up to the second floor. "Just get her. Or I'll do it myself."

Janelle turned around and Cindy, looking terrified, appeared in the doorway. Janelle stayed right next to her.

"Cindy Carpenter?" the younger man standing with Newland asked. When Cindy nodded hesitantly, he thrust papers at her hand and she took them automatically, holding them away from her as though she thought they might burst into flame. "You have been served," he said. With a nod to Edward, the man turned, walked back across the gravel and disappeared down the alley.

"What . . . what is this?" Cindy asked.

The taller woman laid a reassuring arm across the girl's shoulders. "It's papers, just papers." She took the bundle from Cindy's shaking hands. "We'll call a lawyer when we get home and sort things out. Go finish packing your things." Cindy did as she was told and Janelle turned back to Edward Newland.

"Really?" she asked. "You didn't even want her baby, and now you're going to put her through this?"

Edward turned outward a bit and looked up at the empty, darkening gray sky as though it were an especially clear night and he was admiring the stars. Instinctively, Ellen moved back from the screen a few inches. "I never said I didn't want her baby, just not *that* one. Because of her actions, my wife has suffered undue emotional distress and put extreme pressure on our relationship. All of her pain and suffering have clearly been predicated by Cindy Carpenter's deception. And Cindy Carpenter is going to make restitution."

Janelle braced herself by crossing her arms and setting her uneven feet. "Look, I'm sorry you're hurt and disappointed, but what do you hope to gain from this?"

Edward Newland put his hands in his pockets and rocked from side to side, smiling like the Cheshire cat. "No more than what we originally contracted for."

"You are not getting my brother's baby," Janelle said, still controlled, but each word was a shard of ice in a strong wind. "And you have no legal right to take her, you know that."

"Oh, I know the law," he snipped. "I did a little research, it seems your baby mama is wanted for some minor drug charges in her home state. Since the DA and I went to law school together, those charges could land her in jail for up to four full years."

"What do you want from her?" Janelle asked coldly.

He shrugged as if it were simple. "A baby, but this time I'll pick the father. I'll give her six months to recover."

Janelle reeled back and stared in disbelief. Edward Newland turned away with deliberate slowness. Then, as though remembering something, he turned back. For the first time, Ellen could hear him struggling to control his own hurt as he said, "Oh, and part of the deal is not a word of this to anyone, especially not to my wife. She's been injured by Ms. Carpenter's negligent actions enough already." His voice broke slightly. He turned and strode away. Ellen watched him wipe angrily at the tears he couldn't control.

"Holy shit," Temerity whispered.

Across the way, Janelle closed the door and they both heard her double lock it as if that would protect Cindy from the threat outside. Ellen turned to Temerity. "Can he do that?"

"Which part? I mean, I'm not sure, but the whole scheme sounds like blackmail, I think. I mean, maybe he can pull off the suing part—you can basically sue anyone for anything, though I doubt many judges would let it go very far. But it sounds like what he's really threatening is to make her life miserable unless she does what he wants. He certainly seems to have both the resources and the revolting disposition to go through with those threats."

Ellen thought about Susan Newland and the way she'd told her husband that he was going home with her and the baby, or alone. "Do you think his wife knows about this?"

"From what he just ended with, I'm guessing no. Plus, she didn't strike me as someone who was without scruples."

Ellen figured it was better to ask. "And scruples, in this case, would mean that she . . . ?"

"Had a conscience that told her not to do something so downright egregious, that's what they mean in this case anyway." Ellen sighed, and Temerity heard it, of course. She added, "'Egregious' means 'really evil,' by the way. Great word."

"Oh," Ellen exclaimed, surprising herself. "I've seen that word in a book." She didn't, however, say that when she had sounded it out, she had thought it was pronounced "e-gree-ghee-ess."

"What's that?" Temerity pointed one finger to the ceiling.

It took a second to shift her focus from below to above, but when she did, Ellen heard the footsteps as well.

"Never a dull moment in exciting Morningside," Temerity commented dryly.

The footsteps moved around the building and in a few seconds Ellen could see the young man on the roof. It was fully twilight by now, but it was plenty light enough for her to make him out; he was headed for the large vent.

"It's him," she hissed. "It's the guy who shot T-bone," she added, reverting to the nickname in her excitement.

Temerity whistled a low note. "Guess he made bail."

From the street below, a police siren erupted suddenly and the man froze, and then backtracked, diving for cover behind a fan unit the size of a refrigerator, rusted with long disuse.

"Why would he come back here?" Temerity seemed stunned.

"Not sure," Ellen said and immediately felt rotten. Was she really going to lie to the only person who'd ever shared her own secrets? She didn't want to say more, she didn't want to free the partially formed thought that had been nagging at her, but it was like a giant hot-air balloon gathering lift, straining at its tethers. Ellen's deeply entrenched reticence to expose herself was holding on to those ropes with its thousand tiny hands, pulling with all its might to keep the idea pinned to the ground. Against every inclination Ellen opened her mouth, and with a mighty wrench, the balloon lifted off, floating up into the open air, broken ropes trailing behind it as Ellen said, "Actually, I think I do know."

"You do?" Temerity asked, and Ellen marveled that a blind face could light up so much.

Ellen checked the roof. The man was still hunkered down out of sight. On the street below, the cops blipped their siren again and shouted something indistinguishable from the other city noise. She went on. "That night, the guy, he stopped and got rid of the bag he was carrying when he climbed up. He didn't have it when he jumped. I kept thinking about that later. Remember the cops said that there were no fingerprints, and no gun?"

Temerity frowned, cocking her head to one side. "Yes, I remember that. So?"

"I'm not exactly sure," Ellen muttered, the tiny spark of courage that had dared to raise its cautious head wavering, "but I think I know where he put the stuff he stole—his jacket, and maybe the gun."

"Which would have his fingerprints!" Temerity exclaimed. "We can call that detective and tell him." But Ellen made a low noise of disagreement.

"I can't talk to them," Ellen said. "If I do, they'll want me to talk to other people, and then a courtroom—they'll all see me." Her throat closed in panic, choking her off.

She swallowed hard and gulped for air, recovering enough to force out the next words. "And you can't say you're me this time either. They need someone to identify the guy." Her voice was wavering with shock. The thought of facing a busy police station full of people had sent her into paroxysms of shuddering. Her upper arm was itching furiously, and she rubbed at it. Outside her window, on the street

.de, she heard the police shout at someone to get out of their car. Apparently, the man on the roof did too. He raised his head and was peering cautiously over the edge. If they were going to do anything, it had to be now.

"It's okay, it's okay," Temerity said, stroking Ellen's back. "Right," she said with less enthusiasm. "Well, we need to do two things."

Ellen groaned, but secretly she was relieved it was only two. "Which are?"

"Scare him off for now, and get the evidence later. Is he still there?"

"Yes, but you'd better hurry." Without pausing to hear Ellen's further thoughts on the matter, Temerity cranked open the slats the whole way and started yelling. "Get off the roof! I'll shoot you if you aren't gone in five seconds. Damn teenagers! Get off of there!"

The man, confused as to the source of the threats, crouched instinctively. His head swiveled from side to side, but he made no move to leave. Ellen picked up a spatula with a metal handle. The plastic tip had come off the end, leaving the handle a hollow metal tube. She stuck this between the open window slats, through a hole in the screen, and pointed it at the far roof. It was the closest thing to a gun she could come up with on two seconds' notice. She whispered, "Okay, a gun muzzle is sticking out the window."

"You have a gun?" Temerity's brow shot up.

"No. It's a spatula, but it's not loaded."

"Ooh, good thinking," Temerity whispered back, then she yelled again. "I'm gonna count to five and then fill your butt with lead!"

The young man spotted the window with the "muzzle" pointed at him. Potential bullets were apparently better motivators than shouting women. He spun, ran across the rooftop and repeated his leap to the next building.

Temerity had heard his retreating run and then the thump as he hit the roof next door. She did a little dance and sang, "Yipee ki-yay! I felt like I was in the Old West!"

"You sounded like it," Ellen told her, still watching the roof nervously. She was pretty sure now that the kid she'd seen throw a rock at the curtain lady's dog had been sent to do this same job and that this guy would be back, or send someone else.

"Now, phase two." Temerity rubbed her hands together and Ellen did not care for the keenness in her voice.

"But . . . it's the roof. It's . . . high. You have to climb to get up there. Climb," she repeated in case Temerity had missed it the first time.

Temerity laughed. "I'm sure we'll manage, my intrepid friend. But I do not want you trying to do this without me."

Ellen looked at the other girl like she was crazy. Which was pointless, of course. She thought that "intrepid" meant something like brave, but either she was mistaken in that or she was absolutely sure Temerity couldn't be serious. The last thing Ellen intended to do was scale a wall onto a roof and then possibly shimmy down a vent, looking for contraband.

"Yeah, you don't need to worry about that," Ellen said.

Temerity said, "It's starting to sprinkle. Okay, so, how did he get up there? I mean, this time. I know how he did it the night he shot J.B."

Sure enough, when Ellen checked outside, a light drizzle had begun to fall, though she had to listen hard to make out the baby-soft patter on the wooden stairs. Impressed again by Temerity's auditory prowess, she answered automatically. "I don't know," she said. "There's a fire escape ladder on the far side that only goes to the second floor."

"So we're at an advantage. We're already on the second floor. Is there a ladder from this side?"

Ellen thought. "No. The flat roof of the first floor is only on the left side of my kitchen, and my fire escape is my back door."

"Which doesn't open."

Though this thought was slightly alarming, the apartment was so small that Ellen had never understood why it needed a second exit.

"Okay." Temerity began to do the thinking rock from side to side. "What we need is a way to get up there." She pointed to the ceiling. "Once we're up there, we can just walk around the front of the building and check it out. Right?"

Try as she might, Ellen couldn't find a way to disagree, not with the assessment anyway. "Right."

"And, since we first heard spider boy above us, he must have climbed up first on top of your apartment. We were looking out the back, so we know he didn't go up that way. So how did he get up on this side?"

Ellen's eyes cut to the second kitchen window, the one over the sink. Its sill sat about four feet above the first-floor roof. Even as she watched, Mouse, his daily sojourn to relieve himself on the tar outside interrupted by the rain, slipped in through the broken pane, shook his head and meowed with disgruntled aversion before noticing Temerity and trotting over, stomach flapping.

The window was barred on the outside, but Ellen had noticed a while ago that the bar's weight had dragged the screws that held it in place halfway out of the crumbling stucco. Still, the thought of hauling herself through a kitchen window did not appeal to her, so she didn't mention that.

Temerity crouched and scratched thoughtfully behind Mouse's

moist, ragged ears. "You just came in that way, didn't you, little buddy?" She turned toward Ellen for an explanation.

Foiled by her untrustworthy feline, Ellen explained about the bars and the fact that, once on that rooftop, there was nothing but the sheer wall of her apartment, interrupted only by the window, up to the higher roof.

Undeterred, Temerity found her way to the sink, explored the window's surface and found the broken pane. Reaching through, she took hold of one of the three wide bars and gave it a shove. There was the sound of crumbling mortar, and the bars moved.

"We can get this off!" Temerity said.

"And then what?" Ellen was eyeing the window, about three by three, with distaste. "I told you, I'm not very nimble, or very small."

"Oh pish," said Temerity. Ellen had never heard that word either, but the intonation defined it perfectly.

Coming to join Temerity, Ellen leaned over the sink and gazed out as she spoke. "Even if we do get out there, how would we . . ." Her words trailed off. As she looked to the left, she could clearly see the base of a very old, very dilapidated wooden ladder leaning against the wall. And then she remembered.

About two years ago, she'd been woken midmorning by the sound of shouting, loud stamping and a horrible stench. Creeping to the kitchen, she'd seen a crew of men with darkly tanned skin, all in red T-shirts, retarring the rooftop outside this very window. The curtain woman downstairs, she'd overheard later, had complained of leaks and stopped paying her rent until they were fixed. The ladder, covered in black drips of tar, the wood splitting in places and with two broken rungs, had been discarded along with half-empty tar buckets by the crew when they left after doing an extremely substandard job.

had lain flat under her window, rotting, since then, and Ellen had forgotten its existence. Now it seemed that spider boy had resurrected the death trap, propping it up next to her window for access to the higher roof.

"Oh" came out of Ellen's mouth before she could clamp it shut.

"Aha," said Temerity. "I knew it."

19

Even with the window pushed all the way open, the space was a tight and awkward squeeze for Ellen. First, she had to climb up onto the counter, put one foot into the sink, and the other out the window while seated, horsey style, on the sill. Then she folded over as best she could and shimmied her bulk toward the outside while clinging to the faucet with one hand and stretching a cautious foot down to the roof outside. With nothing to step onto and a four-foot drop, she slipped and only avoided falling onto the wet tar in a heap by hooking the inside leg against the sill with the back of her crooked knee. It was painful and, she imagined, about as graceful as a drunk on a greased donkey, but she managed to unhook the leg and find footing on the tar roof at last, knowing she'd be scraped, sore and sorry later.

Temerity came next. Ellen talked her through the procedure, but she didn't really seem to need it, swinging both legs out, turning onto her stomach and dropping neatly. When Ellen asked her how she had known how far down it was, she responded, "Your voice was right by my head."

"Oh," Ellen said again, reminding herself to not forget her friend's perspective.

The ladder was a different story. Never one for leaving the ground unless it might be to escape a life-threatening situation, a rabid animal in pursuit perhaps, which, thankfully, had never come up, Ellen eyed the decrepit object with extreme distrust. She tried her weight on the first rung and the wood creaked threateningly.

There were some things she just couldn't do. "Nuh-uh, can't do it," she said, backing away. "Sorry."

"Why?"

"It's old, it won't hold my weight." Ellen thought that was most likely true anyway.

Temerity threw her arms out. "Fine. So I'll do it."

The rain was a light mist, but it was substantial enough that, within minutes, both of their hair and faces were dotted with specks of moisture. Minutes filled with Ellen first trying in vain to talk Temerity out of the risky venture, giving up, and then explaining both the perils of the ladder and the lay of the land.

"So, once you're up you'll have to go straight, turn left twice and then I'll tell you which way to go."

"Like Marco Polo," Temerity said.

This was the second time she'd mentioned him. To clear up the connection, Ellen asked, "You mean because he was an explorer?"

Temerity's brow furrowed in what looked like confusion. She opened her mouth, then shut it. The corners of her mouth twitched. "Well, yes . . . that, but also because of a game that kids play in a pool."

Having never been to a pool, Ellen asked, "And why is that important now?"

With a huge smile, Temerity said, "Because if it weren't for him, the Italians wouldn't have pasta."

Ellen felt an immediate affection for the man. "Well, thank him for me."

"I will, next time I see him. Get it? Okay, up I go."

"One more thing," Ellen said, stopping her. "The roof is flat, but the edge around it is only about two feet high, so stay low. If you trip over it, it's a long ways down."

Temerity grasped the ladder. "And your confidence in my bounciness is even lower. Got it."

"And I won't be able to see you until you get to the front of the building. So I can't tell you where to go until then."

"And I won't be able to see you at all."

"Which brings up another point. How are you going to look for anything in the vent once you're up there?"

The blind girl held her hands in front of Ellen's face and wiggled her fingers. "I'll use my antennae. Okay, here we go."

Ellen watched, holding her breath, as Temerity started up. She maneuvered her way over the third missing rung, but tested her weight on the cracked fifth one. It gave and she dropped, one foot jamming behind the fourth rung as her hands slid down the slippery side supports. Ellen yelped and clapped her hands over her mouth, but Temerity wrapped her arms around the supports in a bear hug and stopped herself from flipping off backward. She was hanging by the back of one knee, not as ungracefully as Ellen in the windowsill, but with a great deal farther to fall. Her arms were so tight around the ladder she could have been giving it the Heimlich. Temerity grunted, rested her brow against a higher rung while she caught her breath, and muttered, "Ouch. You might have let me know that was one of the broken ones." It was the only time Ellen had heard her sound annoyed, and she did not blame her. With a strong pull,

ity worked her way up again and reached the lip of the roof
e.

"One more rung, and then you can step over the ledge," Ellen
called up. "Be careful!" In another five seconds, Temerity disappeared onto the roof and Ellen found that she was frantic with worry.
Was she insane? Letting the sightless girl negotiate a vent and wire-
strewn obstacle course thirty feet off the ground. But another glance
at the ladder convinced her that, out of the two of them, Temerity
was the only girl for the job. Like she could have stopped her anyway.

Rushing to the edge of the roof, she strained her neck to see
around the corner of her own apartment and up. In a few moments,
she spotted Temerity. Crouching, with one hand on the roof's raised
ledge to guide her, she was moving toward the front of the building. She made the first turn and kept moving until she reached the
far side of the U-shaped roof. When her fingers had found that corner, she straightened up and called out in as low a voice as would
carry, "Ready? Let's play pin the crime on the guilty party."

"Turn a little to your right," Ellen called out softly. "Okay, go
straight about five steps." Temerity took two of those steps confidently then lurched forward, disappearing from view beyond the
roof's ledge. Ellen's hands flew up to cover her mouth. "Oh my God,
I've killed her," she mumbled.

"I'm okay!" Temerity's muffled voice announced, and in a moment she was up again, but this time she stayed low, arms extended
in front of her, and moved more cautiously.

"A few more steps, almost there! Okay, reach out your right hand
a little farther."

"Got it!" Temerity said, running her hands over the aluminum
exhaust vent. It stuck up about four feet, was maybe a foot and a half

in diameter and had a peaked cap to keep the rain out. The conical cap sat over several large openings in the cylinder, each maybe ten inches square, meant to vent whatever furnace was in the basement below. Ellen watched as Temerity circled around it, feeling the ground behind it and then up the sides.

"Anything?" Ellen called, glancing down nervously to the empty courtyard below. She had been afraid curtain lady would hear them, but her back door remained closed and the courtyard deserted. Odd.

"I think that there's something tied onto this strip part between the openings. It's holding something that's hanging down on the inside."

There were twenty seconds of silence and then Temerity straightened up, holding a bundle over her head like a trophy. "Got it!" she said. "Does this look like it could be it?"

The light had grown too faint for Ellen to make out the color, but it did indeed look as though it could be an item of clothing tied into a bundle.

"Come back," Ellen said. "And we'll see. Go straight, be careful!"

Tucking the bundle under her left arm and extending her right, Temerity started forward in her spider crouch, back toward the inside corner of the roof. She rounded it and continued along the front third of the building. Ellen was watching her so intently, it wasn't until her friend turned the second corner and disappeared from her line of vision that she saw the man.

He had come back, up the metal ladder this time on the far side, so that in the dying light his silhouette was outlined by the streetlights behind him. A scream froze in Ellen's throat. He was clearly fixed on Temerity. Though Ellen couldn't see exactly where she was, he began to advance toward where she must be, moving slowly to stay silent and stealthy, and Ellen realized he was going to sneak up on her from behind.

Ellen ran to the ladder and grasped the rough, rotting wood in both hands. She stepped up onto the first rung; it gave slightly, creaked, but held. The second one also took her weight. The third rung was gone, so Ellen twisted sideways to clear enough space to raise her knee high enough for her foot to reach the fourth rung and pulled herself up, her arms shaking with the effort. The whole ladder bowed with her weight, and she heard it groaning and cracking threateningly beneath her. Her heart was pounding in her ears, and the rain was coming in earnest now, so she could not hear her friend's approach, and spider boy had a lifetime of experience creeping silently across rooftops. Ignoring the distance to the ground, Ellen continued on up, clearing the edge of the roof with her head and shoulders. One more rung and her waist was level with the ledge. She could see the man, only twenty feet behind Temerity. Getting up the ladder had been challenge enough, but maneuvering her bulk around it, by stepping over open air onto the higher roof, seemed impossible, and for a second, Ellen's resolve wavered. She wrapped both arms around the ladder and clung there, her courage frozen like a rabbit caught out in an open field.

The man, his attention telescoped on Temerity and the bundle, began to move faster. She was only five yards away from the ladder, still moving steadily but cautiously toward Ellen, one arm sweeping the air in front of her as she advanced, bent almost in half. Her stalker was closing the distance between them. Ellen gritted her teeth and tried to force her muscles to unclench, but she was paralyzed with fear.

Then Ellen saw him reach under his loose shirt, and her eyes focused hard on his right hand. She noticed a semicircle of small scabs on the back of his hand, between his finger and thumb, that resembled a bite mark. As the hand emerged, she saw the knife in it. The timid animal in Ellen morphed into a predatory beast. She threw herself sideways with a great lurch, angling her upper body onto the roof and landing hard on her forearms just inside the ledge, the rest of her body flopping onto the tar behind her. Temerity halted. "Ellen?"

"Behind you!" Ellen called out as she struggled to her feet. Temerity, just in front of her, spun, still crouched, and listened for the unseen threat. The man hesitated, then started forward again with more determination. Ellen got the rubber soles of her Converse firmly against the tar and rushed around Temerity at the man, who spun toward her in alarm. He was no taller than Ellen, and considerably thinner. She hit him hard from the side and he went down, the hand with the knife smacking onto the rough surface, sending the knife flying. It landed near Temerity with a dull metallic clunk. She dropped to her knees and began to fumble for it.

"Get off me, you fat fu—" the man began, but Ellen rose up and slammed down on him again, aiming the bulk of her weight at his stomach, and his rude demand concluded with an "—oof."

"Stay away from my friend," Ellen screamed in a rage. One of his hands came free and found her face, he dug his fingers into her cheek, and Ellen twisted to protect the good side of her face. Grabbing at his wrist to pull his hand away, she vaguely registered that the arc of bite marks was matched on his palm side. She glared down at him and his eyes went wide with horror. He yanked his hand away as though it had landed in acid, and squirmed to get free of her. She rose up to slam down on him again and he rolled away, his face filled with shock and revulsion as he gaped at her. Temerity had found the knife and was clutching it in her free hand, but she was obviously sightless and uncertain which way to turn. The man dragged his eyes from Ellen's scar and began to sidle toward Temerity, inch by inch. Ellen shifted to put herself between them. The man stared at Ellen with a sickened expression and breathed out, "What are you?" as he clutched at his injured stomach.

A ball of pain formed in Ellen's gut, rose to her chest like a flaming catapult, and she released it, hurling it at him with a scream. "I'm the person who's going to stop you from hurting anyone else!" She could feel tears of rage from her bruised life stinging her eyes, but the reaction only made her more determined to hurt this bastard, to hurt everyone who had ever looked at her with disgust. Moving to Temerity, she snatched the knife from her friend's hand, put her head down and rushed him, an animal roar emerging from her chest, catching him in the side with her shoulder and sending him flying. She stood over him, raising the knife to strike. She lunged, but he evaded her as he fumbled to his hands and feet, already scrambling back across the roof. "And don't come back, you little termite!" Ellen had fallen onto her knees. They were scraped, her pants were torn, but she felt nothing but fury. "Run away!" she screamed. "Back to your hole, you mean, horrible, hateful cockroach. You're not better than me! You're an insect!" Ellen put her head back and screamed up at the sky, tears mixing with the rain.

She felt an encompassing presence. Temerity had wrapped her arms around her and she was shushing her, cooing and soothing, but Ellen was shaking and sobbing. "Go away," she said brokenly. "I don't want you to know about this. I don't want to be this. Just go away." She pushed at Temerity, but the girl locked her wrists and held on tight. They stayed there, struggling and rocking until Ellen's strength gave out and the rocking won. "Leave me alone," Ellen moaned.

And Temerity laughed.

The sound stunned Ellen so sharply that it deadlocked her hysteria. She looked up at Temerity's face in a half sob, completely at a loss.

"Nuh-uh, can't do it," her friend said. "Sorry."

20

The arms of the lightweight jacket lay flung out across the floor of Ellen's room as though it had collapsed there, exhausted, staring up at the ceiling. They had unzipped the jacket and on the body of the fabric lay three objects.

The gun, which they'd been careful not to touch, had its business end pointed toward the sofa, but Ellen kept one eye on it as if it might spontaneously go off. The large brown paper bag, reeking of marijuana, rested near the gun's handle. The smaller paper bag was right in front of Temerity's crossed legs.

Temerity felt for it, picked it up and tested its weight.

"Feels like money," she said. "Lots of it."

"Should we open it?" They were the first words Ellen had spoken since her breakdown on the roof. She was cowed, ashamed of the outburst, shaken by her loss of control. Temerity had said that it was a good thing, and she'd actually sounded impressed when she'd said it, as she coerced Ellen down the ladder and back through the window with a constant stream of encouragement and praise. Ellen could not agree. She was disturbed that so much pain and anger had been exposed, and even more disturbed that it had even been there. Though she had to admit that the injection of fury had proved useful, she did not ever want to feel that much again. She'd thought she was through being impaled on that kind of spiked, cold metal pain. She'd worked so hard to put it all aside and just exist, floating in a mushier, neutral place. Temerity had told her, in the course of her soothing monologue; that Ellen should not feel badly about having such a reaction, that it was brave for her to allow that anger and hurt to come out. She'd actually said she was glad it had happened, that it was a good thing, but Ellen would have chosen numbness over that insufferable anguish any day; in fact, she did choose numbness *every* day. But a half hour of Temerity's ministrations had smoothed her razor-slashed nerves enough to go on.

When Temerity ripped away the paper from the smaller bundle, Ellen saw a two-inch-thick stack of bills, and she couldn't stop a gasp; she'd never seen so much cash except at the Costco. "It is money, isn't it?" Temerity said. "Is it ones or twenties or what?" She held it out for Ellen to investigate.

Ellen squinted at it. "It looks like mostly twenties. There are some tens and—wait." She took the bills and flipped through them. "There are quite a few hundred-dollar bills. This is a lot of money." She handed the cache back to Temerity. "Was it J.B.'s, you think?"

"More likely it's the money the kid was supposed to buy the drugs with, but he thought maybe he'd keep them both. That's the occupational hazard of dealing with someone whose business ethics aren't exactly exemplary."

"What do we do with it? Give it to the police?"

"Mmm, I don't think so. It makes J.B. look pretty guilty of selling drugs. He says he's going to start a new life, and while going to jail would certainly be different, I don't think it's the change he had in mind."

"I don't want it," Ellen said.

"Me neither." She hummed. "Maybe we'll give it to a drug rehab charity. I do love irony. I'll take it home and hide it for now, we can figure out what to do with it later. First, though, the gun. We need to put it somewhere obvious, then we can call the police and tell them where it is. We'll say we spotted it, but we don't want to touch it, something like that."

Ellen took a deep breath. She just wanted the nasty thing out of her house. "How about under the back steps? He could have dropped it and they could have missed it. Do you think they looked there?"

"Even if they did, so what? They need to look again."

"I'll do it, just give me a little more time to . . . stop shaking."

Temerity set the stack of money aside and felt for Ellen's leg. "You were magnificent," she said. "I'm sorry about what that guy said."

Ellen shrugged, but it was more of a spasm than a gesture. "I got used to that a long time ago."

But Temerity shook her head. "Nobody gets used to that. I had a few times . . ." Her hand tightened on Ellen's shin, and Ellen sensed a shift from offering strength to drawing it. "I don't like to talk about it, or even remember those things; besides, not many people can relate. But this is you, so I'll tell you about this one time because I want you to know I understand. I mean, sort of, at least.

"I used to take swimming lessons at the Y, and there were swim teams that practiced there." She cleared her throat and shook her head before she went on. "Anyway, one day I went into the locker room to change after my lesson, and the girls' team was in there. One of the girls started talking to me, being friendly, I thought. She was thirteen, my age. I remember I was excited that I might be making a new friend." She snorted a sad laugh. "Anyway, I got in the shower, and then, while I was washing my hair, I heard laughing." She paused again and tears welled in her eyes. She brushed them away angrily with her free hand. "Boys laughing. The girls had brought in the boys' team to watch me take a shower."

Ellen put both hands over her mouth. Blue-hot anger sparked in her again, all the more frustrating because this had been long ago and there was no way to defend her friend. "They all started making these horrible comments," Temerity went on, "and . . . I couldn't get away, or find my clothes. They'd taken them, and my towel. Finally, my instructor came in looking for me. They all got in trouble, but I never forgot it, and I never went back. I wouldn't leave my house for a month."

For Ellen, who had a mortal fear of anyone ever seeing her naked, this was a manifestation of a nightmare. She knew firsthand how cruel adolescent girls could be. Her frequent moving in the foster care system had made her a constant outcast and forced her to repeat the sixth grade, which labeled her as "stupid" to some particularly vicious specimens. She'd been using the toilet in a stall at her new overcrowded public elementary school when a small group of popular sixth-grade girls had kicked open the door and begun pelting her with wet paper towels, calling her names and laughing at her. She had actually tried to crawl into the small space behind the toilet to hide, which had provided the girls with a wealth of excrement-based nicknames to call her. Those names, ridicule, and cruel taunts had followed her when she slunk through those hated hallways, praying to disappear, to not be there.

Remembering that Temerity had used the term to describe Ellen's own past once, she selected it now and said quietly, "That sucks."

"Yeah. It did." Temerity shook her head as though it would loosen the memories and send them flying. "But you know what?"

"What?"

"Those little bitches were petty and mean, probably still are, and I don't believe that cruel people are ever happy. Do you?"

Ellen considered it. It made sense. Her mother had been cruel and miserable. She thought about the Loretta woman she had seen pick a fight with the nice mom at the thrift store, insisting on smoking in the entrance of the door when she could have easily moved away. That was clearly a wretched person, and her resulting behavior was vile. "No," Ellen said, feeling stronger. "No, I don't think they are. If they were happy, they wouldn't even think about being mean."

"Exactly." Temerity smacked her leg. "Enough of this pity fest. Let's get busy!"

"Wait." Ellen looked down at the largest item on the floor in front of them. "What about that?" she asked, and picking up Temerity's hand, she set it on the bag of dope.

Temerity smiled. "I'll ask Justice, but I think I know what he'll want to do. There's a hospice where he sometimes volunteers. I know they use marijuana to help people who can't eat and are in chronic pain; I'm guessing he'll drop it off there."

"It that legal?" Ellen was surprised.

Temerity tilted her head to one side and smiled wryly. "'Legal' becomes more of a suggestion when someone is in constant pain with no hope of getting better. If something can relieve their suffering, and it certainly can't hurt them any worse, then obeying an antiquated law might be considered more of a luxury than they can afford."

This logic sat easily on Ellen. So they decided what to do. Using rusty barbecue tongs to carefully lower the gun into a paper bag, Ellen carried it down the stairs, around the back of the building. She stopped at the edge of the curtain lady's apartment. It was completely dark inside; no light seeped through from behind the fabric. She must have gone out—that was unusual. Ellen heard a scratching at the base of the back door and a pathetic whining. It sounded like curtain lady would have a little extra cleaning to do if she didn't get back soon. She moved out into the courtyard and slipped the gun out of the bag next to J.B.'s steps, then kicked it underneath. She pounded back around the building, up the stairs, and slammed the door behind her.

"Done?" Temerity asked.

"Done," Ellen said, breathing hard.

"Good. I'll call from a pay phone and say that my kid thought they saw a gun when they were playing, but I don't want to get involved. That must be common enough around here." Ellen said she thought that was probably right, both the not wanting to get involved and the seeing the gun parts.

"The last thing is this"—Temerity put her hands on her hips— "will you be all right here tonight?"

Tonight. Work. "What time is it?" Ellen looked at the clock as she said it. It was the first time she had ever forgotten about work. Almost eight. "I won't be here. I have to go to work."

"Perfect. After that guy saw you, I don't really want you here alone until he's safely tucked into the back of a patrol car."

Ellen hadn't considered this, but she still didn't think she was in danger, and she didn't have anywhere else to go anyway. "I know he saw me, but I don't think he'll come back now. There's no reason for him to. He knows we have this, and this is what he wanted." Ellen rustled the bag a little so Temerity would know what she was referring to.

"Yeah, I'm still not all right with that. At least not until the cops find the gun tonight and hopefully pick him up. I'll wait for you, then we can take the bus together and I'll have Justice meet me at the stop, since I'll be carrying contraband. Do you have a few plastic bags? We'd better zip-lock this up airtight or I'll either be arrested or smoked before we get to the corner." She too referenced the brown paper bag around which waves of rich, skunky scent rose, clung, and refused to disperse.

So they repackaged the cash and wrapped the marijuana in several layers of plastic grocery bags, then Ellen put the whole thing into a canvas tote bag. "There, that should do it."

They walked to the corner and while they waited for the 12, Ellen took repeated deep sniffs over the grocery bag but she couldn't detect the telltale odor.

The ride was uneventful, though Ellen couldn't help feeling that everyone on the bus was watching Temerity suspiciously. *It's my guilty conscience,* she thought. *My perspective.*

Justice was waiting for Temerity at the stop. He gave Ellen a little nod through the window but his face was drawn and concerned. As the bus pulled out, Ellen could see the siblings launch into a heated discussion. Temerity looked both annoyed and abashed.

Ellen's knees were beginning to ache. She had put some ointment on them when she changed into dry clothes but she could feel the scrapes stiffening up as they scabbed, making bending and straightening excruciating. When she stood to exit at her stop, she could only rise into a crouch, so she had to walk in a crooked, bent position, which made her feel like a fat spider.

Fortunately, the more she moved, the easier it became. The pain lessened and by the time she reached the loading dock she was limber enough to function almost normally. Inside Costco, Ellen was going through her usual preparations when she saw Irena. This surprised her; she hadn't expected the woman to be there. And the Crows were obviously thinking the same thing.

"What are you doing here?" Rosa asked her. "Shouldn't you be at the hospital with the baby?"

"I cannot stay there." Irena hung her head and focused on her locker. "I must to work. And doctor says he must go home in a few days, maybe." She leaned into her locker and pulled out her battered CD player.

There was something in the way she said the word "maybe" that caught Ellen's attention. It wasn't a "maybe he can go home," more like a "maybe I'll take him home." Kiki hadn't missed it either. Her eyes narrowed and she said, "You don't want him, do you?"

Irena shot a glance at Kiki, fear of discovery in her eyes. Kiki pursed her mouth, waiting for the answer. She crossed her arms and drummed her long fingers against her elbow. Irena tried to draw herself up but the attempt failed and she collapsed forward, exhaustion and worry folding her like an accordion. "He is not my baby. I do not have money to take care." Her hopelessness was hard to witness.

Except for the Crows. This year, Christmas had come again right before Easter.

Rosa said, "I'm sure the hospital can contact social services for you." Elbowing Kiki aside, she patted Irena's shoulder. "They'll find him a nice foster home while they work out the legalities. Don't you fret, sweetie."

Ellen clenched her jaw and ground her teeth. Maybe it wasn't fair that Irena had been deserted by the father and was stuck with the baby, but discarding the child to what, even with her limited knowledge, was almost certainly a grim fate touched Ellen's rawest, bleeding nerve. She didn't know much, but her time in the foster care system had taught her a few of its legal obstacles. Without the birth father or mother to sign off, the baby couldn't be adopted and would most likely be sent back to Russia and an orphanage. She wanted to shout at Irena, *Don't do it!*

"But I cannot give him up. If the father find out," Irena continued in a terrified whisper, "he will kill me."

"Now, why would you say a thing like that?" Kiki asked as though reprimanding a child for exaggerating.

"Because he did before." Irena had spoken so softly that Ellen almost didn't catch it.

For just a second, the Crows were speechless. This was more than entertaining gossip. This was scary and real. "He killed someone?" Rosa asked in a horrified whisper. "You can get a restraining order, it's the law—"

From her crumpled depths, Irena laughed mirthlessly. "Georgi don't care for law," she said. Ellen's ears pricked up at the mention of the father's name. "He do what he like," Irena said.

"Can you go somewhere he won't find you?" Rosa asked almost timidly, clearly out of her realm.

Irena's hands, limp by her sides, rose an inch then flopped hopelessly back to the bench. Ellen was reminded of the death throes of two small, pale fish desperate for water.

Kiki cocked her head at Rosa, indicating that they should move on. "Well, try not to worry. Something will come up."

Irena sighed and nodded weakly. She lifted her earbuds and inserted the tiny speakers, canceling out the world. Then she slammed the locker shut and left without acknowledging the other women further.

The Crows watched her go, clucked a bit, and then Kiki said, "Poor thing."

They'd said it before, but this time Ellen believed that they meant it.

They retreated from the locker room. Ellen sat motionless until she thought the other three would be done in the supply room, and then she pulled herself up, wincing at the pain in her knees.

Checking the assignment list, she saw that she had the front. That meant the checkout registers, followed by the public restrooms. She wrinkled her nose. The "public" was habitually disgusting in its bathroom abuse. The extra-strong cleaning supplies would be necessary.

The last few checkers were finishing up their final counts when she got to the registers, so she started with the lanes that had been shut down. Staying away from the balding, red-haired manager and the two slowest cashiers adding their totals at the far end, Ellen swept out under and around the register station farthest from them. She cleaned the conveyor, which she enjoyed, because it involved using the foot pedal to make it turn as she wiped. She emptied the trash bin, then moved on to the next register station. When she'd finished it, she made her way toward the customer restrooms. She'd start those while she was waiting for the area to empty of employee habitation.

She blocked the restroom door open with the cart and was pulling out the toilet cleanser when she saw the Boss rounding the camping display. He called out, "Billy," and raised a hand in greeting. Following his gaze, Ellen saw the red-haired manager look up in surprise from the register.

The Boss waited until he had closed the distance between them. In the doorway of the women's restroom, Ellen wasn't more than twenty feet from them, and the small anteroom that led to the bathroom made a perfect sounding board for their voices.

"Hey, maybe you already have tickets, but one of our suppliers gave me two for Saturday's game, and I don't want them, thought maybe you might."

"Really? Oh damn! I work Saturday."

The Boss pulled the two tickets from the breast pocket of his suit and slapped them against his hand as he regarded them thoughtfully. "Ah, too bad. They're supposed to be really good, and I don't want to give them to just anybody."

Billy took the tickets from him and peered at them through squinted eyes. "These are courtside!" he exclaimed. "You have to wait for somebody to die to get these seats. Why don't you go?"

"Oh, never liked basketball. They'd be wasted on me, and besides, with all this, you might have heard, divorce stuff going on, I'm just not up to going out, especially in crowds, you know."

"Yeah, I heard. I'm sorry, man."

"Well, too bad. I guess I can try to sell them online." The Boss took the tickets back and started to turn away, and Billy's face had the look of a kid who'd had his all-day sucker ripped from his sticky little hands.

"Wait, maybe I could get someone to cover for me," Billy suggested.

"Hey, hold on," the Boss said, turning back. "I don't work this Saturday, but I could come in for a few hours. Better than sitting in a hotel room alone." He shrugged, making a show of shaking it off. "So—just an idea—if you want, you could leave early, in time to get to the game, and I can come in and cover for you. You usually get out of here about, what? Ten thirty, eleven? Hell, that's an early night for me. I mean, if you thought I could handle it."

Billy grabbed at the suggestion. "It's just collection and deposit. The checkers give you the totals from each register, you add them up, record them on the master ledger and put the cash in the safe."

"Whoa." The Boss's hands went up as though Billy had pulled a gun. "I don't know if I want to be responsible for the safe combination."

The balding man laughed. "It's on a time lock. You just open the slot in the top, drop the bag in, and when you release it, it rolls back up, like a mailbox, only made of two-inch-thick iron. I can give you my key card for the office door. Are you sure?"

The Boss laughed sadly. "Yeah, I'm sure. I'd just be miserable, might as well work."

He handed over the tickets, got a grateful slap on the back, and strode away toward his domain in the back of the store.

Saturday, Ellen thought. That was no coincidence.

And speaking of coincidences . . .

21

It was light when Ellen got off the bus on her street. She had been nervous about coming home alone after Temerity's warning, but there was a police car parked in the entrance to the alley, so she felt better. Still, she opened the door to the apartment slowly, poking her head in cautiously. Mouse got up and meowed loudly, but other than that, no living thing stirred. Ellen reached down and patted Mouse on the head twice. He twisted away and looked from side to side, then pushed his head up again, his tail raised and twitching. So Ellen patted him twice more, allowing him to stroke his cheek against her fingers. His fur felt soft and slightly greasy, but she enjoyed his vibrating purr on the pads of her fingertips. Then she put food in his bowl and went to check the now barless kitchen window.

It was undisturbed. She had left a note for the super last night, telling him that the bars had fallen off and needed to be replaced. She hoped it wouldn't take long. Then she looked through the back door's small window.

The place was swarming with police, though they were so quiet she'd had no indication they were there. It was as though whatever excitement had brought them here was past. They seemed to be focused on the curtain lady's apartment, of which Ellen could see only the steps to the landing. So that was where she saw them bring the body out.

Not that she could see a body; it was just a black plastic bag, secured with three straps to a gurney. Ellen watched, silent and appalled, as it was carried down the steps, across the courtyard and loaded into a nondescript van that Ellen could now see bore the words COUNTY CORONER.

"Oh my God," she whispered. Then watched as a white truck with vented side panels parked in the space vacated by the van's departure. A woman in a light green uniform got out, opened one panel and removed a crate. Ellen saw now that a policeman was holding the dead woman's miserable little poodle under one arm. He passed off the shaking creature to the animal control officer, who cooed to him and petted his head reassuringly before placing him in the crate and loading him onto the truck. Grabbing the binoculars, Ellen read what was printed on the side. ANIMAL CONTROL, EAST CITY SHELTER. Snatching up one of her notebooks, she hurriedly recorded the information.

Below her, Ellen noticed the same detective that she had seen at the hospital draw aside a man in jeans and a jacket—his partner, Ellen assumed. They stood in the shadow of her back stairs for a conference.

"Preliminary coroner report says he thinks heart attack is what actually killed her, brought on by extreme physical distress. She also had heavy bruising on her upper torso, she'd been roughed up. But the coroner doesn't think the blows themselves were fatal. She'll let us know after the autopsy. What do you think?"

"She may have had a heart attack, I don't doubt it, but somebody broke into this old lady's apartment and beat her up. If she died of heart failure, it was because she was literally scared to death."

"And she was the only one who could have ID'd the shooter." He sighed, and Ellen remembered the man with the pierced eyebrow, who had overheard this information at the hospital. The detective went on. "Besides our victim, Tunney, who doesn't seem inclined to butt heads with the Germenes gang."

"Smart guy."

"Yeah, not smart enough to stay away from them. He didn't take a bullet in the shoulder by steering clear of trouble."

"So, he's what? Dealer? Fencer?"

"Most likely, but we don't have any product—no drugs, no stolen goods, nothing to hold over him to make him testify. Says he just wants to get out of town. Claims he never got a look at the guy."

"He let him in the apartment!"

"I know."

"Have we got the report back from forensics on the gun from the tipster?"

"Prints are a match to the kid we released on bail. Ballistics aren't in. They're backed up, big week for shootings. Should get to it tomorrow. But five will get you twenty that it's the weapon that shot J. B. Tunney. We'll send someone to pick him up on an illegal possession charge. If I'm right, and he hasn't skipped bail, we'll get him for the Tunney shooting. But Tunney was only injured, and juries can be a little lenient about shooting a drug dealer, so the shooter will get five and walk in two. But beating up a little old lady and causing her death is another ball of wax, and I'd love to tie the old lady's death to him. But, so far, I got nothing."

"Was she the one who called in the tip about the gun?"

"Don't think so. The informant wouldn't give a name. This lady couldn't wait to have her name stamped in capital letters on the crime report last time."

"Who found her?"

"A state health worker who comes by twice a week to give physical therapy to the guy in 1C. She saw the officer who responded to the call about the gun. She told him she was concerned about the dog whining, said that was unusual. The uniform checked it out, noticed the lock was broken and found the body."

"What about the neighbors? Anybody see anything?"

"We haven't talked to the girl upstairs—works nights, apparently—but everybody else says no. Not surprising."

Ellen drew back from the window. Quickly, she collected a few things, snatched Temerity's card from the wall above her bed and went to the door. Cracking it open, she peered out and then hurried down the stairs, merging into the sidewalk foot traffic just as one of the officers returned to the patrol car. She walked to the corner, crossed the street and booked it.

She didn't slow down until she had put several blocks between herself and the apartment. Then she pulled out Temerity's card and looked around. Pay phones were scarce these days, when even the guys selling fruit on the corner had mobiles, and there were none to be seen. With no other idea, Ellen kept walking. She looped back around to the main thoroughfare and picked up the bus.

When she got to Temerity's building, she stood in the alley looking at the door for a moment. It was so solid, so metal, so intimidating that Ellen turned away, but as she stared blankly at the Dumpster against the alley's dead end, she knew that any place she went would end in a thicker brick wall than the one in front of which she stood.

Ellen turned back to the door and pressed the buzzer.

"Hello?" Temerity sounded surprised to have an early visitor, but Ellen was relieved that she didn't sound like she'd been sleeping.

"It's me," Ellen said. "He killed the old lady."

There was an audible gasp, and then the door buzzer sounded. Ellen pushed it open and went up the stairs, taking them far more easily than she had the first time she'd been there.

The door at the top of the landing was standing open and Temerity had come out to the railing.

"What happened?" she asked when Ellen was still on the flight below.

Breaking the words up to allow for the mandatory sucking in of air, Ellen said, "They think she . . . had a heart attack, because . . . he, or . . . somebody broke in and attacked her."

"How horrible," Temerity said. Her face was grim and set. "It *had* to be him. Of course it was. I hope they get him soon. Did they find the gun?"

"Yeah, they found it, but . . . they are waiting for some kind of test results."

"Ballistics," Temerity said. "You know, like in a detective story. They can tell if a bullet was shot from a particular gun. And they'll have to get the fingerprints."

Ellen knew from her reading what "ballistics" meant, but it was strange to use the word in her life. "Yeah that, but they do have the fingerprint results. I heard the detective say that they match."

"Well, one mission accomplished, I suppose," said Temerity with a sigh. "I'm only sorry we didn't get fifteen seconds to feel good about it."

"I know," Ellen said. "And they took the dog."

As though the word "dog" had produced the real thing, Runt bounded onto the landing and jumped up, placing both paws on Ellen's chest. She braced herself against him and felt an odd cheering sensation at seeing the funny, shaggy head so close to hers. "Hello, Runt," she said.

"I was just going to take him out," Temerity said. "Want to come?"

Ellen looked back down the three flights of stairs, thought about going down and then up them again, and was surprised to hear her voice say, "Sure."

Temerity grabbed a leash from near the door and made the dog sit while she clipped it to his collar. "I don't usually do this," she said, "it being a little unpleasant for me to locate his public offerings by sense of smell, but Justice had to leave early. I was going to just take him in the alley, but now that you're here, we can take him to the dog park."

After a short walk, frequently interrupted by Runt lifting his leg on no less than a dozen streetlamps, they closed the gate to the dog park behind them. Trying to sound conversational, Ellen asked Temerity, "Do you know anything about Russians?"

Temerity unclipped the collar and Runt bounded off to join a thorough mutual sniff from a handful of fellow canines. "You mean Irena?" she asked.

"Sort of."

"Well, I'm no expert on the Slavic peoples, but what did you want to know?"

Ellen considered how best to phrase her question. She settled on, "Is the name 'Georgi' common?"

Temerity made a *puh* sound. "Common? I think it is. In fact, the translation is 'dirt.'"

"What?"

Temerity smiled. "Haven't you ever heard the expression 'common as dirt'?" When Ellen didn't answer, she said, "It's a joke. Never mind. I don't know for sure, but judging from the number of Georgis in the considerable Russian population of this city, I'd guess that it's a very common name. My butcher is named Georgi, so is Justice's mechanic, come to think of it, and they're both Russian. There was a famous conductor in Minnesota named Georgi, a defector from way back when. So it can't be that unusual."

"Oh," said Ellen. "I thought it might be."

"What does that have to do with Irena? Is that the baby's name?"

"Don't know," Ellen said. "But it's the baby's dad's name."

"Father of the Year." Temerity turned her face up to the weak sun and breathed in the smell of the trees and the air around her.

Ellen watched Runt creep up to a small dog, who snapped at him. Runt tucked his tail and bolted for the far side of the dog run. "So," Temerity said, "maybe we should go by the store on the way back. I'm guessing you'll need a few things."

"What for?"

"Well, you are not going to that apartment alone until we're sure the guy is not coming back, so that means you'll stay with us."

"What?" The word was sucked from her in a gasp.

"It's okay, we've got a room. It's not very big, but it's private, has its own bathroom and you won't have to hang out with us unless you want to."

Ellen remembered something she wanted to ask Temerity. "Is Justice, uh, okay?"

"Sure," Temerity said, a little too quickly, and Ellen saw her mouth purse slightly.

"He wasn't mad or anything, was he?"

"Well, let's say he wasn't brimming with enthusiasm about our physical altercation on your roof. Check that, he wasn't enthused that either of us was on the roof to start with. I told him he has no sense of adventure."

"And what did he say?"

"He said people die all the time having adventures."

"And what did you say?"

Temerity's face cracked into a huge grin. "I said people die all the time *not* having adventures. Alone in their apartments." She sighed again. "As witnessed by this morning's sad happenings. I told him, 'You're always after me to get out more. So I did. At least we're living life.' "

Ellen was glad that Temerity couldn't see her grimace. Though she admired Temerity's gusto, she wasn't sure that what had happened yesterday fell under the category of "living life." She would have put it more under the heading of "dancing with death," and the merest wisp of the memory set her core shivering.

On the other hand, she didn't remember ever feeling quite so alert before. She gazed around at the brighter colors, trying to put a name to the phenomenon. It was, she decided, as though she had been asleep, curious and interested but watching through lazy eyes while dozing her way through life. The events of the last few days—and, to be honest, Temerity's continued presence—had affected her nervous system like downing a triple shot of espresso. She was aware of things now, things she would have dismissed as remote before. The problem was, she wasn't sure if this new alertness, this waking up, was worth the shocking sensation of being doused by a bucket of cold water and the slap on the face that accompanied it. On the other hand, she didn't feel exhausted all the time, which was bizarre really, if she considered how much more she was doing. *Weird,* she thought.

After a few more minutes, Temerity called Runt back and fastened his leash again. "Let's go home," she said. "I'm depressed, and you know what I want when I'm depressed?"

"Breakfast?" Ellen asked, hoping she could read minds.

"And lots of it!"

Runt barked to show that he too was psychic.

After visualizing a meal of sweet buns and bacon the whole way back to the loft, Ellen was surprised when Temerity started pulling vegetables out of the fridge. She set Ellen to work washing and slicing tomatoes, green and red peppers, and onions, and then had her whisk four eggs in a bowl while she heated a pan. Ellen stood savoring the smell of the sweet onions with her mouth watering as Temerity sautéed the veggies into a kind of sauce, then added in the eggs and some shredded cheddar cheese and folded it all together. The result, Temerity announced as she slid it from the pan onto a plate, was a Spanish frittata. She cut it into triangular slices like pie and they ate it with their fingers, using dish towels as napkins.

Vegetables, Ellen was discovering, were not just the pile of green pond scum slopped onto a plate in her group home or school cafeteria. Those overcooked frozen vegetables hadn't been something that could be readily carried off to closets to eat while reading. Snack foods wrapped in cellophane had been much easier to secrete away for later, thereby avoiding mealtimes. It came as a surprise to her that vegetables could be tasty and portable, but a good surprise. By the time the last bite had been wiped from their fingers, Ellen's eyelids were drooping. She yawned.

"Sleepy?" Temerity asked.

"Yeah, I haven't slept since yesterday."

So Temerity took her to what she called the choir loft. The door off the main living area opened onto a short hallway. Next to a double door, which Temerity opened to show Ellen her own bedroom, was a narrower single door, not much bigger than a linen closet. It opened to reveal a flight of steps. They went up, single file, to a small, long room with a round window at the end. There was a desk, a shelf with lots of books, a lamp, a closet, a bathroom, a queen-size bed, which seemed huge next to Ellen's single mattress, and a pile of pillows that seemed to wink at Ellen, as though they were saying, *Come on, you know you wanna.*

Waiting only long enough to make sure that Ellen had everything she wanted, Temerity said she had to go and practice, and left her alone.

Cautiously, Ellen sat on the corner of the bed. It gave, but supported her firmly. She bounced it a bit, and it bounced her back. She kicked off her shoes, climbed up into the piles of white comforter and cushions, wrapped herself in a nest of them both and passed out.

When she woke, her eyes focused on the charming wall clock. Ellen smiled, feeling no confusion about where she was or why she was here. *How nice,* she thought, *to have something just because it was charming.* It was two thirty. She'd been asleep for only six hours, but she felt refreshed. She decided that this must be because the room had been so quiet and, for the first time she could remember, she had not woken, not even once. A normal day's sleep for her was interrupted more than a dozen times.

She washed her face and brushed her hair, keeping her eyes away from the mirror. She was amazed to find that there was not only everything she needed in the small bathroom's cabinet, but everything she could have wanted. She looked with longing at the actual bathtub, big enough for even her bulk to lie back in, but she knew that Temerity wanted to go visit J.B. before the day was over, so she cautiously promised herself that treat later.

As she made her way down the single flight, she remembered Temerity telling Cindy that maybe her luck had changed, though she hadn't used those words exactly, and Ellen thought, *Me too.* She'd spent her life living day-to-day, hoping for nothing more than to get through each one unnoticed and unscathed. But she'd cooked breakfast with Temerity, had a wonderful sleep and would treat herself to a warm, maybe even hot, bath tonight.

She smiled. It was so much easier to expect nothing and be all right than to expect something and be disappointed. Still . . .

Temerity was sitting in the huge open room in a square of sunshine streaming in through one of the windows. Just sitting. Her face was turned up to the warmth and her palms rested, turned up, on her thighs. She heard Ellen approaching and turned her head slightly, speaking in a lazy, relaxed manner. "Sleep well?"

"Yes, thank you," Ellen told her. "Did you, uh, practice?"

"Yes, I'm glad it didn't disturb you."

"Oh, I forgot to ask, how was your concert the other night?"

Temerity smiled and got up. "Fun. We play the same program again next weekend. Some guy's cell phone went off in the middle of the second movement. Antoine was pissed."

Having no idea who Antoine was, Ellen made no comment.

"I made you a sandwich. Why don't you have it while I find my shoes and get my stuff, then we'll head out. Okay?"

"Sure." Ellen looked for the sandwich. She saw a plate on the counter, covered with a dish towel. That must be it. She started over.

"I hope you like chicken salad with nuts and apples!" Temerity called out as she passed by the sofa.

Ellen lifted the towel. Underneath was a fat sandwich, but the bread was suspiciously brown and looked like it had seeds in it.

Cautiously, Ellen picked up half and sniffed at it. It smelled surprisingly sweet. She looked at the filling: chunks of chicken, some kind of nut, and little dices of green apple. "I like apples," Ellen called after her, though she didn't mention that she had only added them in their raw form to her list of eligible foods a couple days ago.

"Oh, and I used nonfat yogurt because we were out of mayo," Temerity called as she vanished into the hallway.

Ellen took a bite. The bread was firm but yielding; it had more substance than the white bread she usually ate, which mushed immediately into the doughy paste from which it had come. The nuts and the chicken were satisfying, and the apples were crisp and sweet in the light sauce. She took another bite, and then another.

There was a lot more to this food thing than just salty and sweet, she decided as she finished off the first half of the sandwich. Temerity had left a glass of cold milk next to the plate, and she drank it, amazed at how well it quenched her thirst.

Ellen patted her stomach with contentment. She felt the luxury of not immediately wanting to eat something else, and it hadn't been, for her, very much of a lunch. Maybe these seeds and fruit and stuff filled you up more; she thought she'd read that somewhere.

"Okay, let's hit it." Temerity was back, wearing a dark jacket over jeans and boots with thick soles, like she was in the army. They looked both solid and comfortable. Ellen glanced down at her only pair of shoes, the Converse. One lace was dirtier and shorter than the other. "I should get some boots like that," Ellen said. "I'll bet they last a long time."

"At least you got some new sneakers. I like them," Temerity said.

Ellen just grinned. "Me too," she said.

"Much quieter," Temerity added. "And a better tread, I'll bet."

"That's what I was going for," Ellen told her. Then added experimentally, "Stealth and traction."

"Your nimbility factor," Temerity said, "has definitely improved. I told you it would."

Ellen felt the tingling, pleasant sensation of little bubbles in her chest, like when you drink a soda too fast after you open it. She nodded in agreement, but only for her own benefit. She had somehow known it would too.

22

The guard at the hospital was, thankfully, the same one from before, and he remembered Temerity. *Who wouldn't,* thought Ellen. "Go on through," he said and gestured when Temerity and Ellen approached the desk, though, of course, only to Temerity. For a second, his eyes wavered in Ellen's direction, and then he called out to someone approaching behind her.

"I think we should take J.B. something," Temerity said, pausing near the open doors of the cafeteria. Ellen didn't need to ask how she knew that they were outside the food court because the smell from the hot food was wafting liberally out into the lobby. "What does he like?"

"Cigarettes?" Ellen suggested, her nose wrinkling at the idea.

"No, silly. I mean like some soup, or candy maybe. What do you think?"

"Soup is good for sick people. Right?" Wasn't that what TV moms always gave their kids when they stayed home?

"Let's do it."

They went in, Ellen filled a to-go container at the self-service line with something thick and creamy that had green flecks in it, then she gave it to Temerity and they went up to the cashier. "Hi," Temerity said.

"Hello there, missy. That will be four fifty." The man, an elderly gentleman, was perched on a stool in front of the register. He watched with kindly eyes as Temerity selected the bills, separated into different holders in a special wallet, and handed them to him. He made change and they started off.

"Have a nice day, ladies," the man called out.

Ellen froze and turned back, but the checker was already chatting amiably with the next customer, a nurse in Winnie the Pooh scrubs.

Temerity drew in a breath. "Did he see you? Did you drop something or bump into him?"

"No," Ellen said. "He looked in my direction. People do that sometimes, but he didn't stop smiling or look shocked. When people do have to see me, there's always a reaction. Maybe he was talking to someone else."

"Maybe," Temerity said, but she sounded thoughtful.

Across the lobby, Ellen spotted someone that made her draw up short. "What's she doing here?" she asked.

"I'd tell you," Temerity said, slightly annoyed, "but that would involve my being able to see who you're talking about."

"It's Susan Newland." Thoughts and possibilities began to swirl and compete in Ellen's head. Was she here for a different child? Was she ill? Maybe she had found a way to make Cindy give her back the baby. "She just went past the entrance toward the elevators."

"Change of plan," Temerity said. "We're going with her."

"But . . ."

"We're going where she goes," Temerity insisted. She held up the bag with the soup container. "This should keep for twenty minutes or so, and there's always more where this came from."

Resistance, as Ellen had noted before, was useless. So they fell in behind Susan, who seemed uncertain of her destination. She kept referring to a piece of paper in her hand. Eventually they found themselves in a large, very busy waiting room. On the door it said PEDIATRIC CLINIC.

Susan went straight to the receptionist and murmured something they couldn't hear. The young man checked his computer while Ellen and Temerity took a seat just inside the door in the large waiting room, which was filled with thirty or so members of various families. The receptionist told Susan, "We'll call you." Looking decidedly nervous, Susan sat, clenched her hands firmly in her lap and watched the door.

They didn't have to wait long. Within five minutes, the door opened and Ellen looked up to see Cindy and Janelle coming in. With them, a tall, handsome man was holding a detachable car seat with the baby inside. Ellen assumed this must be Janelle's husband and told Temerity as much.

"She's scrunching up her face," Cindy was saying as she peered anxiously at the baby. "Do you think something is hurting her?"

"No. All babies scrunch up their faces," Janelle said with a laugh. "It's not like they—" Her words died midsentence as she spotted Susan rise to her feet and start toward them.

Her husband followed her look and immediately placed himself between the two women, handing the carrier off to Janelle. "This has to stop," he said calmly but firmly. It was clear he had the same class and self-possession as his wife. "Please don't make me file for a restraining order. Your husband has already—"

"I know, and I'm here to apologize for that," Susan said quickly, laying a gentle hand on the tall man's wrist to disarm him. "I'm so sorry. I wanted to tell you that I didn't have anything to do with that.

I didn't even know anything about it. When I found out, I—well. He won't bother you anymore. I'm sorry," she said again, as though repetition would underline it. Her eyes were moist, and she could barely keep her voice steady.

"How did you know we'd be here?" Janelle asked. The question was stern but gentle.

"The hospital hasn't corrected the records yet. I got a call to confirm Samantha's blood test. That's how I knew. Is she all right?" She sounded so genuinely anxious that Janelle visibly relaxed.

"She's fine. There was a tiny bit of jaundice, and they just want to make sure it's all cleared up."

"Oh thank God." Susan exhaled. "I was so worried. I know it's not my . . . well. I'll go now. I just wanted to tell you that you won't be hearing from Edward anymore." She said this last to Cindy. "And I'm so sorry that he put you through that."

The girl smiled at her. "Thank you," she said. She reached out and took Susan's hand. They held on like sisters who had been separated for a long time. "I could see how much he wanted this, for you, I mean, and I know it's hard for some men when they can't control something. You know what I mean?" Susan looked so grateful, but she only nodded and Cindy went on. "My dad was like that, he got mean and angry when he was really scared. I want you to know that I'm really sorry too about how things worked out, I mean for you," Cindy said. "I know you'll be a great mom someday. You and your husband will have a family."

But Susan's eyes had dropped at the word "husband," and her mouth, lips pressed tightly together, quivered. She cleared her throat and spoke. "That's very kind of you to say, but Edward and I have separated for good this time." She shook her head, closing her eyes for a moment. "That's why he overreacted. He thought maybe I would stay if he could fix it . . . but . . . well, this whole situation, I saw a side of him that . . ." She paused. ". . . that I guess I knew was there, but I pretended wasn't, or that I convinced myself was something else before. I can't . . ." She broke off again, squeezed Cindy's hand and then released it. "But enough about me." She laughed awkwardly. The other three were all watching her with sympathy. "You've got your hands full. Take good care of her. And be happy," Susan said, forcing joviality that clearly wasn't in her grasp at that moment. Then she turned and walked toward where Ellen and Temerity were sitting next to the exit.

Ellen felt a rising panic. This was wrong. Something needed to happen that wasn't happening. This woman shouldn't leave this way. She meant well, and she was really hurting. Someone needed to help her. In a flash, it came to Ellen.

"Stop her," she whispered to Temerity. "You have to stop her."

"What?"

"Just do it!" Ellen couldn't remember ever giving someone an order in her life, and it didn't come easily, but somehow she felt a part of her would die if she let Susan Newland walk out of this hospital alone and broken. "Please?" she added.

"Okay, then." Temerity jumped up. Turning her back to the room, she pulled the soup from the plastic bag and loosened the cap. "Say when," she whispered to Ellen. Susan came level with them and Ellen gave Temerity a little shove in the small of the back.

Temerity took a confident stride forward, right into Susan Newland, and the still-hot soup went careening all down the front of Susan's perfectly pressed white blouse and gray slacks. Susan gasped and tried to swipe off the hot soup with her bare hands.

"Oh my gosh, I'm so sorry," Temerity said, using her own hands to feel for Susan's bent-forward position. "I didn't see you."

Susan was gazing down at the wreckage with her mouth agape. She shook some lumpy bits off her hands and said almost hysterically, "How could you not see me? I mean, you walked straight into . . ." She looked up at Temerity's blank eyes and her admonition throttled itself with a gulp. "I'm sorry. It's all right," she said, the tears in her voice choking her now. "I'm sorry I was rude. It was an accident. I'm just having a really, really, really bad day."

"I'm really sorry to hear that," Temerity said. "Let me help you. There must be a restroom nearby."

"No, no, I'll find it. Thank you, though."

"I insist," Temerity said. "And I'm going to pay for your clothes to be dry-cleaned. It's my fault. Blindness is no excuse for throwing a perfectly good chowder at someone."

In spite of herself, Susan laughed a little and then moaned, "And I've got to be back in court in forty minutes. What else can go wrong today?"

"Are you a lawyer?" Temerity asked as though she was both surprised and impressed.

Susan was looking down the hall. "Oh, there's the restroom. I really need to . . . go pull myself together." The last thread restraining her fragile grasp on self-control snapped and she broke down completely, covering her face with her cream-of-broccoli-saturated hands.

Temerity said softly, "Come on, let's go clean this up and you can tell me about your really, really, really bad day." She grasped Susan's arm with one hand and stroked it reassuringly with the other.

"That would be nice," Susan said in a muffled sob. She sounded like she was four.

Excellent, thought Ellen. Temerity would work her personal magic and Susan would feel better before she left. On top of being smart and funny and caring, Temerity had the incontestable benefit of reminding people to keep a sense of perspective. It was like the universe put a dialogue bubble over her head that read, *Sure, you have soup on your Armani, but I'm blind. Wanna trade?* Ellen turned to see if Cindy and the others had noticed the collision, and saw them at the reception desk. Only Janelle was looking back at Temerity, a suspicious frown on her face, as the two women sort of helped each other out the door.

Oh boy, Ellen thought. But at that moment, the door to the procedure rooms opened and a child's loud wail commandeered the room. Everyone turned toward the commotion and saw a young dad coming out, making shushing noises to his toddler. Seeing so many eyes on him, the boy buried his head in his father's shoulder. Then he snuck a peek at the Band-Aid on his arm, where, no doubt, he'd received a shot, and fresh howls of hurt and betrayal ensued. "You promised it wouldn't hurt!" he wailed. Ellen fell in behind the treacherous father and his loud, unwitting victim as they left the waiting room.

She went to the restroom door and listened for a moment. The voices inside were muffled, but she could make out enough to know that Temerity had gotten Susan to give her a summary of her recent trials and she could hear Temerity soothing and reassuring her. "They say it's always darkest before the dawn. Noon is dark for me, of course, but I get the point. It sounds like you're due for at least six months of daylight. Maybe you should move to Alaska."

Pushing the door open a crack, Ellen could see the women at the sink with their backs to her. Temerity was wetting a paper towel and she held it out to Susan, who had exhausted quite a pile in an effort to expunge the soup. Her blouse and the front of her pants were damp, but the cream and broccoli bits were no longer apparent.

"Maybe I should," Susan said. "I just don't know how much more of this I can take." She sobbed once, but got it under control. "You've been very kind. I'm sorry to dump on you like this."

"Hey now, who dumped on who?" Temerity asked. "I'm the one who's walking out of here soup-free."

Susan laughed, sadly at first, but it grew into genuine amusement. "Oh, thank you," she said. "I really needed to laugh at myself. What a mess I am."

"I'd laugh at you too, probably, if I could see you. I bet you look funny."

"I do," Susan said. In the mirror, Ellen watched Susan study Temerity. "What do you do for a living?"

"Oh, I'm a violinist, with the symphony."

"Really?" Susan paused in her wiping, genuinely impressed. "I remember you!" she exclaimed. "I have season tickets." Her face fell. "Or I *did*. I guess we'll have to find out who gets them now." She frowned severely.

"How about this?" Temerity put her hands on her hips. "If you give me a card, I'll leave you some tickets, good ones, at will-call for this weekend, and then you won't have to ask . . . What did you say his name was? Dickhead?"

Susan snorted with laugher. "Close enough," she said. "You don't have to—"

"I know, but I want to," Temerity said. "And I want that dry-cleaning bill."

"You know what?" Susan said. "I think I'll throw these clothes away when I get home. I hate this outfit anyway."

"Yeah," Temerity said, pretending to scrutinize the ensemble. "It makes you look like a lawyer."

"Horrors!" Susan said with a smile. "But, speaking of"—she looked at her watch—"I've got to get going. Listen, here's my card. I'd love to come to a concert; I could use a diversion. And you are absolutely right. I don't want to ask dickhead for anything right now. I don't even want to talk to him. I still can't believe you took the time to listen to me blubber."

"Why? Let me ask you something," Temerity said soberly. "If someone were hit by a car right in front of you, would you step over them and keep walking? Or would you stop to help them?"

"I'd stop," Susan said, sounding a little surprised at her answer.

"Well, girl," she said, "from what you just told me, you were hit by a train. I'm only too glad to dust you off."

Susan stopped wiping and turned to face Temerity. "You're a very special person. Thank you for reminding me that they're out there. I needed that."

"Just try to stay off the tracks," Temerity said.

Susan promised to come to the concert, straightened her sadly wrinkled and moist blouse, and said good-bye.

Ellen retreated a few feet down the hall and watched Susan leave, then she went back to the restroom. She opened the door. "What did you think?"

Temerity sniffed, held her head up high and said, "I think she's next."

"For what?" Ellen asked.

"On our list."

"We don't have a list."

"We do now. Let's go see J.B." Temerity unfolded her stick and they started out.

They'd only gone a few feet down the hall when a voice called out from behind them.

It said, "Did you ever find a rug you liked?"

Ellen walked a few feet on, hoping that if they ignored Janelle she'd think she was mistaken. But Temerity had stopped and Ellen turned to see her facing the regal woman.

"Sorry?" Temerity asked.

"You're the one who came in the store and asked about the rug, then the next day I got a note telling me about Sam's baby. Now I bring Samantha in for a checkup, and here you are, talking to Susan Newland, no less."

"Oh, you must be Janelle," Temerity said without apology. "Sorry, I'm not very good with faces."

"You want to tell me what's going on? Are you in cahoots with Ms. Newland?"

"Never met her before today. We just happened to, uh, run into each other."

"I see. And you are here why?"

"Well." Temerity held her stick up straight and propped both hands on it, settling in. "To tell you the truth, we came to see Cindy's neighbor, J.B. He got shot, as I'm sure you know. And then we saw Susan in the lobby, recognized her from when she came to talk to Cindy, and wondered what was going on, so we snooped. And then, when I heard how upset Susan was, I thought she could use someone to talk to."

At the word "we," Janelle's eyes scanned the hallway. Ellen turned away. "How do you know Cindy?" she asked.

"Oh, I don't," Temerity said. "But my friend is her neighbor, and your letter got delivered to her by mistake. She opened it without checking the name, and once she'd seen it, well, we thought it deserved a little help, so we slipped it under her door. Plus, Cindy—we called her Heidi then, 'cause we didn't know her name—seemed like she could use a little assistance deciding what to do, what with going into labor suddenly and all, so we sent you the note."

Janelle looked as though a brace of squirrels had moved an exercise wheel into her skull and they would not stop running. She shook her head. "I'm sorry, I don't understand. What are you, some kind of masked citizen's brigade?"

Temerity smiled wryly. "More blindfolded than masked, but whatever," she said. "Listen, we didn't mean to make any trouble. Finding out about Cindy and you was accidental, but it seemed like a good idea for Cindy to find out about you too—once we'd met you anyway—and for you to know about the baby. So we butted in. I apologize if that caused you any kind of distress."

"Actually," Janelle said, clearly processing the information and finding that it checked out, "I'm glad you did." She did not, however, look completely convinced. "But whatever possessed you to get so involved?"

Ellen turned back, moving directly behind Temerity, who said, "That's a fair question. I guess it's all about timing. Someone helped me when I was in serious trouble a few days ago, someone I didn't even know. Then, right after that, well, your letter showed up and it seemed like a good idea to pass on the favor, even though you didn't know me. Besides, I always find that focusing on helping other people makes my problems much more insignificant, don't you?"

Perspective bubble activated, Janelle opened her mouth to speak, then seemed to think the better of what she was going to say and shut it again. She stood thoughtfully for a few moments. "What about Susan Newland." It was a statement.

"She's in a bad way, don't you think?" Temerity asked. "But other than just listening to her vent a bit and inviting her to hear a concert this weekend, I'm not real sure what more I can do. She strikes me as a resilient little warrior, though."

Janelle smiled, a big smile that showed two rows of perfect white teeth. "Yes, that she does."

"How's the baby?" Temerity asked, and started closing the distance between them.

"She's perfect." Janelle's smile lit up the corridor. When Temerity stopped in front of her she said, "Thank you. I don't know what Cindy would have decided in the long run, but I'm really grateful that you 'butted in,' as you put it, and we can know and take care of Sam's child." She paused, looking over her shoulder through the glass wall into the waiting room, where her husband was gesturing that they'd been called in. Next to him, Cindy was cooing to the baby. "And the girl who Sam loved too," she added quietly. "I can see why he did. She's very sweet."

"She really needed you," Temerity said just as softly. "She misses him too."

A spasm of sorrow passed over Janelle's face at the mention of her brother's death. "I've got to go; they're taking us in," Janelle said. "Stop by and see me sometime. I'll get you that handicapped discount." She started away with her syncopated gait and then stopped and looked back over her shoulder. "You're telling the truth now, right?"

"Actually, I lied," Temerity said, hanging her head. She mumbled, "I already have a rug."

Janelle laughed and went to join her family.

Temerity let out a long, slow whistle. "Whew," she said. "I'm really glad she took that well. I'm not sure what I would have done if she'd jumped me."

Ellen just laughed. She knew what she would have done if someone went after her friend. Check that. She knew what she had done, and it was hard to believe that she was the same person who, just a week before, had sat and meekly watched the world go by.

23

J.B. had visitors when they reached his room. From the hallway, through the open door, they could hear male voices inside, and both of them recognized the detective and the doctor in addition to the patient.

"Yeah, I know," the detective was saying. "And I get it. These guys are scary. But the longer he goes away, the safer you'll be."

J.B. hummed a bit dubiously. Then he said, "I'm really sorry to hear about Connie. She wasn't the friendliest gal, but she never hurt anybody and she kept an eye on things. Guess that was a mistake this time, huh?"

"Something like that," the detective growled.

"What happened to her little dog?" J.B. sounded genuinely concerned.

"Animal control took him. He'll go to the shelter, maybe he'll find a new home."

There was a long sigh. "What a shame. He was a faithful little guy."

Ellen thought, *Yes, more than you know.*

"A crusty old guy like him won't get adopted, and he won't last long. Sounds like me. We both just want to get out of Dodge before somebody turns out our lights. If I can get some money together, then I'll go stay with my son."

"How about this," the detective said. "You come in and ID the guy, if you can. He won't see you. We can take a statement from you, and you can move on into your new life. If you do need to go to court, which I seriously doubt, we'll give you protection while you're back in town."

"Well . . ."

"You think about it," the detective said. "I'll be back to discharge you on Sunday. If you decide you can do it, we can schedule the lineup for then. Just promise me you'll give it some thought."

"Yes, sir," J.B. said. "I'll do that."

"Get some rest," the doctor told him. "I'm dropping you back from the morphine to codeine, let me know if the pain gets bad."

"It's bad," J.B. said without pausing to consider it.

"Of course it is," the doctor said automatically. "I'll send the nurse in with one more morphine dose, but that's it."

Ellen and Temerity decided this might be a good time to fetch more soup. That would give J.B.'s other visitors time to clear out.

"What about the rest of the Germenes gang?" Temerity whispered as they began to retrace their steps to the cafeteria. "I mean, they don't have them all in jail, do they?"

Ellen didn't answer, but she was thinking about what had happened to Curtain Connie. And there was no question that J.B. could identify his attacker if he chose to, and the other gang members knew it.

The cafeteria was mostly deserted in the late afternoon, and Ellen picked a different soup, a clear one that would be easier to clean up, just in case. They were starting to leave when Ellen heard a raking cough she'd heard before. It was such an unpleasant and unwelcome sound that it made her muscles seize up tightly, causing the lid to pop up off the soup she was holding in both hands. She stopped abruptly, pulling Temerity up next to her.

Temerity half whispered, "I know. You'd think somebody with that cough would refrain from visiting a hospital. I mean, they've got enough germs here without that guy shoveling them around like steer manure on a winter lawn."

Having nothing to contribute conversationally about lawns, of which she knew nothing, or steer manure, about which she was glad she knew even less, Ellen turned slowly toward the sickly sound. To her astonishment, but not her surprise, there was Georgi in the far corner. Draped over his shoulders was the trashy Loretta, glaring across the table at a rigid and obviously frightened Irena.

"Let's sit down," Ellen said. Before Temerity could object, she led her to a table along the back wall, only a couple tables away from the improbable trio. As she pulled out the plastic chair for Temerity, she whispered to her, "That's Irena and her, uh, fake husband and his fiancée."

Temerity's eyebrows went up in surprise. "No way," she breathed, almost silently. "I thought you said he left the country."

"That's what she thought, but . . ." Ellen wanted to hear what was going on, so she said only, "There's more to the story, I'll explain in a minute."

At first Ellen thought that eavesdropping would be pointless because Irena was saying something in Russian. But Georgi brought a massive hand down on the tabletop, making Loretta's drink cup and Irena jump.

"You are in America. Speak English," he ordered. "You want to stay here. I am trying to help you."

Ellen had put Temerity's back to the group and taken the chair across from her so that she had a view of the menacing couple and Irena's trembling face.

Irena dropped her eyes to her lap and made a visible effort to rouse herself but landed back in the same protective crouch. "Georgi, please, is your boy."

"You will care for my son until I come back," Georgi said quietly, but the threat in his voice was unmistakable. "I have business for a few months. Big business. When I am finished, we will come for Ivan. Then my family will live in a big house on a lake with a boat." He leaned back in his chair and patted Loretta's hand.

"Georgi, I have no money, I cannot keep . . ." Irena began.

The big man leaned forward and hissed menacingly through his teeth. Irena cowed back, raising her hands to her face as though conditioned by the sound to expect an assault. He coughed, the phlegm churning deep in his lungs, thick and rough. Temerity pulled a face and mouthed, *Pass me the Lysol.* "I will give you money for my son on Sunday. There will be enough for Ivan to have a good home and a decent babysitter when you are working," Georgi proclaimed. Irena seemed frozen, but she managed a curt nod.

"Good. You will stay here and wait to hear from me. If anything happens to Ivan, you will answer to me." He paused to let the image of whatever brutality he was referring to sink in. Irena blanched and shuddered. "Understand?" he rumbled.

Irena nodded again, one quick jerk. He stood. Loretta was dragged up with him, looking down her nose at the woman her fiancé had just dismissed so cruelly. Ellen watched her, thinking, *I wouldn't be so smug. You're next.*

"You are strong. You will be all right. Take care of my son," Georgi said, and stalked away. Still clutching the huge man's arm, Loretta turned to look over her shoulder at Irena and made a childish face.

Irena waited for them to go, then leapt up as though the chair were suddenly electrified, shoving the seat back so forcibly with the movement that it fell over and clattered on the floor, then ran from the cafeteria.

Temerity was sitting with her mouth open. For a few seconds, she didn't speak, and then she asked, "What fresh hell is this?"

So Ellen told her. About overhearing Georgi's conversation with the Boss in the parking lot, about the way the Boss had arranged to get the other manager out of the way so they could rob the Costco. About the rumors that Georgi had killed his last wife and the fact that once he had his citizenship papers, Loretta too was almost certainly a goner.

"My, my, what a tangled life you live," Temerity commented, sounding awed.

Ellen thought about it. "I used to just hear stuff I knew was wrong and write it down. I mean, it's hard not to hear things when people don't know you're there, but it never occurred to me to do something about it. Until . . . well, until . . . I met you."

Temerity put her head back and laughed. "So I'm the spider who caught you in that sticky web."

"Yeah," Ellen said. "Kind of."

"Well, let's get weaving!" So they talked it out. Discussing whether or not Irena would be safe even if she did everything Georgi asked. The vote on that was a double no. They speculated on what the kid's life would be like with the world's most despicable parents. The prognosis was bleak. They puzzled out that Georgi and the Boss had obviously met through Irena; the Crows had said so. They speculated on what the "big noise" that Georgi had promised would be. Nothing good. And then they naturally shifted into discussing what, if anything, they could do about it. They talked until the soup got cold and the cafeteria began to fill up for dinner.

So they went back for a third container of soup, then took it upstairs to find J.B. snugly cushioned in the blissful ignorance of state-sanctioned narcotics. So Ellen wrote a note dictated by Temerity: "Came by, will try again." As an afterthought, Ellen added two sentences of her own and placed the folded paper on top of the soup.

When they got home, Justice was standing in the kitchen and the smell of something in the oven grew more enticing as they crossed the big room.

"Hey, bro," Temerity called out. "Ellen is staying with us for a few days."

"Cool," Justice said. "I'll get out the life vests and the inflatable rafts."

"Are we expecting a flood?" Temerity asked.

"I think it would be unwise to rule out anything when you two get together, including—no, *especially*—natural disasters."

She ignored him. "Smells good, meat loaf?"

"Turkey meat loaf. You want to make a salad or set the table?"

Temerity picked the table, volunteering Ellen for the salad. Ellen tried to confess complete salad ignorance, but Justice walked her through it. It wasn't that hard, just washing and chopping. He encouraged her to try the vegetables on their own. The sweet snap of the crunchy, juicy pepper had Ellen rethinking her prejudice against vegetables once again. She felt she had some catching up to do.

While they ate, Temerity told her brother about Georgi, the Boss, the plot, and poor Irena.

When she finished the sad story, he just sighed and shook his head. "Is it too late to choose the flood?" he asked. "One shooting wasn't enough for you? I think you should stay out of this one. In fact, as your attorney, I strongly advise not getting involved."

"You're not an attorney."

"I'm the closest thing you've got to sane advice. Dropping a note off to help out a scared pregnant girl is one thing, insinuating your-self in the middle of an armed assault is another."

Temerity just waved a hand. "Done that. Right, Ellen?"

But Ellen was with Justice on this one. She wasn't eager to get in-volved in anything to do with either Georgi or the Boss, if she could avoid it. "Do you think you should just tell somebody—you know, authorities—about the plan?" she asked Temerity, deliberately leav-ing herself out of the suggestion.

Justice frowned. "Unfortunately, there are two problems with that idea. First, you don't really have anything to tell that's not specu-lation. Nothing illegal has happened yet, which brings us to the second thing. The only way to tell the police, or the store, is for you, Ellen, to come forward and tell the right people what you've heard."

Before Ellen had finished shaking her head no, Justice went on. "And the sad fact is, at this point, it's all hearsay. He could call you a liar and sue you for libel. It's his word against yours and once he finds out that someone's on to him, it is highly unlikely this theft would happen, but you would officially be on record as spreading false rumors that were damaging to his good reputation."

"But he doesn't have one," Ellen said.

"I hear you, but strictly speaking, gossip and undocumented harassment accusations of his female employees don't count as evi-dence against him. I repeat, I really don't think you should get in-volved in this."

Temerity was drumming her fingers on the tabletop, her mouth screwed up sideways while she thought. Suddenly she smacked a fist on the table, clipping the tines of her fork and sending it spinning up in the air. Justice reached out, snatched it from the air and set it back on her plate.

"We have to catch them in the act!" she announced.

Justice groaned. "Okay, that would fall under the category of getting involved," he said. "Which, in case you missed it, I strongly advised not doing."

"Well, we can't just stand by and let them get away with this!" Temerity insisted. "If you could have heard that Georgi guy talking . . ." She shook a little in anger. "Somebody needs to put him in jail."

Justice settled down a bit. "And I'm sure somebody will, eventually, but it's probably best if it isn't you two, for multiple reasons."

"What about Irena?" Ellen asked quietly. "He might hurt her, and the baby will grow up to be like him."

Though he looked like he wanted to argue, Justice grimaced and nodded his agreement. "Hard to argue that. Okay. Let's look at our options. Ellen, could you take one of the security guys aside and let him know what might happen, so they could be alerted?"

Before he'd finished, Ellen was already shaking her head furiously. "I can't talk to anyone there. I don't want to. Plus, the security guy on for that job is, like, seventy, and he's related to the Boss. He might just tell him what I said."

"Then somehow you have to get the police there as it's happening, so they can witness it and stop it. But . . . do it from a distance. Stay away from these guys! Do you understand?"

Temerity picked up the fork, felt for a vegetable and speared it. She munched thoughtfully. "We'll have to wait until they start—"

"Okay, hold on!" Justice came to his feet and reached across the table. "You"—he tapped his sister's hand—"are not going to be there.

You don't work there, for one thing, and this is going to happen when the store is closed, as I understand it. For another thing, you're blind. You don't make the best lookout, or witness, no offense."

"None taken," Temerity told him. "Ellen, can you get me in?"

Several possibilities presented themselves. "Sure," Ellen said. "It would be easier if you were already in the store before it closed, then I could hide you until after. No problem."

Justice pushed his plate away and let his body fall forward until his forehead thunked on the wooden table. "Great," he muttered into the grain. "You know that list I have? The one titled 'stupid things I've done for my crazy sister'?"

With a cherubic smile, Temerity asked, "The one you blame me for?"

"Yes, that one. Add to it 'trespassing' and 'vigilantism'—put them right up at the top. That will really round it out nicely."

"Excellent!" Temerity exclaimed, and Ellen realized that Temerity had been planning all along to get Justice to help them, and her friend had just pulled off what she had heard referred to as a "fast one."

A glance at her watch told Ellen that she needed to get moving if she was going to get to work early. She thought with longing of the tub upstairs, but it would have to wait.

24

That night at work Ellen kept an eye on a listless Irena who worked with mechanical dullness, twice stopping in mid-swipe to slump despondently as though stabbed with a shunt that drained her body of its life force. Ellen knew that posture; she'd seen it before in the second-floor apartment directly across from her. Before the blanket, there had been a man who sat list-lessly, staring down at the morbid, vacuous courtyard for endless, almost unblinking hours. A man who, though Ellen watched for signs of animation, never laughed, never spoke, never raised his eyes to the charcoal outline of the city or the sky itself, only sat, his body slumped and abandoned. Then he had disappeared from his bleak perch, and a few days later, the firemen had come and cut the body down. The ensuing occupant had sealed off that melancholy view with the blanket.

When she arrived back at the loft around six a.m., Justice greeted her and asked if they should go and get her cat. They found a card-board box and drove to her apartment. She told him to wait in the car, but he flatly refused.

She watched his face nervously when they went in. He glanced around, taking in the tiny room and its grubby contents in a single pass. Though she couldn't imagine Justice being deliberately cruel, Ellen felt a twisting pain in her chest as she waited for the inevitable censure, raised eyebrows, a distasteful twisting of the nose and mouth. But Justice's eyes swept the room with nothing but interest, and then he smiled. "So this," he said, "is where it all began."

Mouse trotted up, mewing loudly. His stomach, swinging precariously from side to side, resembled a fuzzy hammock filled to bursting with mashed potatoes. He'd missed a meal and, though he could easily afford to, he was not happy about it. Justice crouched down and scratched Mouse's ears roughly; the mews turned to a raucous purr. Then he scooped him up and dropped him in the box, to which the fat cat objected soundly. Justice shushed him and scratched his head to calm him while Ellen grabbed her laundry bag and gathered up a few items of clothing, the cat food and an unused notebook.

When she was ready, she found Justice standing in front of her shelf of journals. "Is this the writing you were telling me about?" he asked.

Ellen nodded, blushing.

"May I?" He reached out and touched one of the spines.

She felt a frosty finger trail down the back of her neck, but she couldn't refuse him. "I guess, if you want. It's not really interesting to anyone else, probably."

"Ah, but you forget that I am a student—soon to be a doctor—of human behavior. To me, this collection of recorded history is like the Rosetta stone."

Ellen sighed, she had no idea what kind of stone that was, and she was too tired to ask right now. Justice pulled out a book, opened it at random and began to read. Ellen felt short of breath, and her scalp prickled with heat as she watched him. A light sort of came on in his eyes, and his lips began to move as he followed from one entry to another. After a few moments, during which Ellen's face felt so hot she thought she might burst into flames, he looked up at her.

"You," he said, "have an amazing sense of morality, meaning right and wrong. It's really very developed. Why do you think that is?"

She shrugged, inwardly pleased. "I guess because so many bad things happened to me, so many people were, you know, mean— worse than mean. Sometimes they were really, truly cruel." She stared at the floor. "I mean, no biggie, it's all okay now, but I knew it wasn't right." She hoped she was making sense. "I experienced a lot of things that I could feel were wrong, so now I know." She had never had this confirmed, but it seemed logical.

Justice nodded. "And something else"—he smiled at her with what looked like pride—"you notice things the average person doesn't. You're very smart, Ellen. I don't suppose you know your IQ?"

Ellen rubbed at a stain on the floor with one toe. "I've heard of that, but I've never been sure what 'IQ' stands for, I mean, exactly."

He laughed. "It means 'intelligence quotient.'"

She frowned and looked at her feet. Of course, she could have looked it up, but it had never come up, or seemed important, until now. "Oh. You mean, how smart I am? Not very. I didn't even finish tenth grade. I . . ." She hesitated, unable to find the words to say that the very act of attending school had been beyond her. "I just went to the library and got my GED online. I repeated a grade, so I was seventeen already, and . . . well, independent, you know."

"IQ doesn't have anything to do with education. It has to do with learning potential and natural intelligence, and you have a great deal of both." He closed the book with a snap and replaced it on the shelf. "But, of course, we knew that much already." He ran a finger along the neat row of spines almost longingly, and Ellen marveled that her simple comments would make him think she was smart. It was a mystery. She didn't know about anything. Then he turned. "All set?"

They went out and she locked the door behind her, as usual. But what wasn't usual was the feeling that went with it. Usually, she closed that door with a distinct reluctance, fighting the impulse to go back in and lock it from the inside. But today, she felt like she was putting the little room away for a while, up on the shelf with those notebooks. It would be here, she would return, but it could wait.

Back at the loft, Runt spotted the box and the hair along his spine, though too long and curly to actually stand on end, got all ruffled. He sniffed at the mystery container and Mouse growled a threatening, ragged tone from inside, a tune he'd sung in his past life on the streets.

"He won't hurt him, will he?" Ellen asked a little nervously.

"No. I'm not sure which animal you're referring to," Justice said, "but either way, no. Just let them get used to the smell of each other, then we'll open the box." He set it on the floor and Runt, after sniffing all around the base of it, planted himself on his haunches and stared at the mystery package with zealous interest, cocking one shaggy ear to listen to the sustained *rurr-ur* coming from within. "Besides, if there is an altercation, my money is on Mouse. Runt barks like a girl and runs away from squirrels."

"But chases buses." Ellen smiled.

"It's a wacky, ninja-squirrel, dog-eat-bus kind of world in his floppy puppy brain," Justice agreed.

"Justice? Uh, thanks," Ellen said.

Justice looked up from where he was pouring another cup of coffee. "For what?" he asked, looking surprised.

"For . . . you know, everything. Letting me stay here."

"Glad to have you," he said with a little bow. "And you know I owe you. Twice now. You want coffee?"

"No, thanks. I need to get some sleep."

"Oh, that reminds me." Justice opened one of the kitchen cabinets and took down a single key on a tiny violin keychain from a row of hooks. "Here. I'll probably be gone when you wake up. Tem is at rehearsal but she'll be home around five."

Ellen took it, admiring the tiny instrument and the shiny silver object that meant "permission to enter" in her palm. She had to hide her crooked but wide smile.

She did need to sleep, but there was something else she was going to do first. Ellen went down the hall, up the hidden stairway and into the bathroom. She turned on the water for the tub, nice and hot, then poured in a generous dollop of pearly pink syrup that bubbled and filled the humid air with the scent of roses so strong that Ellen sneezed. When the tub was halfway filled, she hung a towel over the long mirror on the back of the door, took off her clothes and lowered herself into the silky bubbles.

She felt the joy of her muscles relaxing, the luxury of the cushioning water and the utter pleasure of being cocooned, sustained and supported by the cradle rock of the rose garden–scented bath. She closed her eyes and felt her body rise, float and sink with each full breath.

Two hours later, she was rudely woken to find that she'd fallen asleep in what still smelled powerfully like the stockroom of a florist. Her head, lolled to one side, had slowly slipped farther and farther down until her right nostril was an inch above the water, then a centimeter above the water, and finally, contact. She had sucked in a drop with a snort that distributed it liberally into her objecting sinuses, triggering a violent sneeze. The water was still warm, but only just, and she climbed out, wrapping herself in a towel so thick and plush that she wanted to sleep with it.

So she did, climbing up into the bed and taking the towel with her.

The light was dimming when she woke again, and instead of her customary relief that another day had passed, Ellen had an unfamiliar rush of frustration that she had missed what must have been a beautiful day. She reminded herself that it was Friday and she didn't have to go to work tonight, and that consoled her somewhat.

Ellen climbed from the soft, sweet-smelling sheets and stood for a moment, stunned that she was naked. She could never remember sleeping naked before, and it pleased her to find it liberating. She dug out her clean clothes: a huge black T-shirt and drawstring pants, which, it seemed to her, she had to cinch in more than usual, and some socks, then reached for her shoes but stopped herself.

She remembered the first time she had come for dinner. It seemed like a year ago, and Temerity had worn the mismatched pink and green socks. Ellen rocked on her stocking feet and felt the pile of the carpet beneath her unbound toes. It was so tempting, but . . . no, it felt too exposed. She put on her shoes and went down.

When she opened the door to the main living space, Ellen heard hushed voices speaking. Across the great room, under the far windows next to the grand piano, Temerity sat holding her violin across her knees. Facing her in a second chair was the large man with the cello whom Ellen had seen at rehearsal. They were clearly in an intense discussion of their work and Ellen shied back, watching them through the partially open door.

And then they stopped talking and began to play. The music pulled at Ellen like a crooked finger beckoning her out. She moved slowly, almost against her will, fascinated not only by the melody and the graceful twisting and blending of tones, but by this person, so ungainly in size and shape, who was yet able to produce such delicate and intricate sound.

Incapable of resisting, she crept out and sank down on the rug behind the high back of the sofa, which blocked the rest of the room from her view. The piece went on for several minutes, and when it finished, she heard someone clapping. And then Justice called out "Bravo!" from just inside the door.

He must have let himself in during the piece, Ellen realized now, and he had been standing there listening, as she had, for the last few minutes. Afraid that her presence would be interpreted as intruding, she started to pull herself up to beat a hasty retreat.

But as she rose, she found herself face-to-face with Runt, who had been napping on the couch. Spotting a familiar face a foot from his, he barked once and panted with enthusiasm at his clever discovery. On the other end of the sofa, to Ellen's amazement, sprawled an excessively languid Mouse. The tom raised his head and hissed briefly at Runt's disruption before laying the burden of his heavy head back on his front paws. Runt nosed at Mouse's backside and whined, earning a second lazy hiss and a lethargic raised paw. The feline's message was clearly *Don't make me come over there.*

"Runt, shush!" Temerity called out.

"That was splendiferous," Justice said, crossing in now and laying his bag on the counter. "Hey, Rupert."

The big man mumbled a hello but, Ellen noticed, didn't seem inclined toward social exchange. Encouraged by that, she stood up, smoothing her hair down over the left side of her face, and patted Runt awkwardly with a flat hand while she kept an eye trained on the other three humans.

Justice spotted Ellen and said softly so only she could hear, "You're up!" Ellen saw his eyes cut to Rupert and then back to her, but he said nothing, thoughtfully shifting his attention back to the two musicians. "Are you guys about done? I was going to order Chinese for dinner. Who's in?"

Ellen nodded to him but made no sound. Rupert offered a clumsy excuse and began to wipe down his instrument, packing it into its formfitting case as gently as if it were a baby going down for a nap. Ellen liked that. She folded herself into the corner of the sofa behind Runt and waited for him to leave.

Temerity was putting her violin away now too. Justice poured a glass of wine and then pointed to the bottle in question to Ellen. She shook her head no. He smiled and raised his glass in a mock toast.

The extra-stout Rupert made his way hastily to the door, where he turned around and spoke without looking up. "I'll see you guys on Sunday night. You're coming, Justice?"

"Wouldn't miss it."

Clearly a man of great talent but few words, Rupert looked at the floor and rocked his substantial weight back and forth in a nervous, antsy dance. "Well, good night." He reached for the doorknob, then stopped and patted at his pockets with his free hand. "My keys," he muttered. From across the room, Ellen could see his face go splotchy red with distress.

She spotted the errant ring on the coffee table just in front of her. Rupert was still fumbling and muttering as he slapped his pockets and turned in a circle, keenly embarrassed.

Almost without thinking, Ellen reached out, picked up the keys, and stood. "Here they are," she said. Her voice came out soft, almost shaky. Rupert looked up and saw her across the big room. He started, blinked. For a moment Ellen thought she had made a terrible mistake and her hand flew up to resmooth the hair over her scarred face. But when the large, round man started ambling toward her, he looked so lost and uncomfortable that Ellen wanted to pat him on the head and tell him it would all be okay, the way J.B. had done with Curtain Connie's faithful little dog. When he finally arrived on the other side of the coffee table, he looked into her eyes fleetingly, reddened, and looked down, as though it pained him for her to see him, and Ellen almost dropped the keys. She ran the thought through her spongy mushroom brain again. It pained him for *her* to see *him*.

"Thanks," he mumbled. "I'm always losing stuff, sorry. Um, I'm Rupert." It was more of an apology than an introduction. He took the keys, stuck them in his pocket, and offered his hand. His eyes never once strayed to her ravaged cheek but flicked again and again to her eyes, as if trying to make them stick there but finding himself lacking the bonding adhesive. It was clearly an effort for him to make any kind of contact at all, and Ellen saw no disgust or fear, only timidity. She was stunned.

"I'm Ellen," she managed to whisper.

"Nice to meet you. Thanks," he said shyly, his spots reddening to a deeper shade of crimson, and then spun and moved away with surprising alacrity, as though safety was on the other side of that door in the protective camouflage of a sheltering thicket.

She could relate.

25

Rupert was gone in twenty seconds. Neither Justice nor Temerity said anything. Ellen walked over to the kitchen and sat down on one of the high stools at the counter. After a moment of trying to solidify the thought, she said, "He didn't seem to mind my face."

Justice drank his wine and appeared to be applying considerable effort to keep from grinning. "Lots of people, like Rupert, are too self-conscious about their own appearance to even notice anyone else's." He sipped, the corners of his mouth twitched and he sipped again.

Temerity also gave the impression of trying to contain herself. She shifted from foot to foot and rubbed her hands together. She said, "Rupert is very gifted but very shy." She tried to busy herself in the kitchen, but her curiosity was palpably animating her, and after a minute it burst out. "Did he see you before you spoke?" she asked in a torrent.

"I don't think so," Ellen said.

"What made you decide to let him see you?" she pursued.

"Uh, I didn't really think about it. He just seemed like he needed help, I guess. So, I said, 'Here they are.'"

Justice was watching her over his wineglass. "You want to know what I think?" he said.

"Not really," Temerity said.

"Well, we don't always get what we want, do we?" he quipped back. "I think that the more Ellen realizes and uses her own strengths, the more visible she is. I think she's materializing."

Ellen shuddered, then remembered the cashier who had said, *Have a nice day, ladies*, and wondered if it might be true. The idea felt like an assault to Ellen. It was one thing to speak to a shy individual in a safe place, another thing altogether to say *Ta-da* to the general public.

"I don't want that," Ellen said quickly.

"Then you won't." Justice shrugged. "I'm just saying."

"Well, I'm saying this," Ellen said, and the siblings both reacted slightly at the confidence in her voice. Ellen announced, "I'm buying dinner tonight."

"Okay, thanks," Temerity said.

But Justice pretended to be offended. Shaking his head, he said, "You are so bossy!"

Was she? It was, after all, the second time she had given a command. Ellen discovered that it was a relief to be decisive for a change.

After dinner, Temerity went to her room and Justice said he had some reading to do. He asked Ellen if she wanted him to set her up with the TV or a movie, but she said no. But she knew it would be hours before she could sleep again, and it had started to mist lightly outside with the promise of heavier precipitation. She was standing near one of the big windows that had been cracked open to let in the fresh air, and she breathed in the soft, exhilarating weather. Ellen had always loved the rain. She didn't understand why people rushed through it, avoided it and ducked out of it, but she was glad. It left the sidewalks and the parks blissfully deserted, just for her.

"I think I'll go out for a while, actually," Ellen said.

Justice squinted at her. "You're going to walk in the rain."

She tilted her head and tried to justify what she assumed Justice would find a silly impulse. "I just like to. It feels like . . . I'm a part of it."

He nodded. "That's what I like about it, blending right into the air and water around me."

Her breath caught, surprised that he understood. "Exactly." It was strange, almost threatening, to have someone claim as their own a sensation Ellen had thought of as so uniquely personal, but the unpleasant gust of possessive jealousy faded quickly away, dissolving into a warm, breezy sense of companionship.

Justice offered her a big black umbrella, checked to make sure she had her key, and told her to be careful. Ellen took all three suggestions, thinking this is what it must be like to have a big brother, or anyone, who worried about you. The responsibility of his concern made her uneasy because she wasn't used to accounting for anyone but herself. So she told him she wouldn't be too late and he said she'd better not be or she'd be grounded.

Ellen went down the stairs at a good clip and opened the heavy fire door into the alley. Her first deep breath of the moist air surprised her with its cloying sweetness, and then she realized that the heady smell of musky blossoms was not coming from outside but from under her huge army jacket. The perfume had marinated into her skin during her two-hour bath and had intensified as her body warmed from the walk down the stairs. When she paused it wafted about her like a cloth of fragrant garden swathed around her shoulders. The image of a scarf knit of roses made her giggle as she stepped out into the night.

She went along, admiring the way the light danced on the wet sidewalks and how beautiful the city looked washed clean and glimmering. She wandered to the little park where she had gone into the dog run with Runt and Temerity and sat on a bench, still dry, under a huge weeping willow. The sound of the rain on the branches was lush and full of some mystery that felt sacred to Ellen, who knew no religion except this, but she knew that it was true.

After a while, she was jogged by a niggling sensation that there was something she should do, or maybe had forgotten. The feeling wasn't specific, so she got up and started walking again. Letting her feet carry her where they wanted to go, not thinking about it, just feeling and following the vigorous currents of the shiny world around her.

So it seemed completely natural when she found herself outside Saint Vincent's Hospital, though she recognized with faint surprise that she had walked so far.

Through the glass front, she could see into the lobby. The guard's desk was deserted. On the counter, a printed sign was propped up that read BACK IN FIVE MINUTES. DO NOT ENTER WITHOUT A PASS.

Ellen glanced around. No one. She went in, hurried past the security desk and went up in the elevator. The halls were almost empty and only the stray nurse or doctor passed her with purposeful strides, absorbed in their concerns and responsibility. Having been there once before, Ellen found the room she was seeking without difficulty. She listened at the closed door for a moment but heard nothing, so very slowly she pushed it open a crack.

It was muted and dark. The only light came from the monitor and a silvery, filtered sheen from outside lights glowing through the wet glass. Ellen could make out a ghostly silhouette in front of the window. The person's back was to her, the hands raised and laid flat against the glass and forehead pressed between them, as though willing her body to flow through it and escape.

Ellen pushed the door open only enough to slip through and advanced inside, closing it behind her. When she was a few feet in, she stood in reverent silence, recognizing the desperation that pervaded the small room.

Then the form at the window spoke softly. "You smell of Peterhof garden in spring."

Ellen smiled in spite of being caught out. "Irena?" she asked.

The woman did not turn, but her silver-gray figure lowered her hands and pressed them against her face.

"Yes?"

"Are you doing okay?"

"I'm want for sleep, that is all. Is it time for medicine?" she asked, her voice exhausted and befuddled.

"I don't know. I'm not a nurse. I'm . . . I know you, from work. My name is Ellen."

Irena turned now, but Ellen could make out nothing of her face except a gray featureless oval, deep with shadows, and Irena couldn't have seen much more of her. The announcement didn't seem to have any effect on Irena, or maybe, Ellen thought, she just didn't have the will left to care. So it was a shock when the Russian woman said the last thing she expected: "Yes. I know you."

"You do?" Ellen was taken aback, but not as much as she thought she would be.

"Sit down, if you want." Irena sank into the chair next to the crib. She reached in almost automatically and adjusted a blanket. "He is breathing okay now," she said.

"That's good." Ellen moved through the dimness to the other side of the raised cradle and looked in. Her eyes were adjusting to the low light and she could make out the outline of tiny fists and the tubes that led under the blanket. Remembering what Irena had told the Crows, and wanting to understand the situation, Ellen asked, "Where is his, you know, real mother?"

Irena twitched slightly. "Dead," she said quietly. She drew a sharp breath and added, "His father don't want complication." She shivered slightly.

"Oh." She didn't press Irena for details. It was obvious anyway. Curious about what bond might be between them, Ellen asked, "Do you love the baby?"

In the gloom, Irena sighed. "I don't want for him to be sick, but I don't want to be mother." It was simple and honest, but not complete.

"And you can't give him up, because, well, because of what happened to his mother," Ellen said, then went on, "and you can't let yourself love him, because he won't stay."

"They never stay," Irena said, her voice distant and detached.

"That's true," Ellen said. "Or, it has been for us, hasn't it? I don't think it's that way for everyone."

"Why did you come here?" Irena asked.

It was Ellen's turn to shrug. "I'm not sure. I guess I wanted to see how you're doing. I knew it was your night off too, and I thought you'd be here. I know you don't know me."

"You don't like for anyone to know. You don't want to be seen, but some small times, I do. I understand, so I say nothing."

"You see me?" Ellen asked.

"Sometimes, but then I forget you are there. You are not like the others. You always watch, so you know."

Ellen wasn't sure what to make of that. "I don't know much," she said with a deep breath, looking down at the crib and feeling very ignorant indeed.

"You know that I am . . . too much . . . uh . . . like a bird . . . in cage."

"'Trapped.'" Ellen fed her the word. "I was too," she added. "I guess I still am. Maybe that's why I came tonight, to tell you that sometimes something can happen in a minute, and then everything is different."

From the shadow in the chair came a long, ragged exhale. "Not for me," Irena whispered. "One way only . . . to get away . . ." She trailed off, leaving the dark thought unspoken. Then she said, "I want, I try to hope, but . . . it is . . . too much pain."

"I understand," Ellen said. And she did, she had lived with so much anguish and so little hope her whole life that she really did know what it was to shut that off because the hurt was just too heavy, too dense to carry if she acknowledged its massive presence. She had survived her isolation by looking outside herself. But her advantage, ironically, had been that she was alone. She'd been able to slough off her tormentors by shutting them out. Irena did not have that option.

They sat in silence for a few moments while the drizzle pattered softly at the window. Then Irena said, "I don't want to go on."

"I know," Ellen said. She didn't plead with Irena not to end it. She didn't say she should hold on or believe that things would get better.

Because she didn't know if they would. And it wasn't for her to judge how much pain someone else could live with before they had to make it stop.

So she said nothing, only sat quietly and listened to the constant consolation of the rain. Much later, when she heard the deeper breathing of Irena's fitful sleep, she got quietly to her feet and went out, leaving only the lingering perfume of roses.

26

When Ellen arrived extra-early at work on Saturday, she went to her locker, put on her smock and then went straight to the storage closet to get a cart. She took all of the supplies off its lower rack and added several of the extra-large black trash bags to her supplies on top. Then she headed out onto the floor.

The store was still in full swing, but this close to closing, people were moving quickly around the aisles to finish their shopping and get home. As they had arranged, Ellen went to the far end of the paper goods aisle, where she spotted Temerity and Justice. They had a cart with two items in it: a pack of diapers and a paper shredder, neither of which would be of any use to them, nor would they be purchased. Ellen angled the cart to block a small triangle of space next to the shelves in one of the camera's blind spots and handed one of the trash bags to Justice.

"Commencing operation lawn bag," Justice said with a smirk. "In you go." He opened the bag and helped Temerity step into it like a sack-race contestant while she stooped down behind the cart, then guided her onto the bottom of it. She lay down on her side in a ball and held the giant bag loosely gathered over her head.

"Remember," Justice quoted the labeling, "this bag is not a toy."

"Be back in a minute," Ellen whispered, and she wheeled the cart, much more unruly with its added weight, through to the back. She deposited Temerity in an oversized broom closet, where she had turned two buckets upside down for seats in anticipation. As she closed the door, Temerity said, "Hey, it's dark in here." Ellen automatically started to reach for the light before she heard Temerity giggle. She shushed her and shut the door.

As the process was repeated with Justice, the announcement was made to bring all purchases up front, as the store was closing in five minutes.

After depositing him with his sister, Ellen hurried back to the floor and began to empty the trash bins near one of the sample stations so she could keep an eye on the two security guards sweeping the store. One of them unzipped the tent in the camping display near the registers, looked in and then moved on. The only customers left were now in the checkout lanes. As soon as the guards had completed their check, she returned to the closet.

"Okay," she said, pulling the door shut behind her and switching on the light, causing Justice to squint and cover his eyes. "Let's go. I've picked spots for you. Temerity, you'll be in a tent display between the cash registers and the office, where you can hear what's going on. Justice, you can actually go on top of the roof of the front office. It's like a block built into the corner next to the front door. Did you see it?"

"Reconnaissance complete."

"Whatever that means." Temerity snorted.

"It means I checked it out," he said with a sniff of his own.

"Did you learn that from your G.I. Joe doll?"

"Action figure," Justice snapped automatically, "and I wouldn't talk if—"

Ellen cut them off. "There's a ladder built into the wall on the back side. You'll have to be quiet so no one hears you up there, but it's the perfect place for you to be. None of the cleaners or the security will bother to look up there, and it will give you a perfect view of everything going on. You've got your cell phone?"

He held it up. Temerity displayed hers as well. "Okay. I'm going to be cleaning the camping display, so I'll be close to you both. We all know what to do?"

"Yes," Justice said, licking his lips nervously. "It's the 'why' that still evades me."

"Shut up," his sister hissed in the tight air of the closet. "We're catching bad guys."

"I know that," he snapped, then puffed his cheeks out and made a raspberry sound as he released the breath. "Sorry, I get sarcastic when I'm about to break the law. What's the most important thing to remember?" he asked.

"Never back into a radiator when your pants are down?" Temerity suggested.

"Nobody gets involved, do you hear me? All we do is wait, and the second it looks like something is going to go down, we call the police."

Ellen took a deep breath. She nodded.

The relocation process was repeated. Ellen wheeled the cart into the corner behind the office and after a quick check around, she whispered, "Okay, now!" Justice fought his way out of the bag and went up the metal rungs fastened into the wall. The second he disappeared over the ledge, she went back for Temerity.

This was more excitement and exercise than Ellen usually had in a week, and she was relieved that, though she was breathing hard and perspiring, she was not finding it overly taxing. Once Temerity was loaded, she pushed the cart to the camping display, where foldable chairs, a portable barbecue complete with accessories, coolers, fishing gear and a tent were all set up around a fake fire. The tent had two entrances, one of them facing the registers. Ellen pulled the cart right up to the other side of the tent and unzipped the door enough for the slim girl to get through, then she pretended to be dusting the equipment while Temerity slid, snakelike, through the opening. Ellen rezipped it, parked the cart along the side of the tent and pulled out a rag to wipe down the chairs just as the older security guard locked the sliding glass doors behind the last customer, then took up his next position, standing outside the office door to watch while the cashiers began to count out their registers. The junior guard retreated to his post on the loading docks for the evening deliveries.

The Boss was distinctly sweaty, Ellen thought as she watched him pace around the front, trying to appear busy. He continually passed the glass doors at the front and scanned the parking lot outside, as though expecting someone, and he checked his watch obsessively. Ellen frowned. This guy was a joke. Even if she hadn't overheard him plotting, she would have known he was up to something. For that matter, she thought, even Temerity would be able to see he was up to something.

Several of the cashiers were securing their bundles of various bills with rubber bands and recording their totals. The Boss went into the office, using the magnetic security card lent to him by Billy the sports fan, and came out with the empty cash bag. It was a simple thing, heavy cream canvas with a zippered top. He started with the register nearest the office, taking the cash and recording the amount onto a clipboard, waiting for the clerk to sign off for the amounts. The security guard stayed a few feet behind him, looking bored but competent.

When the Boss reached the farthest register, the young checker was not ready yet. He apologized when the Boss clucked and shook his head, snapping at him to get a move on and glancing nervously to the door every time a car's headlights flashed past it in the dark parking lot.

Moving around the back of the tent, Ellen reviewed everyone's positions. Only the Boss, the slow checker, and the security guard were still milling around the front. The rest of the daytime employees had gone by now, disappearing to the locker room to collect their things and claim what was left of their Saturday night. Two cleaners were working down the first aisle near the pharmacy. Ellen recognized Rosa and Irena, but they were a good distance away. From where she stood, Ellen could barely make out the shape of Justice's head and shoulders where he was lying almost flat on the roof of the office, watching the Boss. It was reassuring to know he was there, cell phone in one hand at the ready.

It was quiet, everything was happening as it normally did, and Ellen was just beginning to wonder if the Boss had lost his nerve after all, when she saw it.

Through the front window, headlights were coming straight toward the doors. This in itself was not unusual, but in the darkness outside, Ellen could see that the lights were moving too fast and getting faster. She could hear the gunning of the car's engine as it grew close, neither turning nor slowing as it reached the end of the parking aisle. The lights glared brighter and hotter through the glass, and the car whipped into and through the cross lane that ran directly in front of the store. There was a grating scrape of metal on cement as the car's wheels bounced up over the curb. The security guard and the clerk spun in unison toward the alarming sound, then instinc-tively shielded their faces with their arms as the car smashed right through the glass doors, dragging the metal frame for a few feet be-fore the frame won, restraining the revving car. The car's single-wheel drive was still spinning the front left wheel, but the puny, bald tire was unable to grab enough traction to pull the car free from the metal net. A thin woman was slumped over the steering wheel.

Recovering from the initial shock, Ellen checked to see what was happening. Justice was already on the phone. He lowered it and gave her a quick thumbs-up. Then he crawled right to the edge of the office roof and crouched, watching what was happening below.

The Boss had started yelling, "Somebody help that woman!" He spun on the young clerk standing next to him with his mouth gaping open. "Call an ambulance! Is there a doctor anywhere?"

The clerk ran for the office. The security guard started cautiously toward the car because the engine was still emitting a furious whine and the spinning tire was producing a dark, acrid smoke. The metal strips holding the car in place could give at any second, releasing it straight into the registers.

The minute the guard's attention was distracted, the Boss stepped quickly over to the camping display and, opening a large cooler, he dropped in the cash bag and pulled out another, identical one, then moved quickly back to the fray, clutching the fake bag in his hand.

Meanwhile, people had begun to gather as though from nowhere. A few dozen customers had still been unloading their heavily laden carts into their cars, but most of them left their purchases to goggle at the accident. The employees still in the store had hurried back toward the front to see what the commotion was.

"Is there a doctor anywhere?" the Boss called out again. "This woman is injured!"

A man stepped forward from the group outside and made his way cautiously through the smashed doors. He was in dress slacks and a jacket, but his thick motorcycle boots crunched on the fractured glass.

Georgi. Ellen felt her throat clench and glanced up to Justice. He looked over at her and she pointed and mouthed, *That's him.* Not understanding, Justice made a hopeless face, turning his hands up like he was holding an empty tray.

"I'm a doctor," Georgi said. "Get back, I'll help her." His Russian accent was thick enough that Ellen saw Justice register understanding. He dialed his phone again, and she saw him whispering furiously, passing on the information to the police.

Georgi opened the car door and looked in. "Her foot is jammed against the gas pedal," he called out loudly, almost theatrically. He leaned down and, in a second, the engine stopped revving. Then he pretended to take the woman's pulse. As he put his fingers on her neck, the head jerked back and Ellen saw it was Loretta, her eyes open but rolling in their sockets to expose the whites, drool running in a thin line from one corner of her mouth.

Ellen shuddered. She did not have a second of doubt that even a drug addict like Loretta would not have done this of her own accord. But she didn't have the luxury to think that through right now. The guard had backed up next to the Boss to give the "doctor" room, and the Boss thrust the fake cash bag at him. "Put this in the safe!" he ordered. "I'll see if I can help them." He gave the guard a shove and the man ran the few yards to the office door, opened it with his card and disappeared inside.

Ellen came around the tent and stood next to the cooler with the real cash bag in it, right in front of the tent. "They crashed a car through the front door," she whispered to Temerity.

"You seriously needed to tell me that? Nobody's *that* blind," Temerity hissed back.

"And he dropped the cash bag in the cooler right here." Ellen thumped it with her heel so that Temerity could hear its location.

"I'll keep an eye on it," Temerity said and sniggered.

The guard returned from the office and went to keep the employees who had come running and were standing gawking at the wreckage from getting too close. There was a good crowd of people outside by now, and a cluster of maybe twenty around the car inside.

Among them, Ellen saw Irena. She was staring at Georgi with fear and loathing, both so extreme she wondered that the two emotions didn't cancel each other out.

"She's only unconscious," Georgi announced, straightening up. "Looks like a drug overdose." He shook his head as though it were all too sad for words, then he spotted Irena. His mouth went to a thin, mean line and one eyebrow raised just enough to send a message. He went on with his no-doubt-rehearsed speech. "She must have had a seizure and pushed the accelerator. She needs an ambulance. No one try to move her, she's had trauma to her chest. I'm going to get my bag out of my car." Ellen knew what that meant. He was leaving, and they would never find him. She felt a rising vexation, an anxious heat in her chest. Somehow she had to stop him.

But even before Georgi had started to turn away, Loretta coughed and jerked. The Boss jumped back as if she were a coiled snake, but not the mean-faced Georgi. Loretta stared blurrily up at the big man, whose expression had gone distinctly furious. "You son of bitch," she slurred. Then she seemed to gather strength. "He tried to kill me," she said shakily, pointing a trembling finger at him. "He put me in here and put a brick on the . . . the . . . go thing." She was struggling, too drugged up to find the words she wanted but lucid enough to be understood. She was trying to get out of the car, but she seemed to have only partial control over her muscles. Everyone was staring at Georgi now.

"She's hallucinating," he said, but the faces regarding him coldly made it clear that no one was buying it.

"Liar!" Loretta slurred, and the crowd began to mutter. "He's not a doctor!" she shouted thickly. "He's a crook! His name is—"

Georgi punched Loretta in the face and she crumpled, unable to say any more. Then he turned to face the guard.

Ellen watched as first the truth and then fear dawned on the security guard's face and he swallowed and reached to pull his nightstick from his belt, but he was too old and too slow for the seasoned criminal. Georgi charged him, knocking him flat to the ground. His skull made a solid cracking sound that made Ellen wince. The Russian started toward the ruined entrance just as the first police car pulled up, sirens screaming. He stopped short, spun, and a gun appeared from beneath his jacket.

Moving faster than Ellen imagined possible for such a meaty man, Georgi rushed straight into the group of stunned employees. Irena screamed and turned to run, but he snatched her by the hair and half dragged her back to the front. "Everybody mind your own business, and she won't get hurt," Georgi said almost calmly as he moved away. "She's just going to show me out."

"Oh please, no," Ellen breathed.

Irena had gone catatonic. Her eyes, wide, stared up at the ceiling as she was manhandled through the glass and wreckage. The cops got out of their car, guns drawn, and hunched down behind their open doors, muzzles trained on Georgi and his hostage.

"Ah, ah, ah," Georgi said to them, pointing the gun at Irena's head. "We're just leaving, and if you want her to live, you'll drop your weapons."

The Boss was taking advantage of the drama to move toward the hidden cash bag, backing up a half step at a time. The cops held their positions. Georgi shifted the gun from Irena's temple to a few inches in front of her face and fired a blind single shot past her nose into the store. There was an outbreak of screams and panic as everyone dropped to the floor or scuttled for cover. Ellen felt a painful, hot hollowness in her chest and looked down. There was a small hole in the front of her shirt that she hadn't noticed when she got dressed, but she was so terrified for Irena and so caught up in the unreality of the whole situation that she dismissed it and the burning sensation. Georgi inched toward the door, keeping Irena's body in front of his. He was almost through the doors when suddenly a shape dropped from the sky.

Justice caught Georgi in the back as he landed, yanking him off of Irena, who stumbled a few feet and fell onto the shattered glass on her hands and knees. The powerful man twisted toward Justice, who was outweighed and clearly no match for a desperate criminal. The cops took aim again, but in the struggle, there was no way to fire without possibly hitting Justice. The ache under Ellen's right shoulder had grown into a piercing pain, she fleetingly wondered if she was having a heart attack.

Suddenly, the confusion was sliced by a high, shrieking scream of rage. Irena had risen from the ground, a thin shard of glass clutched in one hand, and as she screamed, she lunged, thrusting the makeshift dagger into Georgi's back. He howled with pain and released Justice, who fell off to one side. Georgi turned, raising the gun at

Irena. She did not flinch, only opened her arms as though to welcome the bullet. A shot rang out. Irena's body jerked. Then a volley of shots ricocheted and echoed through the huge space, and Georgi fell to the ground, where he lay in an unmoving, crumpled heap.

Irena swayed precariously and looked down at her tormentor. Blood was running down her hand where the glass had sliced it open, but she seemed oblivious to anything but him. She was staring down at the body like it was a monster in a nightmare, which, Ellen thought, he surely was. Ellen's chest was hurting so badly now that she tilted forward and reached one hand to the apex of the pain. It was wet with warm liquid.

The cops were shouting and moving in, more cars raced up and screeched to a stop. In the confusion, the Boss made a lunge for his prize.

He tore open the cooler. It made a sucking, vacuum sound, like Tupperware, and he stared down in astonishment at the empty container. Confusion was instantly replaced by rage. Almost immediately, his gaze fixed on the partially unzipped tent door and the movement inside. His face twisted in fury and his hands clenched. In spite of the twisting pain and throbbing in her chest, Ellen reached out with her right hand and took hold of the only weapon she could find on her cart.

"Looking for this?" Temerity asked, emerging from the tent and holding up the bag. "Hello, police officers! Over here."

The Boss's face seethed with frenzied rage. He locked his eyes on the bag and then lunged for Temerity. Ellen's hand holding a spray bottle flew up between them, and she released a long stream of toxic green cleaning liquid directly into his face.

He screamed, backing away and clawing at his eyes as he dropped to his knees. One of the officers hurried over to them. "What's going on?" she demanded. Her gun was drawn but pointed at the ground in front of her.

"He was trying to get this." Temerity held up the canvas sack. "That's what this was all about—the car crash, the whole thing. They were robbing the store together."

The cop's gun was redirected at the Boss. "Get down on your stomach," she shouted at him, moving in closer. "Down on the floor!"

More police officers were coming in now and everything started to happen very fast, though it seemed to be blurring together for Ellen. She was panting, but she couldn't get a deep enough breath, and she wasn't sure why. The Boss was handcuffed, his eyes squeezed shut and streaming tears. Ellen suspected not all of the tears were from the cleanser. At the same time, the female officer took the cash bag from Temerity, but as she did, she looked past her in Ellen's direction. Her eyes wavered up and down, fixed on Ellen's face, then dropped quickly to her chest. She looked vaguely sickened. That didn't surprise Ellen, but what came next was unexpected. Instead of turning away, the officer stepped toward Ellen and addressed her.

"Ma'am, are you all right?" she asked, her voice full of concern. She turned and shouted over her shoulder. "Let's get a paramedic in here!"

Ellen was watching the police officer, confused. Had the woman spoken to her? Did she see her? Everything seemed to be pulling farther away. She glanced down at her front, to check if her body was there, and saw the blood streaming from between her fingers where they were pressed against her chest. Everything started to dim. She reached forward and grasped the barbecue grill to steady herself.

"Just stay calm, ma'am," the cop said, holstering her gun.

Ellen's head spun, and the ceiling above her circled, slowly, then faster. The floor rushed up toward her, and her face hit, unrestrained against the side of the grill, but there was only a second of fleeting, tearing pain as she dropped into a dark, silent void.

27

"Ellen? Ellen?" Someone was calling her name through a thick fog, but she was distant from the sound, as though there were a cushioning barrier of foam between herself and the speaker.

Then, very slowly, she opened her eyes. Temerity was leaning over her.

"What happened?" Ellen managed to whisper as an onslaught of images rushed her. Her face and jaw felt locked stiff, her lips swollen, and it was hard to speak through the numbness and narcotics.

"You got shot," Temerity said, squeezing her hand tightly. "So you've got a great story to tell! The good news is the bullet went through the fleshy bit next to your arm, so it just grazed you. It bled a lot, but didn't do much damage. Thank heaven you have some extra padding." Temerity was stroking her hand, and Ellen noticed that, though Temerity spoke with her familiar confidence, she was crying.

Ellen tried to sit up, but it sent her head spinning, so she only made it a few inches before collapsing back. "What's wrong?" she slurred through slightly parted lips that wouldn't fully function. "Why are you crying? Is Justice . . . ?"

"He's fine—he's right here."

"Present and accounted for," Justice's voice said from her left. "A bit sore, but nothing a fistful of Advil and a hot shower didn't improve."

Ellen tried to turn her head but found that she was prevented from doing so by thick bandaging on the left side of her face. "What's wrong with me?" she asked, raising a tentative finger to touch the bulky gauze.

The painkillers in her system kept Ellen from feeling her previous aversion to any kind of scrutiny, but they also made it difficult to comprehend what was happening.

"You took a little spill when you saw your own blood. Happens to some people," Justice told her, coming around to stand behind his sister so that Ellen could see him. "And you hit your face on the grill tongs that were hooked on the side of the barbecue, sliced it open pretty good. The doctors cut off quite a bit of scar tissue before they stitched it up and then they decided to do a skin graft, so you might look a little different when we get that off." He beamed down at her. "That's why you've been out for such a long time. Two surgeons, friends of Dr. Amanda, heard about what you did and they both came in to work on you. I don't want to say much, but they were pretty cocky about how well it came out. You are now officially a surgeon's work of art."

This was far more information than she could process, so Ellen fumbled for something simpler to grasp. "What day is it?" she asked. Her tongue felt bloated and her teeth were locked together.

"Sunday morning. You've been here all night. Two hours of surgery, a few hours in recovery, and now you're here with us in this beautifully appointed private room," Temerity said. "I *think* it's beautifully appointed anyway. It is, in my mind."

"Yeah, hang on to that," Justice said, glancing around at the grubby room with a comic grimace that fleetingly made Ellen want to laugh, but the impulse was smothered in pillows of opiates.

"So . . ." Ellen wanted to lick her lips—her mouth was so dry—but her teeth wouldn't open. Justice held a cup of water for her to sip from a straw, and that helped. "So," she began again, "Georgi?"

"Dead," Temerity said. "And I can't say I'm too broken up about that."

"Oh," Ellen said. She wasn't sure what she felt, if anything. Her emotions were fluttering somewhere outside her body like frantic butterflies.

"Better him than me," Justice added.

"Irena?" Ellen asked, her eyes flickering wide as she remembered.

"She's okay. She's here too. She had to have her hand stitched up; she wants to see you when you're ready."

"See me," Ellen muttered. "That's weird."

Justice laughed, then said seriously, "That boss of yours is in custody. The police told us he'll get put away for a long time for being an accessory to attempted murder and robbery. Oh, that Loretta woman is pretty banged up, but she'll be back to her old self soon."

"Loretta's old self," Ellen mumbled, remembering how appalling the woman had been of her own accord. "That's not good."

Temerity laughed. "I'm with you there," she said. "Justice means she'll be okay."

"'Okay' would be an improvement," Ellen muttered.

Temerity and Justice both laughed, and Ellen was mistily aware of wishing she could join them but too lost in the fog to feel disappointed. "Oh yeah," Temerity added. "J.B. is being released this morning."

Justice pulled out a familiar small package wrapped in brown paper and held it up so that Ellen could see it without having to turn her head.

"I'm on my way up to give him a little parting gift. It's his anyway."

Ellen tried to smile, but only half her face worked. "That's good." She sighed.

"He might not have been a model citizen, so far anyway, but he's an excellent capitalist, and I think that quality needs to be supported by his fellow Americans. We'll call it venture capital for his new start-up."

"Very patriotic," Temerity noted.

There was a soft knock from behind Justice, and he turned to the source. "Hi," Ellen heard him say. "Come on in. She's awake, barely."

Someone appeared next to him, and Ellen found herself being peered at by a third person, which wasn't as bad as she thought it would be because it was Irena. Her right hand was a club of white gauze and was held against her chest with a sling. She smiled down at Ellen, some, though not all, of the haunted look having left her eyes. "Thanks you," she said.

"Not me," Ellen replied, raising a limp finger half an inch to point at Justice. "Him," she said.

"Yes, thanks him too. But if not for you, he would not be there, and I would not be here."

Ellen watched her through her druggy, silver haze. A thought floated into her fuzzy brain. "See? I told you that something can happen that changes everything. Now you can rest," she said.

Irena's smile was distracted. "Yes. That horrible man will not come back." She ran her good hand through her hair. "But I must to decide about Ivan." Ellen could tell from Irena's voice that she *did* know, that she too had been unwanted. "I am afraid for him." Tears came to her eyes.

Ellen did not speak, only shifted her eyes so that she could see Temerity, who was grinning widely in the general direction of the Russian woman. Temerity said, "Irena, do you like Mozart?"

Irena started and stared at the blind girl. "Yes, very much. I was one time, how do you say? Pianist."

Temerity's smile was so smugly contented that Ellen half imagined a feather protruding from the edge of it. "If you're up for it, I'd love for you to come to my concert tonight," she told Irena. "I have two tickets and only one is taken, by a nice woman, a lady whom I would very much like you to meet."

Irena had drawn back a bit, her fine but exhausted features veiled with distrust. "I don't know, people who are new, I am not so much interesting to people, friends."

"Oh, I'm confident she'll find you fascinating." Temerity stood up and moved around to Irena. Locating her good arm, she hooked her own through it and started to lead Irena out into the hallway. "So you were a pianist," she was saying. "Tell me about that."

They were out the door and Ellen felt the encompassing warmth of knowing that Irena was securely in Temerity's thrall.

Justice leaned over and put the back of his hand on Ellen's unbandaged cheek. "You rest now," he said softly. "I've got to go strew largesse." Then he tucked the blanket in under her chin and slipped quietly out.

Ellen was fading away, falling into the clouds that drifted and shimmied around her. "Strew largesse," she mumbled. As she succumbed to the allure of the floating fog and was borne away, her last thought was, *Whatever that means.*

But she knew it was something good.

28

Ellen stood gazing in the small mirror she'd uncovered above her sink. Her dark hair was pulled back and her round brown eyes stared with awed disbelief. Two round eyes. The left brow, which had been cruelly drawn downward by the burn, half closing her left eye, was now released and reshaped. The scar lines from the surgery six months ago were still red but growing fainter, and between them—though she still couldn't quite fathom how—smooth skin was healing. Her cheek and eye were whole again. The many weeks of not being able to chew solid food properly, as well as a diet supervised by Temerity and Justice, had made her drop almost eighty pounds, and she found that she had gained a face but lost a chin. Now she was down to one, still plump but strong enough on its own to support her new look.

There was a knock on her door. "Yeah?" she called out, turning self-consciously as though she'd been caught doing something naughty.

"It's me!" Temerity called through the door. "Dr. Amanda's here. Dinner's almost ready, and I want you to hear the piece I'm working on."

Ellen shifted her weight. Though she'd endured months of doctors, nurses and other strangers studying her and had learned to suffer the exchanges without too much awkwardness, it was still a conscious skirmish for her to knowingly interact with anyone besides Justice and Temerity.

"Uh, sure. I'll be right down."

She glanced up at a corner of the mirror, where a snapshot, taped to an index card, was fixed. The picture was of a small, wiry poodle, looking far more furry and fat than when last she'd seen it, held by tobacco-stained hands, across the top of which were visible the fangs of a snake tattoo. On the card under the picture were scribbled the words "Loving life in Arizona!"

Ellen had been bewildered to find the envelope, addressed to her, at her apartment when she'd gone to move her things out. J.B. had apparently known more about her existence than she'd realized, and the note that she had left on top of the soup container that day so long ago, telling him where the little dog had been taken and to try matching the bite mark on the shooter's hand to the dog's teeth, had not gone unheeded. The detective had been able to prove that the same man who shot J.B. had attacked and killed Curtain Connie. The little dog had bitten his mistress's attacker, providing proof of the crime and of his faithful, canine heart.

J.B. had found out about Ellen and her efforts on his behalf when Justice had told him all about it the day he delivered the welcome package of cash.

Ellen brushed her straight hair and then refastened it back with a clip. Turning her face from side to side, she stared, incredulous, at the face she had never imagined she would have.

Then, taking a deep breath and clapping her hands together to muster some courage, she went downstairs—in her stocking feet.

Temerity was standing under the window, tuning her violin. Justice was cooking, chopping and tossing green beans into a pot, but he paused to listen to the pretty blonde doctor sitting at the counter. Amanda turned and smiled at Ellen's entrance, but her wave turned to a pointed finger, which she used to accentuate a point in her spirited argument with Justice. He leaned across, snatched the hand, and kissed it.

Embarrassed by the show of affection and still hesitant to join the group, Ellen made her way to the sofa, but no closer, and stood on one foot as she twisted a strand of hair with her left hand, fighting the impulse to pull it down across her face.

"Hello," a soft voice said from a foot away.

Jumping slightly, Ellen looked down to see that the high-backed armchair was occupied. Rupert too, it seemed, had cozied himself away from the others, preferring to sit and listen and watch at the edge.

Ellen took up her spot in the corner of the sofa, pulling a half-asleep Mouse into her lap. He opened his mouth in a silent *eh-eh-eh*, looked up at her, and then closed his eyes and leaned his head hard against her hand as she began to scratch that special place behind his ears. She smiled shyly at the cellist. He blushed and looked away, suppressing a self-conscious grin.

They'd become tentative friends in the last few weeks. Their awkward exchanges included a number of conversations consisting of more than a dozen lines, in which they found they had several things in common. They both liked music, of course, rain, children who leapt fearlessly from swings, and food, especially bacon.

"Okay, listen up!" Temerity called across the space and began to play. The strains of her violin joined into the music of the conversation, adding a new voice, longing and benevolent and demanding to be heard all at once. *Huge,* thought Ellen with great fondness. Temerity and her life were huge, and she was in it.

Ellen sighed, settling in. She felt at last that she was here—still timidly, she knew, still in the shallows of that vast shared ocean, but definitely wading now, knee-deep, into the warm, scary, lapping waves where everything, even promises, were uncertain and unknown.

And she was all right with that.

ACKNOWLEDGMENTS

This book says something I feel in my heart and have always wanted to express. I'm so grateful to those who gave me the opportunity to put it in print, especially Paul, Nita, and Meaghan. It's been my nature all my life to speak up for others who might not have the strength or the skills to do so. That said, I have to thank a few unique friends who helped me down that road. Larry Clayton, you taught me that spirit and kindness have nothing to do with appearance. You will always be beautiful to me. Desi Geestman, your presence in heaven has had such an effect on my life on this earth, and the courage of your family inspires me daily. David Beard, you helped teach me to see others through different eyes and opened my world. The many children and teens I've worked with for years through the Desi Geestman Foundation, my sense of perspective is magnificently altered because of your remarkable journeys and I am forever changed for the better.

And, of course, to my extraordinary family, especially Joseph, Creason, and Calee, who give me inspiration and support every single day, I thank you. It's not the result but the experience that counts. I'm grateful for every moment.